# Love
### AND
# Lavender

A MAYFIELD FAMILY ROMANCE

# Love AND Lavender

PROPER ROMANCE

# JOSI S. KILPACK

SHADOW
MOUNTAIN

Library of Congress Cataloging-in-Publication Data

Names: Kilpack, Josi S., author. | Kilpack, Josi S. Mayfield family ; bk. 4.

Title: Love and lavender / Josi S. Kilpack.

Other titles: Proper romance.

Description: Salt Lake City : Shadow Mountain, [2021] | Series: Mayfield family; book 4 | Summary: "Hazel Stillman and Duncan Penhale agree to a marriage of convenience in order for them both to claim their inheritances from Elliott Mayfield, but as part of the agreement, Hazel and Duncan must live together as husband and wife for one year before parting. During that year, the couple learns that perhaps what started out as a business relationship might actually turn into a deep and abiding romance."— Provided by publisher.

Identifiers: LCCN 2021018068 | ISBN 9781629729299 (trade paperback)

Subjects: LCSH: Marriage—Fiction. | Man-woman relationships—Fiction. | Heirs— Fiction. | Great Britain—History—Regency, 1811–1820—Fiction. | BISAC: FICTION / Romance / Historical / Regency | FICTION / Romance / Clean & Wholesome | LCGFT: Romance fiction. | Historical fiction.

Classification: LCC PS3611.I45276 L68 2021 | DDC 823/.92—dc23

LC record available at https://lccn.loc.gov/2021018068

Printed in the United States of America

Lake Book Manufacturing, Inc., Melrose Park, IL

10  9  8  7  6  5  4  3  2  1

## Lavender

The lavender flower is made up of many small, spiky, purple blooms that grow from a long, straight stem, with several stems per plant. The value of lavender flowers exceeds that of most flowers due to their use over the centuries for healing as well as for their fragrance, which is both floral and earthy. The purple color lends further association with royalty and spiritual connectivity. When given as a gift, lavender flowers represent purity, devotion, and grace.

# Mayfield
## FAMILY PEDIGREE
### 1822

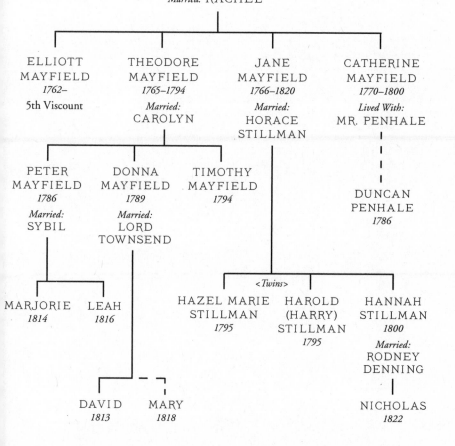

HAROLD MAYFIELD
4th Viscount
*Married:* RACHEL

ELLIOTT
MAYFIELD
*1762–*
5th Viscount

THEODORE
MAYFIELD
*1765–1794*
*Married:*
CAROLYN

JANE
MAYFIELD
*1766–1820*
*Married:*
HORACE
STILLMAN

CATHERINE
MAYFIELD
*1770–1800*
*Lived With:*
MR. PENHALE

PETER
MAYFIELD
*1786*
*Married:*
SYBIL

DONNA
MAYFIELD
*1789*
*Married:*
LORD
TOWNSEND

TIMOTHY
MAYFIELD
*1794*

DUNCAN
PENHALE
*1786*

MARJORIE
*1814*

LEAH
*1816*

*<Twins>*

HAZEL MARIE
STILLMAN
*1795*

HAROLD
(HARRY)
STILLMAN
*1795*

HANNAH
STILLMAN
*1800*
*Married:*
RODNEY
DENNING

DAVID
*1813*

MARY
*1818*

NICHOLAS
*1822*

# Chapter One

*March 23, 1822*

Hazel had not slept well. Her crippled foot ached, despite it having been propped on a pillow all night to help manage the swelling induced by traveling. However, the discomfort was little in comparison to the ache that lingered in her heart after Uncle Elliott's bestowal of a dowry.

The offer had circled around and around in her mind like a pack of wolves until she thought she'd go mad. Or maybe she had gone mad. Or maybe she'd been mad to begin with. Or maybe Uncle Elliott was mad. That seemed likely in Hazel's opinion; he must be mad to think that a decent husband could be "bought." Even for fifty thousand pounds. And yet, Uncle Elliott was one of the kindest and most generous men Hazel had ever known.

Could he be kind and generous *and* mad?

Possibly.

She sighed at the ceiling and threw an arm over her forehead. Life had proven to her over and over that people were complex creatures with complicated motivations and confusing intentions.

Why should Uncle Elliott be spared such humanness? Though prone to the frailties of virtue, as all people were, Uncle Elliott was also part of her *family*.

A family who had routinely overlooked Hazel—why should he be so different?

Discarded by her parents, baited by her twin brother, pitied by her younger sister, and ignored by all of them. Not one of them had ever known her. Not one of them had ever tried. Why should she expect Uncle Elliott to see her any more clearly than they did?

Before yesterday, though, Hazel had thought Uncle Elliott was the family member who understood her best. Apparently, she had been wrong. And, oh, how that hurt.

The sky began to lighten toward dawn, and despite the miserable night's sleep, Hazel kept to her usual schedule of taking an early breakfast. With any luck, eating so early would prevent her from encountering Uncle Elliott until she knew how she should act.

As she dressed for the day, she thought of how just yesterday, the Gold Room, which had been prepared for her stay at Howard House, had seemed bright and elegant; a lovely place to spend the spring holiday between school terms. After Uncle Elliott had presented the dowry, however, Hazel had limped back to the Gold Room and found it tacky and overdone. She had cried herself to sleep in the gaudy room over long-buried dreams.

Morning had not offered as much of a remedy as she'd have liked, and the hurt lingered with her as she made her jerky way through the halls, down the stairs, and into the empty morning room where breakfast had been laid out on the long sideboard that spanned the entire west wall. Hazel was used to being surrounded by students and other teachers most of the time, which made the room feel even emptier.

She chose a soft-boiled egg and a single slice of toast from the sideboard, then sat in one of the chairs at the long table that faced windows overlooking the Howardsford estate. The picturesque fields of Norfolkshire and countless shades of green still draped in morning mist could have been those of her childhood home in Falconridge some fifteen miles west. She had lived at Falconridge, the Stillman family estate, only until she was six, so her memories of that place were soft and faded.

Hazel looked away from the representation of a life denied her and returned to the task at hand: determining whether to make amends with Uncle Elliott and stay the week as planned, or leave today and return to the teacher dormitories at Cordon Academy and her tiny room on the second floor with a single window roughly the size of her breakfast plate.

Using the edge of her knife, Hazel swiftly sliced the soft-boiled egg in half, shell and all. She used the spoon to scoop the contents of each half of the egg onto the single piece of buttered toast. The liquid yolk soaked into the bread as she mashed the rest of the egg with the back of her fork. She was cutting her first bite and thinking about the long trip back to King's Lynn after she'd only just arrived, when the door to the morning room opened and a dark-haired man with equally dark eyes stepped over the threshold.

They'd never met, but she knew he was Duncan Penhale, her sort-of cousin. Duncan had been raised by Hazel's scandalous Aunt Catherine, whom Hazel had never met either. He had been expected yesterday afternoon, and had Hazel not been unraveled in her room after her conversation with Uncle Elliott, they'd have been formally introduced at dinner. Instead, she'd skipped dinner and wallowed in a rare bout of self-pity.

Duncan took three long steps toward the buffet, saw her, and came to an abrupt stop. He inclined his head, looked at the floor, clasped his hands behind his back like a schoolboy prepared to give a recitation, and cleared his throat. "Forgive me, ma'am. I had not thought anyone else would be up at six o'clock for breakfast."

*Ma'am?*

"Neither did I," Hazel replied with the same even tone he'd used. "Though you owe me no apology."

He continued to stare at the floor. His boots were not new but showed a recent polish. His trousers and coat were those of a working man, and his dark hair was combed smoothly back from his forehead. The tips reached his back collar with determined curls, the ends not entirely controlled by whatever substance he used to keep his hair in place.

It was not such a bad thing to have something—or, rather, someone—to distract her from the howling thoughts still omnipresent in her mind. Never mind that it was a someone she'd always been curious about.

"You must be Duncan." She smiled at him the way she smiled at new students in hopes of putting them at ease. "I am your cousin, Hazel Stillman." She held out her hand without standing, palm down, and after a moment's hesitation, he crossed the remaining space between them.

Instead of bowing over her hand as she'd expected, he took it as he would a man's, gave two solid pumps, and let go before stepping back with almost military precision. "Duncan Penhale. Nice to meet you, Miss Stillman."

"Please call me Hazel." She heard plenty of "Miss Stillman" at school, though that was preferable to "Ma'am."

"I do not think that appropriate, Miss Stillman. We have only just met."

"But we are cousins."

Duncan shook his head, his gaze still on the floor. "You and I share no blood relation."

The rigid posture and the way he spoke without looking her in the eye reminded Hazel of some of her former students, one in particular. Audrey Mathews had been solitary and analytical in ways that set her apart, though the girl had never minded her isolation. She excelled at mathematics, which had put her and Hazel in accord.

Relying on her skill of reading people rather well and rather quickly, Hazel took a chance and spoke to Duncan in the same upfront way she'd found effective with Audrey. "My mother, Jane, and Catherine, your . . . guardian, were both Uncle Elliott's sisters, and he has been your benefactor just as he's been mine. Therefore, I feel it appropriate for us to continue on a first name basis due to our shared connection. Also, Uncle Elliott considers you his nephew as though you *are* a blood relation."

His tight eyebrows made him appear unconvinced.

"Would it be more comfortable to call me Cousin Hazel?"

"It is a false relational title."

"As I have never met any of my blood cousins and know as much about them as I do you, I think calling one another 'cousin' is appropriate. It at least gives us a distinction between any other person we might address more formally. Does that not seem reasonable?"

Duncan pondered a few moments, then nodded. "That is a reasonable distinction. May I breakfast here, or would you prefer to dine alone?"

Hazel celebrated the victory internally. "I am not opposed to company, *Cousin Duncan*. You are welcome to dine here with me."

He nodded and continued to the sideboard, filled his plate to heaping, and chose the chair two seats away from Hazel. Whereas Hazel's plate contained a single slice of toast with egg, Duncan's plate was full. Hazel did not eat that much food in two days' time. She watched the way Duncan focused on his plate, the way he employed his fork and knife to cut exacting bites. He'd chosen three of each item—three links of sausage, three quarters of potato, three hard-boiled eggs, three slices of kidney pie, and three slices of ham. He had not served himself any hash or beans; perhaps those things were difficult to count?

"When did you arrive at Howard House, Cousin Duncan?" she asked when half of his plate had been cleared. He had eaten one slice of pie, followed by potato, ham, sausage, egg. Then he'd started over in the same order.

He finished chewing the egg from his second pass and swallowed before he spoke. "Yesterday afternoon. I shall stay until tomorrow morning at nine o'clock, which is when the carriage will fetch me for the return journey. I do not like to travel." He continued to cut and eat his food, chewing each bite carefully and not talking with his mouth full.

Though Hazel's students were usually gentry of one level or another, she learned a lot about their upbringings by observing their manners when they first arrived. Duncan's manners were excellent—aside from his having shaken her hand instead of bowing over it—and above what Hazel would expect from the son of a laborer raised by a disgraced woman who, though the daughter of a viscount, had abandoned her privilege for reasons Hazel had never been told. Aunt Catherine was not the only scandal in the Mayfield line, but her fall from grace had taken a fair amount of the family reputation with it—people did not give up what she had given up.

"And where do you live, Duncan?"

He swallowed before he answered but still did not look at her. "In an upper apartment of the Burrow Building on Providence Street in Ipswich, number four."

"I have never been to Ipswich," Hazel said conversationally

after giving adequate pause to allow him to expand, which he did not. "Do you like it there?"

"Yes." He paused in his breakfast, then looked up at her. He held eye contact for only a moment before turning his attention back to his plate. "You live in King's Lynn, the once-famous port city, and you teach mathematics at a school for girls."

Hazel startled slightly. "How did you know?"

"Lord Howardsford told me. He also said you are a twin with your brother, Harold, who was birthed ten minutes after your birth, making you the eldest child of Jane Mayfield and Horace Stillman." He went back to cutting and eating his perfect bites.

"Yes," she said, watching him surreptitiously while taking another bite of her egg on toast, which had gone cold. "I will have you know, however, that I am not only the older twin, but also the smarter, better behaved, and better looking one."

He paused a moment and then lifted his eyes to her chin. He smiled, revealing a dimple in his right cheek and a slight gap between his front teeth that gave him a boyish look that belied his years. "That is a clever answer, Cousin Hazel. I have never met your twin brother and therefore cannot prove whether or not you are joking."

She no longer needed the forced teacher-smile. "Well, then I hope you shall never meet him so that my pronouncement shall remain uncontested."

He held her eyes another moment and then went back to his breakfast.

They were quiet for some time, her eating as slowly as possible in order to prolong her reason for staying in the room. "You also *work* in Ipswich, do you not, Cousin Duncan?"

He nodded and took a drink of his ale. "I am a junior clerk at

Perkins & Cromley Accounting. It occupies office number nine also located in the Burrow Building, which is highly convenient."

"You enjoy numbers, then?"

"Numbers are unchanging and only need formulation to be understood," he said without looking up. "You teach mathematics, which is a rare subject for a girl's school to offer but even more rare for a woman to teach." He looked up. "Do you enjoy numbers?"

"I do like numbers, but I also like teaching. The two of them together is highly satisfying."

Duncan took a bite of ham, paused in his chewing, and then resumed, his jaw moving slowly and carefully while he stared at the table with fierce concentration. Was he counting how many times he chewed?

After he swallowed, he looked up at her, though he did not meet her eye directly, and pointed at the ham on his plate. "You must try this ham, Cousin Hazel." He laid his silverware on the edges of his plate and stood.

"I usually only have an egg on toast for my breakfast."

He moved to the buffet and returned with a piece of ham on a fresh plate without acknowledging that she'd spoken. He set the plate in front of her and nodded toward it as he sat down at the table again. He did not resume his own meal but instead looked expectantly between her and the plate.

Hazel hesitated, then pulled the plate closer to her and cut a bite of ham. She chewed it slowly and swallowed before smiling at him. "It *is* very good."

He nodded, apparently satisfied with her reaction, and returned to his meal. She hesitated before deciding to finish the ham. It *was* quite good, though she was not much of a critic. Most of her meals these last twenty years had been taken in school dining halls—first as a boarded student and then as a teacher. There was little variety or excitement about the dishes, and over the years, she had come to approach eating with the same rote as sleeping and washing.

"King's Lynn is a fair distance from East Ashlam," Duncan stated.

"Thirty-five miles, I think." The ham tasted better and better with each bite—was it flavored with maple? Who thought of such things like flavoring ham with maple? "I had to wait for the winter term to end before I was able to accept Uncle Elliott's invitation."

Mentioning the invitation reminded her of the reason behind it. Which reminded her that she needed to decide whether or not to stay. Uncle Elliott had hired a private carriage for her journey here, a luxury that had made the trek far more comfortable than it would have been if she'd taken a mail coach that flew across the roads with little consideration to the passengers bouncing around inside like marbles.

It felt presumptuous to expect the same accommodation for the return travel if she left earlier than planned. A public carriage, then. Bounced like a marble. Pressed in among strangers. She would have to pay for the miserable journey herself as well, which would cut into her carefully guarded savings. Had she even brought enough coin with her to cover the expense of a return journey?

"You did not attend dinner last night," Duncan said, drawing her from her thoughts. "Lord Howardsford said you were tired from your journey."

"That was part of my reason for not making an appearance," she said, hearing the tightness in her voice. She eyed her sort-of cousin, wondering if he would be as unfailingly honest as Audrey had always been. It was beastly to take advantage of that possibility, but, well, she felt rather beastly. "What is the purpose of your visit to Howard House, Cousin Duncan?"

He finished chewing and spoke while cutting a bite of his

last piece of sausage. "Lord Howardsford wanted to tell me about marriage inheritances he has drafted for each of his nieces and nephews—and myself, even though I am no blood relation. He asked me here so we might discuss the inheritance he has designed for me."

Even though she'd asked, she hadn't fully expected such an honest answer. She hesitated before choosing curiosity over manners a second time.

"What was his marriage inheritance for you?"

"Should I marry a woman of gentle birth and appropriate disposition, as approved by Lord Howardsford, the title for the Burrow Building will transfer to me, and I shall be the sole owner of the entire office block." He relayed this without the animation he'd displayed regarding the ham and took the final bite of his sausage.

His inheritance was nowhere near the value of Hazel's dowry, yet it put Duncan in a very different economic position than he was right now. It was generous for Duncan's situation in a similar way that Hazel's dowry was generous for hers. But his inheritance would be his *own*, while Hazel's, because of the patriarchal laws of England, would belong to her hypothetical husband. She tried to tamp down her irritation at such laws by keeping her focus on Duncan's situation.

"Uncle Elliott would purchase the building and deed it into your name?"

"He already owns the Burrow Building and would only need to sign the deed over to me."

Duncan lived *and* worked in a building Uncle Elliott owned? Uncle Elliott had played quite a hand in the organization of Duncan's life, it seemed, and was now trying to manage even more of the details.

"You must be very excited by the prospect of owning the building."

Duncan turned his attention to a hard-boiled egg. "Owning the building would be a grand financial security for me and therefore exciting, yes. But I do not want to marry."

"Why not?"

He speared some egg onto his fork and did not answer until he had sufficiently chewed, savored, and swallowed. "I have been told that I am odd, and a genteel woman would never marry a clerk. I, therefore, do not feel my prospects are high in regard to making an arrangement that would satisfy Lord Howardsford's terms."

Hazel's cheeks turned hot at the ease with which he spoke of the sort of things most people never said out loud.

"What did Uncle Elliott create for you to inherit upon marriage, Cousin Hazel?"

Hazel felt instant offense at the impertinence of his question but immediately saw the hypocrisy. It was only fair that she answer as honestly as he had.

"A dowry," she said flatly. "Fifty thousand pounds." She hadn't said the words out loud until now, and the marvel of it shimmered down her spine. Then the offense shimmered back up to her head where it buzzed like an angry hornet.

Duncan straightened, his shoulders drawing back as he looked at her with wide eyes. "Fifty thousand pounds? That is an incredible sum! Is that in addition to your existing dowry from your parents or is it a combination of the two?"

His enthusiasm was surprising, and a little bit gauche. "I did not have an existing dowry."

His eyes moved back to her chin. "You did not?"

"No one has ever expected I would marry, dowry or not. And my father tended to spend any money that came his way, not set it aside for his children." Harry had followed their father's pattern of not worrying about anyone but himself. Gallant men, the Stillmans.

"No one but Lord Howardsford, you mean."

Hazel pulled her eyebrows together. "What?"

"You said no one has ever expected you would marry, dowry or not, but apparently Lord Howardsford *does* expect you will marry."

Hazel would have laughed out loud, but she was still a gentlewoman. "For fifty thousand dollars, a great many men would marry their horses."

Duncan pulled his eyebrows together as though trying to make sense of her statement.

The pause went on long enough for her to feel awkward. "Never mind," she said, shrugging one shoulder to feign her indifference.

Satisfied with her acknowledgment, Duncan returned his attention to his plate, which was nearly cleared. She finished the last bite of her cold egg on toast and took a sip of cold tea, watching him.

It had been Harry who had told Hazel about Duncan several years ago, when they'd been home from school at the same time—a rare event outside of Christmas holiday.

"Did you know we have an illegitimate cousin?" Harry had said, his eyes wide with fascination as he'd plopped down beside her on her bed where she had been reading *Robinson Crusoe* for the fourth time that week. There was a limited selection of books at Falconridge, and she'd not thought to borrow from the extensive library at St. Mary's before she'd left.

"We do not," she'd said in the authoritative tone she used most often when talking to Harry.

"We do." His eyes were bright with anticipation to share his gossip. "I heard Mother talking to Mrs. Moyle about it just now. It seems our Aunt Catherine—she died when we were five years old—took up with a man who already had a child, and Mother called Aunt Catherine 'his mistress.'" Harry had grinned at the delightful scandal. "Catherine promised Uncle Elliott she would marry that man, but she never did, and then *he* died, and she was left with the care of his son, who became *her* ward. He is twenty years old and works as an apprentice clerk in Ipswich. Mother said that Uncle Elliott has paid for all the boy's schooling and helped him find an apprenticeship, and she is furious."

"If the boy's parents were married when he was born, he is not illegitimate," Hazel had said.

"But his father never married Aunt Catherine, and that is how Mother identified the boy to Mrs. Moyle—'Catherine's illegitimate son.'"

How *should* they reference this boy's relationship to their dead aunt? Hazel had wondered. Catherine hadn't been his stepmother, because she'd never married his father. Not wanting to admit she didn't know the answer, Hazel had gone back to her book.

"You are an imbecile, Harry. Why does petty gossip hold such interest to you?"

Harry's cheeks had gone red, and he had grabbed her book and thrown it against the wall, breaking the binding, before jumping off the bed and running from the room while she screamed additional names after him.

Now Hazel watched their "illegitimate" cousin take the last bite of his breakfast and calculated that if he had been twenty years old when she had been eleven, he was thirty-six years old now—the same age as her cousin Peter—and nine years her senior. She wondered what it had been like for Duncan to live in rented rooms above shops with a woman who was not his mother. What a strange life.

Duncan took another drink of ale.

Hazel decided to push for more information. "You do not find the requirement of making a genteel match offensive?"

Duncan leaned back in his chair. "Lord Howardsford said that he hopes to help each of us establish what he himself was unable to have in his youth. His hope may have blinded him to reasonable expectations."

"Did you tell him that?"

Duncan shook his head. "As he has always done me such kindness, I did not want to be rude. I was taught to always say thank you when given a gift."

"You had more manners than I did, then," Hazel said, pushing both of her empty plates aside and feeling foolish for having spoken her mind so directly yesterday in light of Duncan's restraint.

Uncle Elliott had paid for Hazel to attend St. Mary's, a more advanced school than her parents could afford, and he'd arranged to have gifts sent at her birthday and Christmastide, even though he had lived in India most of her life. He had come to see her whenever he was in England, and he was the first person to suggest that a specialty boot might be made for her clubbed foot. Walking had required crutches before then. It had been a wonderous thing to walk on two feet like every other nine-year-old girl, even if she still could not run or play.

"You *were* offended by his gift of dowry for you, then?" Duncan asked her.

"Completely." It felt silly to say so. It was not as though she had anything less now than she'd had before. Somehow it felt as though she'd lost something, though. "I have no marriage prospects, and for Uncle Elliott to try to induce a man to marry me for money was quite . . . painful, really."

"Is your lack of marriage prospects due to your deformed foot?"

Hazel's spine snapped into alignment, and her eyes popped wide. The burn in her cheeks blazed red-hot, and she looked away not only to take a breath and center her thoughts but also to give him ample opportunity to restate his question or apologize. When he did not do either one, she turned back to him and stared at him coldly. He missed the look completely because he was not looking at her.

"Yes, Duncan. My *deformed* foot." Her twisted, grotesque, and mutilated foot that had set the course of her life from the day of her birth.

"Is it so bad? I mean, you can walk, can't you?" He looked around the room. "I see no crutch or bath chair."

Hazel's chest tightened up like planks of a barrel. "I can walk."

"That is *very* good, then," he said with a nod. "As you are of gentle birth, intelligent, and well-featured, a deformed foot is not such a deficit as to interfere with your ability to marry. As there are many men of gentle birth in need of fortunes for one reason or another, you will have no trouble finding a husband."

While Hazel's blood boiled, Duncan finished his ale and then pulled a battered watch from the pocket of his unadorned waistcoat. The footman came in to clear their plates.

"That was a most excellent breakfast," Duncan said, nodding at the stoic footman. He turned his attention to Hazel with an expression free of any awareness of her response to the egregious things he'd said. "I am glad to have met you, Cousin Hazel."

"The pleasure is all mine," she said stiffly. She wanted him to understand that he'd offended her, and yet looking into his innocent expression made her question the right to have been offended.

He hadn't said or done anything that indicated *scorn* of her failing; he'd simply been direct about her foot in ways no one ever was.

*Deformed,* she repeated in her mind. While shocking in its starkness and a completely inappropriate term for casual conversation, Duncan's description of her clubbed foot was not *wrong.* Her foot was *de*-formed.

Duncan stood and straightened his coat, less awkward than he'd been when he entered the room, though still . . . odd. She did not quite know what to make of him. Was he slow-witted or, like Audrey, was he advanced in some ways and unskilled in others, like social graces that determined what one did and did not talk about?

"I am going to take a walk around the back pond before it rains," he announced. "Lord Howardsford showed me the path from the window yesterday evening, and I enjoy walking. Perhaps I shall see you at luncheon, Cousin Hazel. Do you find number riddles interesting?"

"Sometimes," she said, unsure how she felt about the prospect of further conversations with him now that her initial curiosity competed with defensiveness. Even in her offended state, however, she found his directness a bit refreshing in a world where people said one thing but meant something else or often spent hours talking of nothing at all.

"I collect number riddles. They are fun," Duncan said as he straightened his simple brown waistcoat beneath his darker brown coat. "Most people lack the rational ability to factor them for the sake of entertainment. As you are a mathematics teacher, however, I expect you may be up to the challenge. I shall think of some we can entertain ourselves with at luncheon. Good day, Cousin Hazel."

He nodded, smiled quickly as though someone had whispered in his ear that he should, and left the room.

# Chapter Two

April 4, 1822

Dear Cousin Hazel,

I enjoyed the number games we shared at lunch last month when we met at Howard House, and I wish to continue them through written correspondence. It is a rare treat for me to find someone with as much wit and intellect as myself in these matters, and I enjoyed that you reciprocated with challenges I had not known before. The one about the zebras was particularly intriguing.

I am glad that you rectified your relationship with Lord Howardsford before I left. It was a very pleasant visit for me, aside from the travel, due to the excellent food and stimulating company.

A man is climbing a mountain 100 kilometers high. Every day, he climbs up 2 kilometers then sleeps for the night, but every night while he sleeps, he slips 1 kilometer backward. In the morning, he starts again. How many days does it take the man to reach the mountaintop?

Sincerely,

Mr. D. Penhale

✳

*May 28, 1822*

*Dear Duncan,*

*I am also glad that Uncle Elliott and I were able to find accord during my visit. We did not speak of my dowry again for the whole of the week, which is likely the chief reason I was able enjoy the rest of my time at Howard House. I still question his motivations in creating his "marriage inheritances," and I feel they are much more a disadvantage than an advantage. My brother shall marry for his inheritance alone, mark my words. I feel very sorry for the woman he marries, who, without Uncle Elliott's manipulation, might have lived a happy life.*

*The answer to your riddle—which is one I give my own students—is ninety-nine days.*

*What is summer like in Ipswich?*

*It stays rather cool this far north, and the cold fog that rolls in from the ocean, the haar, is often present, which can become tedious. Unfortunately, the haar does not discourage the summer visitors. It seems that when people leave London after the season ends, they all come to King's Lynn.*

*Can you guess the next number in this sequence?*

*27, 82, 41, 124, 62, 31, 94, 47, 142, 71, 214, 107*

*Sincerely,*

*Hazel*

❊

June 27, 1822

Dear Cousin Hazel,

To continue the sequence you relayed in your latest letter, I must use the following formula:

(x*3+1, /2, *3+1, /2)

This results in the next two numbers of the sequence being 322, 161.

Surely, there could not possibly be enough accommodations in King's Lynn for everyone who goes to London for the season to then go on to King's Lynn. I realize you may have been stating an exaggeration in order to make a related point: that more people visit King's Lynn this time of year than they do in the spring. A more precise explanation would lend greater clarity to the recipient, who, in this case, is me.

I understand King's Lynn to be a bit less temperate a climate than Ipswich. The summers here are very pleasant, and though the winters are cold, we do not get a great deal of snow.

You had mentioned over lunch at Howard House that the school you currently teach in is not the first school that employed you. What was your first school? Do you like this one better than that one?

What digit is the most frequent between the numbers 1 and 1,000?

Regards,

*Mr. D. Penhale*

*August 1, 1822*

*Dear Duncan,*

 *Before this position in Lynn, I taught at an all girl's school in Northampton called St. Mary's Female Seminary. It is the same school I had attended for several years as a student; they offered me a teaching position when I completed my education. I enjoyed my time there and was able to move into the position of advanced mathematics teacher when the former teacher retired. Unfortunately, two years ago, a local clergyman took over as headmaster, and he felt that subjects like mathematics and any language other than French were unnecessary. He stated that those topics did not improve the student's abilities to be good wives and mothers. To avoid being imprecise with my language, I will say rather boldly here that I found that decision disheartening.*

 *The Latin teacher at St. Mary's, Sophie Baxter, and I were both fortunate to find positions with Cordon Academy here in King's Lynn. I have liked it here, though there are fewer students than at St. Mary's due to its more remote location. I teach two advanced courses, and the rest of my classes are basic math for the younger students. There are not many girl's schools that offer any advanced subjects, however, so I am grateful to have found a position here.*

 *Many of my students are the daughters of industrialists and successful merchants rather than of nobility. The father of one of my students believes that by 1840, there will be rail lines crisscrossing England and that one will be able to travel from York to London in a matter of hours instead of days. Can you even imagine? Surely in a world of such advancement, women will finally be acknowledged as being as intelligent as men and have equal opportunity to gain the education necessary to participate in the technologies of our age. I like to believe that I am even now educating future engineers who will continue to build our country. It is a nice thought.*

*To answer your puzzle—1 is the most common digit between 1 and 1,000. I had actually learned this one in school many years ago. You must send me more of a challenge!*

*I hope you will not be disappointed that mine is not a riddle: What does x need to be for this following balanced equation to be true?*

$$-4(x + 5) = 3x - 11x - 8$$

*Warm regards,*

*Hazel*

❊

September 5, 1822

*Dear Cousin Hazel,*

*Your letter was very interesting, especially regarding your opinion of women's overall intelligence. I am unsure if women are as smart as men, and I could give you examples of research that would claim to prove that they are not, but in the consideration of your belief, I realized that all my research comes from men. Women have few opportunities to prove themselves as capable as men, and therefore patriarchal tradition can essentially make whatever claim it likes without refutation. There is the example of Theano, Pythagoras's wife, who was herself an exceptional mathematician and is credited with the continued teaching of his system after his death, which proves the potential for a woman to be as intelligent as a man. Sadly, Theano is the only such woman in mathematical history I have ever encountered.*

*You are the only woman with a mathematical mind that I have ever met, but then I have not met many women. It would take significant study and experimentation to prove men and women equally capable of advanced learning, but without opportunity to prove equal intellectual ability by educating equal numbers of girls and boys, we again end with circular logic that cannot be entirely trusted. It is a fascinating topic of consideration.*

*I am also intrigued by your information regarding the railroad as I have followed the development of the locomotive since Trevithick's first completed engine. I have read that there will be steam engines running as soon as 1825. I am eager to see if these predictions come to pass. I do not like to travel even by carriage, and I find the idea of rail travel quite uncomfortable, never mind my respect for the feat of its invention. I have only ever traveled to Bury St. Edmunds, where I attended a school I despised, and to East Ashlam upon Uncle Elliott's invitation to Howard House. I prefer to stay in Ipswich where everything I need is within walking distance.*

*The answer to your variable equation is 3.*

*Here is my puzzle:*

*The day before yesterday Matilda was 25.*
*The next year Matilda will be 28.*
*This is true only one day in a year.*
*What day is Matilda's birthday?*

*(Originally this riddle used the name "Matthew,"*
*but in light of my consideration of the equal representa-*
*tion of women, I chose to change the name to a female*
*variation.)*

*Sincerely,*

Mr. D. Penhale

December 2, 1822

Dear Duncan,

Can you believe we have been writing for nearly eight months? When I received your first letter I had not considered there would be a second, yet our correspondence has become something I look forward to.

Will you be going to Howard House for the Christmas holiday? I will be there for a full fortnight and expect some of my other cousins will be in attendance. I am oddly anxious about that as I have not met them before. Have you heard that both Cousin Peter and Cousin Timothy—they are our late uncle Theodore Mayfield's sons—have married in recent months? And Uncle Elliott too! That is even more ridiculous than my ridiculous nerves. I do hope you will come. I will have much more faith in there being good conversation if you are there.

Now, as for the new junior clerk you mentioned in

*your last letter, it sounds to me that his hire is nothing short of nepotism in the very literal way if one puts Mr. Cromley in the position of "Pope" of this company and Mr. Ludwig in the position of "nephew" given privileges, though I do not believe Mr. Ludwig is an illegitimate son masquerading as a nephew—I digress. Suffice it to say, I am sorry that it has been so frustrating to you. Have you talked to Mr. Perkins? You have spoken highly of him in the past. Perhaps he would intervene.*

 *Here is the puzzle: What mathematical symbol can be placed between 5 and 9 to get a number greater than 5 and smaller than 9?*

*Sincerely,*

*Hazel*

*April 17, 1823*

*Dear Cousin Hazel,*

 *I was very disappointed that you did not go to Easter at Howard House. Lady Howardsford was a very accommodating hostess, and I was glad to meet Peter and his daughters. Did you know that after his first wife passed, he married Lady Howardsford's daughter? The interfamily marriages shall make for a very messy pedigree one day, I'm afraid. Lord Howardsford said that you did not come to Easter because I had been unable to come at Christmas and you were taking revenge. I believe this was a joke but have been rather worried. Did I offend you by not attending at Christmas? It was only that the roads were so poor,* and as I do not like to travel, it did not seem wise to go so far north. Additionally, Mr. Perkins and Mr. Cromley have been frustrated with my complaints against Mr. Ludwig and did not like when I asked to take additional days away from the office. I wish I had been more clear with you regarding my intention to come at Easter. I had not known for sure that I would be able to go until a few days before the holiday, and even then, I only stayed three days.

Because we have corresponded since Christmas and you have not seemed angry, I am hopeful that Lord Howardsford was making a jest at my expense by claiming you were angry with me, but I am not always good at interpreting such things and would appreciate clarification.

Also, do you subscribe to The Review? I have only just received the edition from last November, and there is the most fascinating article about the Bernoulli brothers in France. Have you read it? I am eager to hear your opinion on whether or not they truly turned the tide on modern mathematics and overshadowed other great minds in the process.

Mr. Ludwig tried to convince me that the Greeks were superior to the Egyptians in regard to their understanding of mathematics. I was incensed! It is not necessarily the level of Egypt's knowledge, but the fact that they were superior in their knowledge and understanding thousands of years before the rest of the civilized world. It is one of the world's great mysteries that they could be so far advanced while separated from the greater world culture. Mr. Ludwig is an imbecile and only makes himself appear the worse by trying to pretend he isn't.

*The answer to your puzzle from last month's letter is Queen Elizabeth, and the age of your factor is 45. Very clever.*

*Here is my latest number puzzle for you. I am quite enjoying these algebraic-based equations as I do not have near the algebra involved in my day-to-day work as I would like. Solve this with the numbers currently represented by the letters.*

KAJAK

KAJAK

KAJAK

KAJAK

KAJAK

KAJAK

———

VESLO

*Sincerely,*

Mr. D. Penhale

May 7, 1823

*Dear Duncan,*

*Of course I did not stay away because you did not come at Christmas! Goodness, do you think me such a punishing woman? I will admit that I missed your company at Christmas, but I would not have missed Easter out of spite. Sophie and I stayed at the school with the three girls who were unable to travel home for the holidays. As I had spent Christmas with my family, as odd as that is since I have never done so before, it seemed only fair. Let us both decide now that we will go to Howard House next Christmas. Shall we?*

*Oh, the Bernoulli brothers! You may not like to hear my opinion; therefore, I suggest you sit down before you continue reading as my thoughts might be rather shocking. I have not read the article as I do not have access to The Review, but I shall forewarn you, and perhaps give away my position, with the statement that I believe Euler to be the most brilliant mathematical mind of the last century—not that anyone would know that, thanks to Jacob and Johann Bernoulli. It is my opinion that the novelty of brothers having such advanced minds—I do admit they are brilliant, make no mistake—overshadowed poor Euler, whom I truly believe would have factored much higher in the overall accomplishments of the field if not for the death of Empress Catherine I, which is, after all, what led Euler to become a ship captain for those prime years. He was a man with very bad luck, in my opinion, but an excellent mind. I am now eager to hear what the article stated regarding this topic; thank you for bringing it to my attention.*

*My education of the history of mathematics is certainly lacking when compared to yours, but that can be fully accounted for by your access to teachers and libraries a girl can only dream of encountering. I was one of only two students in the history of St. Mary's who passed the final exams of the advanced mathematics course without a single mistake, and the school's library had only the first volume of Euclid's Elements. Cordon Academy's library has up through volume four, which has been wonderful,* but I am still self-taught to a great degree, which is as much a source of pride to me as it is a source of regret. I have read about lectures given at Cambridge and Oxford and have grown terribly green with envy over all the education sprinkled so generously over the fortunate heads of those students. (All men, of course.)

Here is the solution to your last puzzle:

15451 x 6 = 92706

My puzzle is simple, but appropriate as to the celebration of the developments of the rail system here in England. Each letter represents a number:

CHOO

+ CHOO

———

TRAIN

Your friend,
*Hazel*

※

June 26, 1823

Dear Cousin Hazel,

I am sorry it has taken me so long to respond to your last letter. I trust you will not think it was because I am unacquainted with number variables. The solution to your very simple puzzle is:

5488

+ 5488

———

10976

*The reason for my delay is that Mr. Ludwig is making my life increasingly miserable. I am spending hours every day fixing his mistakes, which has left me in a very poor mood. I often spend additional hours walking in the evening as I find that to be an activity that helps me recover from my frustrations. Mr. Ludwig is not well suited for his position, but Mr. Cromley is even more determined to have him a place as Mr. Ludwig is newly married. Mr. Cromley gets irritated with me when I complain and claims Mr. Ludwig simply needs more time and patience. This belief cannot possibly be true. Mr. Cromley's assertions that continued time and patience will remedy Mr. Ludwig's limitations is ridiculous. At least I am given his work to go over before it is sent out; I find myself rewriting approximately 63% of those submissions.*

*I wish Mr. Ludwig had half your mathematics skills. I find it a shame you do not train up young men so that I might present Mr. Cromley with a truly competent alternative to his nephew.*

*I hope that my delay in replying to your last letter will not turn you off from continuing our correspondence as I find it most enjoyable and would like it to continue. I will improve my response rate so that I might keep to our every month pattern.*

*Find the missing number:*

*7 6 12*

*5 5 7*

*4 6 X*

*168 90 168*

*Sincerely,*

*Mr. D. Penhale*

# Chapter Three

*August 1, 1823*

"Miss Stillman?"

Hazel stopped in the hallway and turned toward the front maid walking quickly in her direction. "Good morning, Gretchen."

"Good morning, Miss Stillman." Gretchen dropped a very shallow curtsy that was little more than an inclination of her head. She held out a letter. "This came for you, and I thought you would want it before your next class."

"Thank you," Hazel said, leaning on her cane as she took the letter with her free hand. Gretchen gave another barely noticeable curtsy and turned back the way she'd come.

Hazel looked at the letter, fully expecting Duncan's cramped scrawl. They had been writing for a year and a half, but she'd had a letter just last week. Perhaps he'd thought of a new riddle and could not wait for her response before he sent it on.

It wasn't Duncan's tight script across the front of the letter, however. Instead, it was Harry's more billowy penmanship that stared back at her. She let out a breath as she turned toward her classroom and limped a little faster, and less decorously, her cane tapping out the rhythm of her steps. She liked to be sitting behind her desk before the students came into class, and with every lurching step, her indignation toward her brother burned a bit hotter in her chest.

It had been a full year since she'd last corresponded with Harry. He'd asked her for money, and had he been there in person, she'd have thrashed him with a belt. Instead she'd had to settle for a thrashing of the pen-and-parchment variety. It had been an ugly letter, and she'd *almost* regretted her words after she'd posted it. Almost.

When their father had died and Harry had inherited the family estate, Hazel had expected him to lead the Stillman family at least as well as Father had, which was not much of a level to rise to, truth be told. Instead, Harry had scampered off to London, where he spent the estate profits—such as they were—on women and wine and gaming tables. Had Harry been a decent man, Hazel would not be supporting herself. And yet, even when fired up with her righteous anger regarding his neglect, she had to admit she was generally happy with her life, which put her at odds with being at odds with her brother. Had she not needed to pursue teaching, the only life left for a gentleman's crippled daughter would have been rotting in front of the fire with no purpose at all.

Harry, Harry, Harry. If her only feelings toward him were bitterness and frustration, she'd have solved this equation in her head years ago. But a tenderness always seeped in behind the anger that she could never fully discount.

Once seated behind her desk, she tucked the letter into the drawer to read later. For now, she needed to review her lessons and choose which girl would scribe today. Other teachers could stand before their students, write on the board, and command attention through their physical presence. What Hazel did not have in physical command, she made up for in well-placed praise, focused lessons, and, when necessary, reasonable discipline. She took pride in knowing that her classes were among the best behaved.

Maybe some of the students' attentiveness came from pity for the poor crippled teacher, but there was something unique in verbally explaining equations rather than relying only on numeric demonstration. Hazel believed that the blending of semantics and numbers made mathematics more accessible, especially to those students who were not naturally inclined toward quotients.

Betsy Schumacher stayed after Hazel's second class to work on her advanced studies; the girl had a mind for geometry, and they spent a happy hour exploring geometric algebra through the numerical representation of line segments. They ended the session with a fascinating discussion of how Newton's binomial theorem led to de Moivre's multinomial theorem and how that affected the growing understanding of analytical geometry.

Once Betsy had left, Hazel removed Harry's letter from the drawer, broke the seal, took a breath, and braced herself.

The letter was an . . . apology. Not only for the inappropriate request for funds he'd made last year, but for all the years he'd not done right by her—financially and personally. He explained that he'd made a mess of everything in London but had learned great lessons. He promised her he would do better and be the brother she deserved him to be. The final paragraph was particularly humble:

*I have great admiration for you and the way you*
*have risen to the challenges life has given you, Hazel. I*

*hope to prove that we have more of those virtues in common than either of us have believed and that one day you will be proud to be the person who has known me best and longest.*

My sincere love and appreciation,
*Harry*

*Best and longest.*

Despite all the times Harry had irritated and angered her, she knew her brother in ways that others never could. The same people who had expected nothing of Hazel had expected everything of Harry. He had been expected to possess every virtue and ability from the time they were both small. When Harry executed anything with less than perfect proficiency, their father had lashed out with verbal attacks that cut Harry to the core. He was the son, the heir, but Father had only ever seen Harry for what he should be, not for what he actually was.

Mother would dote on Harry to make up for Father's meanness, and then Father would turn on her for making Harry soft. Hazel had seen very little of this dynamic before being sent away to school, but it had not been difficult to put the pieces together when she came home and watched how the relationships played out firsthand.

At some point, about when they were fourteen years old, Harry had stopped trying to please their unpleasable father and had instead sought only to please himself. When Harry started getting into trouble at school, Hazel had known it came from a place of needing attention and control—trying to fill the holes left over from their childhood.

She'd done the same thing in a different way: studying harder than anyone, setting herself apart any way she could, besting

Harry in matters of education in hopes that her parents would see some worth in their crippled oldest child. Her efforts had given her success in the academic world but had not filled those holes any more than Harry's dissipation had filled his. She had come to accept that nothing would fill those gaps, and she'd made her peace.

Though her sympathy for Harry was deep, it extended only so far. He was a grown man, with more opportunity than most people—male or female—could ever hope for. Rather than use his advantages, he had squandered the security intended for all three of the Stillman children. Hannah had married beneath her and, from what Hazel could pick out from her younger sister's sporadic and carefully worded letters, was now trapped in an unhappy life she could not leave.

Over the years, Hazel had learned about therapies for disabilities like hers, including braces that adjusted the twisted tendons and ligaments over time. There was even a surgeon in Berlin who could reset some of the bones to improve her ability to properly bear weight on the bottom of her foot. There was no time or money to pursue such possibilities, however, because she was financially responsible for herself.

Harry's course had set her own. And although his letter demonstrated that he had suffered for his choices, it seemed likely to Hazel that someone had—once again—come along to help him out of the mess he'd made, thus instigating this apology. The same way school administrators had given him "one more chance" a dozen times. The way Mother had coddled him. The way Uncle Elliott had paid off his debts. Yet, even with all those benefits, Harry had *still* wasted the profits from Falconridge and years of his life and, far as Hazel knew, had never cared for anyone but himself.

It seemed Harry had landed on his perfectly formed feet the way he always had, and though she accepted his apology and was touched by his expressed admiration of her accomplishments, nothing in their shared history gave her reason to believe he would actually become the person his letter said he wanted to become. She would not lose sleep worrying about his ability to achieve his proposed restoration.

The sound of classroom doors clicking shut in the hallway brought her mind back to the present. Sophie would have finished teaching her class ten minutes ago. Hazel used the desk to push herself to standing, wincing slightly as she adjusted her foot within the heavy boot that had been specially made to accommodate the misshapen appendage. She needed to hurry so Sophie would not think Hazel had ignored their standing appointment.

Hazel hadn't had Sophie as a teacher while studying at St. Mary's, but they'd become friends after Hazel joined the faculty. That friendship had helped make a strange transition less awkward for Hazel and had become even stronger when they'd both found positions at Cordon. Not having to come to a new school alone was the closest thing to a miracle Hazel would ever acknowledge taking place in her life.

Every step out of the classroom and down the hall sent a shooting pain up her leg and into her hip. The foot itself felt as though she were walking on broken glass. This particular boot was more than three years old now and so worn on the inner sole that even the slightest shift in her weight caused different parts of her foot and ankle to ache. Because no one else was in the halls, she let her body lurch and swing so she could use the momentum to help propel her forward. When she was around people, she forced a straighter posture that looked less awkward but doubled her discomfort.

The specialty cobbler she'd used over the years was in Northampton—near St. Mary's—and too far away for Hazel to use again. The prospect of finding a new cobbler here in King's Lynn made her stomach hurt from anxiety. It was such an embarrassment to explain her need, let alone show anyone her twisted foot. She'd looked at it every day of her life and found it repulsive; the toes curled under, and the ankle twisted backward, which required her to walk on the outside of her foot rather than the sole. She could only imagine the horror people felt when they looked at it for the first time.

Unexpectedly, she remembered something Duncan had said during their first meeting that day at Howard House. He'd called her "well-featured," which she took to mean "pretty." It was the only compliment she'd ever been paid by a man regarding her looks. That he'd said it so directly made it worth that much more.

"There you are."

Hazel startled and looked through the doorway of the teacher's parlor to where Sophie stood with her hands on her ample hips, eyes narrowed playfully.

Hazel, hoping Sophie hadn't seen her lurching, adopted her "company walk" and smiled at her friend as she limped the rest of the way into the room. "I suppose I *am* late. Please make my apologies to Her Highness."

Sophie snorted and made a show of checking the time on the watch pinned to the bodice of her rose-colored dress. "Two minutes late, to be exact."

"My most abject apologies," Hazel said, pressing her free hand to her chest and bowing in apology. She moved to a chair across the low table from Sophie and set her cane aside before grasping both arms of the chair and lowering herself into the seat as gracefully as possible without putting weight on her foot. "I shall pour to make up for my delay."

Sophie huffed a breath, remaining in character as she spread her skirts and regally lowered herself into her own chair with enviable ease.

Hazel leaned forward to pour the tea, grateful that Sophie didn't try to take over the task. It had always been important for Hazel to do everything she *could* do.

"Have you heard?" Sophie asked as Hazel handed her a cup, only half full because Sophie would add sugar and milk to the brim.

"What news?"

"Mrs. Cordon is selling the school."

Startled, Hazel sloshed tea onto the saucer of her own cup. She put down the kettle, an instant hollow forming in her stomach.

"You are joking," Hazel said as she sat back in her chair.

Sophie pursed her thin lips together as she shook her head and poured milk into her cup. "Mrs. Phillips told me just this morning. It seems that Mrs. Cordon's brother has convinced her to sell the school and use the profits toward the water projects he's been working on in the north. Apparently he's had a difficult time raising the necessary funds."

The hollow in Hazel's stomach widened. "Mrs. Cordon would be a fool to squander her investments on that man's latest hobbyhorse."

"I agree, but it sounds as though she's going to do it all the same." Sophie continued to share the gossip she'd learned from the school's head cook. Hazel struggled to focus on the details.

When Hazel had left for school at the tender age of six, she had not understood that school would become her residence and Falconridge would merely be a place she visited. By the time she'd become a teacher at St. Mary's, the school had felt like *home* mostly because she hadn't had a real home for such a long time that she didn't have anything to compare it with.

She'd felt the sharp sense of displacement when she'd come to Cordon, but Sophie had been with her, and Hazel believed that in time she would feel as comfortable here as she had at St. Mary's.

The new owner *might* share Mrs. Cordon's philosophy for educating girls at a higher level, but there was an equal chance, or better chance, really, that they wouldn't. What if Hazel were asked to reduce her maths courses to counting money and adding household accounts? What if they expected her to teach introductory embroidery or piano to justify her staying on with a reduced maths schedule? What if they didn't keep her at all?

"Are you alright, Hazel?"

Hazel looked up from where she had been staring into her teacup. "Certainly, just . . . surprised."

Sophie gave her a sympathetic smile. "And terrified, if you feel anything like I do. If the new owner does not keep the advanced programs . . ." Her words trailed off to silence.

Sophie was fifteen years older than Hazel and had buried her husband and child before starting a new life as a teacher. While basic mathematics was considered essential for a girl's education, there was little justification for a wife and mother to know any bit of Latin. Hazel was not the only person who faced trials and worried over an uncertain future.

Hazel tried to smile for the sake of comforting her friend.

Sophie smiled back for likely the same reason.

The silence stretched as they both stared into their cooling cups of tea.

# Chapter Four

"Well, then, I am off to the races."

Duncan looked up from the ledger he was copying to see Mr. Ludwig pop up from his desk on the other side of the room. Mr. Ludwig did not mean actual horse races; rather, it was a phrase he used regularly to explain that he was leaving the office.

Duncan glanced at the clock on the wall. "It is only a quarter 'til six."

Mr. Ludwig reached for his coat and hat hanging beside the door of their shared office. They had been working together for several months now, but it seemed like a much longer period of time due to the way the man increased Duncan's workload and continually grated on Duncan's nerves.

"I have finished my day's work, old boy, and will return in the morning to start anew."

Duncan did not like being called "old boy," but it was another phrase Mr. Ludwig liked to utilize in his regular speech. If the man would speak concisely and not force Duncan to translate the meaning behind the things he said, they would likely get on far better than they did. Oh, and it would be nice if Mr. Ludwig cared at all for accurate accounting practices and did not interfere with Duncan's relationship with the partners.

"Office hours are until six thirty on Tuesdays and Wednesdays," Duncan said slowly, as if he were talking to a child or someone for whom English was not their first language. "If you have finished the Carillon account, you may begin tomorrow's work."

On Mondays, Thursdays, and Fridays, office hours for the junior clerks went to 5:30. Duncan had spoken to the partners on seven different occasions about choosing the same time to end each of the five workdays of the week so as to mitigate confusion, but they did not find the varying times inconvenient since they left whenever they wished.

The varying end time of the workdays was only one of several details that Duncan would change if he were the one making the decisions. But since he was not the one making the decisions, he had no choice but to abide by the stipulations enforced by the partners. He was the senior employee on the premises right now, and therefore it was his responsibility to make sure the rules were followed.

"Hmm," Mr. Ludwig said as he walked to the clock located by the door and opened the glass face.

Duncan shot to his feet. "Mr. Ludwig!" He came around his desk and marched across the room while fumbling in his vest pocket for his pocket watch while Mr. Ludwig moved the hands of the clock.

Duncan was horrified. He wound his pocket watch every evening and checked the time with the clockmaker, Mr. Handlery, every Tuesday afternoon. Mr. Handlery's clock was kept to Greenwich Time and cross-checked monthly.

Mr. Ludwig stood in front of him, the grin gone from his

face. Duncan stepped left in order to move around him, but Mr. Ludwig stepped in the same direction, blocking Duncan's path to the clock.

"I have an appointment tonight, Mr. Penhale, and I will be on my way, is that understood?"

"Changing the time on the clock does not change the time," Duncan said, holding up his pocket watch to prove that he had possession of the actual time of day. The watch chain attached to Duncan's vest pulled tight.

He took a breath and forced himself to look Mr. Ludwig in the eye. Catherine had taught him it was an important social protocol he should use whenever possible, and he found it especially effective when he was trying to make a point, even though it made him uncomfortable.

"Office hours are until six thirty on Tuesday and Wednesdays—*that* is your appointment. Any other personal business you need to conduct must be done outside of business hours or with the stated permission of one of the partners. Since such permission has not been communicated to me, your early departure is a breach of policy."

Mr. Ludwig grabbed the pocket watch from Duncan's hand, snapping the chain, and threw it against the wall. The metal casing hit the wood panel like a stone and fell to the ground.

Duncan stared at the watch, his hands tightening into fists at his side.

"Unlike you, Mr. Penhale, I have a life outside of this miserable office," Mr. Ludwig said, hissing through his teeth, his misty spittle hitting Duncan's face.

"You are obligated by both employment and ethics to remain working until—"

"Go back to your desk, Mr. Penhale, and leave me be." He

moved to go around Duncan, but Duncan copied Mr. Ludwig's earlier practice and stepped to the side, further blocking the man's access to the door.

"You are not authorized to leave early."

"My uncle owns this firm, Mr. Penhale, and he has about had his fill of you. One more complaint from me and you may very well find yourself on the street, is that what you want?"

"That is not what I want nor is it worth my concern. Terminating me would be a serious error in judgment, as you are a very poor clerk and I am a very skilled one."

Mr. Ludwig laughed, but it was an odd sound that did not reflect amusement. He tried to step around Duncan a second time, and Duncan, fueled by his growing temper, once again blocked his passage.

"Take your place at your desk and finish the workday, Mr. Ludwig."

Mr. Ludwig growled low in his throat and shoved Duncan's right shoulder to move him out of the way. Upon the violent contact, Da's voice sounded in Duncan's head: *Never start the altercation, Dunny, but if a bloke hits you first, hit back twice as hard.*

Duncan caught himself mid-stumble, looked into Mr. Ludwig's face to take aim, and punched the other man straight in the nose.

Mr. Ludwig spun around and was beginning to fall when Duncan grabbed him by the arm and pulled him upright so he could hit him again even though a second hit was not justified by anything other than Duncan's anger, which was no justification in and of itself.

After the third punch, Duncan remembered Catherine's additional advice: "If you cannot control the situation by the third hit—run."

He let go, and Mr. Ludwig crumpled to the ground with a groan. Duncan watched carefully in order to assess if he had adequately taken control of this situation or if it was in his best interest to run.

Mr. Ludwig continued to groan for several seconds before rolling onto his knees, the back of his coat comically flipped over his head and his backside stuck into the air. When he looked up at Duncan, his eyes were wide and his demeanor cowering.

Duncan determined he did not have to run. He shook out his hand; he'd forgotten how painful it was to hit someone. He put out his unaffected hand to help Mr. Ludwig stand as a gesture of sportsmanship, even though they had not been sporting with one another.

Mr. Ludwig crawled away from Duncan's outstretched hand. "Good grief, what is wrong with you?"

Duncan lowered the hand Mr. Ludwig had refused and straightened his waistcoat instead, which had ridden up, exposing an inch of his shirt underneath. "You cannot change time by changing the clock, nor can you change rules for your own gratification, Mr. Ludwig." He pointed at the victimized clock. "Both practices cheat the partners of your time. It is my responsibility as senior junior clerk to ensure honesty and punctuality."

He walked to the clock, but then remembered he needed to verify the time on his pocket watch, which Mr. Ludwig had thrown to the opposite side of the room. He changed course, and Mr. Ludwig crawled quickly out of Duncan's path.

Duncan picked up the watch and flipped open the battered cover before raising it to his ear. He smiled with relief and made eye contact with Mr. Ludwig. "You are lucky that it is still working, otherwise I would have demanded you pay for the repair.

This is a verge fusee and was used by my father when he served in the King's navy."

He walked back to the clock and compared it to his pocket watch. He adjusted the hands back to the proper time of 5:49. Duncan preferred clocks with a minute hand and was glad that the one at the office had one.

When he turned back, he saw Mr. Ludwig was standing but still staring at him, in what Duncan interpreted as a slightly cowering posture.

"There is a trickle of blood coming from your nose," Duncan said as he crossed back to his desk. "You have five minutes to see to it in the washroom, then I expect you back at your desk. We will stay until 6:40 to make up for the lost time of this altercation and necessary cleanup." Duncan was entrusted with the office keys, so he would have to stay late as well, but then he usually stayed late proofing and correcting Mr. Ludwig's work.

Mr. Ludwig left the room without saying a word, but Duncan did not understand why he took his coat and hat with him. At 6:08, Duncan went to check on him on the washroom, but there was no indication Mr. Ludwig had even gone to the back of the office. Perhaps Mr. Ludwig had thought Duncan meant that he should see to his injury in the washroom at the apartments he shared with his wife a few blocks away. Duncan should have been clearer in his instructions, but the miscommunication did not change the fact that Mr. Ludwig had still cheated the partners of his time.

Duncan worked until nearly seven o'clock on the Carillon account. Mr. Ludwig had been the original clerk assigned to copy the figures, but he had scratched out two mistakes, which was unacceptable for a clean copy. Mr. Cromley, Mr. Ludwig's uncle, had told Duncan several months ago to stop bringing complaints to him about Mr. Ludwig, specifying that he was running out of patience with Duncan's dissatisfaction. Well, Duncan was losing patience with staying late at the office; Elizabeth was ornery when he finally arrived home and would sometimes snub him for the whole of the evening. Mr. Ludwig was coming to work late more often too, which did not bother Elizabeth but certainly contributed to Duncan's late hours.

More and more often, Duncan found himself considering how things might be different if he were the one setting hours and expectations. If he owned the Burrow Building, he could open his own accounting office and finish his work at the same time every evening. Elizabeth would like that, too.

However, the only way he could own the building would be if he received the inheritance from Lord Howardsford, which required he marry a woman of genteel birth. There were some women at church who fit the parameters, but he had tried several times over the years to speak to them, and it had never produced satisfying results. Women, he had determined, did not generally like him. Elizabeth, Delores, and Hazel seemed to be the only exceptions. He did not want to marry a woman who did not like him, and he was quite sure Elizabeth would not like for him to be married any more than Duncan would. What if the woman he married did not like Elizabeth?

Duncan finished his work and tidied first his desk and then Mr. Ludwig's, which was always left scattered and unaligned. He retrieved his coat and hat from the rack designated for his articles, exited the office, and locked the door.

Three doors down from Perkins & Cromley was Ye Old Pub, where Delores had his dinner wrapped in paper and waiting for him, a daily service for which he paid her weekly each Monday.

He thanked her and went out again—it was very loud in the pub in the evenings.

Delores had been Catherine's friend first, but then Catherine had died, and now Delores was Duncan's friend. She liked to talk to him about his problems and sometimes gave him advice on how to rectify a situation that had gone awry, but she knew that he did not like to linger when the pub was busy so he knew it would not hurt her feelings that he had left so quickly. The door just east of the pub was painted dark brown. He used another key on his ring to unlock it, then walked up the narrow stairs and unlocked the door on the right side of the small landing.

The door on the left side of the landing allowed entry into the rooms rented by Mr. MacDonald, who was a Scotsman. Duncan enjoyed talking to Mr. MacDonald about history as he was very well educated on the subject. Mr. MacDonald was a glover, so he knew quite a bit about fabrics and construction. He also had a fair mind for practical math, though he did not play number games.

Sometimes Mr. MacDonald would drink too much and become very sad about his wife who had left him. Duncan would make him strong coffee and make him eat bread, like he had learned to do with Catherine when she drank too much, and sit with him until he fell asleep. Sometimes it took most of the night, and Duncan would be very tired the next day, but Mr. MacDonald was his friend and very lonely without his wife, so Duncan did not complain and made sure to always have coffee and bread on hand.

This circumstance had not happened for nine days, which meant there was a high probability that Mr. MacDonald would get drunk in the next few days. He rarely went more than a fortnight. Duncan made a note to buy bread tomorrow and plan to eat dinner with Mr. MacDonald.

Elizabeth was waiting when Duncan let himself into the apartment and immediately began vocalizing her complaints at his lateness.

"I know, I know," Duncan placated as he tried to cross the floor despite her determination to prevent it. "It was Mr. Ludwig again. He is as useful as a box of rocks—good for propping open a door but not much else." He smiled at his joke and looked at Elizabeth for a reaction, but she only blinked her green eyes and yowled again.

"I punched him in the nose today," Duncan said, still feeling a bit of a rush about it. Da had started teaching Duncan how to hit when he was five years old, teaching him more techniques of defending himself as Duncan grew older. Catherine had expressed concern over Da encouraging violence, but Da had said, "If there's ever been a boy who needs to stand up for himself, it's Duncan. He'll be drawing the wrong sort of attention all his life." Back then, Duncan hadn't understood how he was any different than other boys, but as he'd grown older, he'd become more aware.

Duncan appreciated routine and rules, he was not shy about sharing what he knew, and he did not feel the penchant for gossip and small talk that wasted so much time. He believed in working hard and finding one's own amusement rather than expecting other people to entertain him, and he was quick to point out when rules were broken. Those differences often led other boys to assault him out of irritation or annoyance or just not understanding Duncan's position.

Duncan never hit first—Da had been very clear on that rule—but he'd used his fists a fair amount when he was young.

Such events had lessened as he'd grown into a man who could more easily choose his associations, but he appreciated Da's foresight in teaching him a skill he could use to defend himself when the situation arose.

Elizabeth jumped onto the counter, and he scratched her behind her ear the way she liked. "I am sure Delores put it right here," he said, unwrapping the newsprint-wrapped parcel. Inside was a jacket potato dripping with butter, a slice of bread, and two thick pieces of fried haddock. He put the smaller portion of fish in Elizabeth's bowl—she was, after all, the smaller of the two of them—and put the larger piece on his plate with the potato. Elizabeth did not like potatoes, though she would sometimes lick the butter from the paper.

On nights when Duncan was late leaving the office, Delores would put his dinner on the warmer, a very kind gesture. Cold fish suited Elizabeth just fine, but he was more particular. On the weekends, Duncan did his own cooking on the stove in his apartment, shopping for ingredients on Saturday morning and enjoying the improvements he made to his favorite dishes. He especially liked fried ham steak and split pea soup.

Elizabeth finished her dinner first, as usual, and began weaving around his legs as he continued eating while standing. The sound of her purring made him smile between bites. Catherine had never let him keep more than one cat at a time, and she had never allowed them into the house.

Duncan had come to appreciate her wisdom after trying to keep three cats when he'd first moved into this small apartment. The transition had been uncomfortable for Duncan as he'd lived in the other rooms for eight years by then; having as many cats as he liked had seemed like a good way to mitigate the discomfort.

Cats, as it turned out, do not usually like each other very much, and cats fighting in a small apartment was very distressing.

He had settled his attention on Elizabeth, the most personable of the three cats, and stopped allowing the other two cats inside. He still saw one of the other two cats from time to time on the streets, but it no longer approached him, and he liked to think the animal understood Duncan's reasoning, even though there was no research to suggest cats had that sort of comprehensive ability.

He'd adapted the window of his bedroom so Elizabeth could come and go while he was at work, which pleased her a great deal and improved the smell in the apartment, which had been foul after she'd been trapped inside all day. They were good company for one another in the evenings, and she slept on his feet at night, which kept his coal use more efficient than it would be otherwise, which made up for the loss of heat due to the window that Elizabeth used during the day.

He cut another bite of his potato and looked out the single window of his main room. He could see the lights of other apartments across the alley and hear the sound of laughter from patrons leaving the pub below. Da had died when Duncan was eleven years old, but he had taught Duncan to count and to fight, two skills that had proven very useful. Catherine had taught Duncan how to write letters and numbers, and how to read. It wasn't until Duncan was a young man that he'd realized his father had been illiterate. Catherine, on the other hand, had been educated by a governess at Howard House and knew all sorts of things, even French.

After Da died, she was often sad and drank too much, like Mr. MacDonald, but she had been a lovely singer and had always been kind to Duncan. It was after Catherine died that Duncan first met Lord Howardsford, Catherine's brother and a viscount in Norfolk. Lord Howardsford had already been paying for Duncan's schooling, but after they met, he'd arranged for Duncan to apprentice with Mr. Perkins and Mr. Cromley. Duncan liked the rudimentary and monotonous work well enough and was glad not to have to work as a laborer the way Da had after the war.

Duncan liked his rooms on the top floor of the Burrow Building. He liked that he could keep Elizabeth inside. He liked to take walks around the city and through the nearby wooded areas, do puzzles or read in the evening, cook on Saturday, and attend church services on Sunday mornings. He liked to read the paper when he could get a copy. He liked to visit with his associates in the village and to buy meat pies from the vendor on the corner. He liked to write letters back and forth with Hazel.

He liked to buy a book every month from the book trader on Essex Street, which he would then read several times to make sure he had learned all he could about the topic. If he got tired of a book before the month was finished, he would trade it for a different book. He owned sixteen books of his own, a small but excellent library if one considered content more valuable than quantity.

Sometimes Duncan wondered if there might be other things he would enjoy, but there seemed little point in trying to discover what those things might be if the attempts interfered with the things he knew he already liked.

A woman laughed below his window, and he thought of Hazel. Besides Catherine and Delores, his interaction with Hazel had been the most enjoyable he'd ever shared with a woman. She spoke to him clearly and had not laughed at him or taken offense through the whole course of their conversations, of which there had been three on the one day they had shared company—one at breakfast, one at lunch, and one in the drawing room after dinner. He found it easier to look at her eyes than with most other people; maybe because her eyes were hazel, just like her name, and he liked the symmetry of those facts.

Delores had been the one to encourage him to write Hazel a letter and continue their number games after he had told Delores how enjoyable their conversations had been. He'd found the correspondence equally enjoyable and always wrote to Hazel on Thursday nights three weeks after receiving her letter. Delores had told him that was an acceptable time between letters; Duncan did not wish to annoy Hazel with too much correspondence.

He felt sure that if he and Hazel were to be in company at Howard House again one day, he would enjoy it even more than he had their first encounter. He wished she'd come to Howard House at Easter time so they could have had more time together. That had been his strongest motivation to attend, as he did not like to travel. He was concerned of her lack of education regarding the history of mathematics and felt that time together would allow him to teach her what she had missed. There was no doubt that a more substantial education would improve her overall passion for the subject. It certainly had improved his own.

Elizabeth jumped onto the brown sofa on the other side of the room and began licking her fur as she did multiple times a day. She often dug her claws into the sides of the couch and stretched, which had shredded the fabric. It was unsightly, but he'd come to think of the sofa as her domain, and so he allowed her to keep it as she liked and focused his attention on keeping the rest of the apartment tidy and organized.

Did Hazel like cats? What would she think about him punching Mr. Ludwig in the nose?

Perhaps he would ask her these things in his next letter.

# Chapter Five

August 19, 1823

Dear Cousin Hazel,

 I hope you will forgive my writing you before getting your response to my last letter and that I did not write to you on a Thursday three weeks after receiving your letter, as is my usual routine, but there have been some developments with my situation that warrant this breach of pattern between us. I wonder if there might be an opportunity for us to speak in person about a potential solution to my current problems, and perhaps to your own as well. Would you kindly write to me as soon as possible with some days that would be most convenient for me to come to King's Lynn? Would you also inform me of the particular process I should take to notify you of my arrival and arrange a private meeting?

 Thank you for your consideration. I hope to hear from you soon.

Sincerely,
*Mr. D. Penhale*

Sophie finished reading the letter and lowered it to her lap, though her eyes remained on the page. "After nearly a year and a half of exchanging letters, he still addresses you as 'Cousin Hazel' and signs his name as 'Sincerely, Mr. D. Penhale'?"

Hazel let out an exasperated sigh. "That is all you have to say?"

"Do you sign your letters to him 'Ms. H. Stillman'?"

"No," Hazel said tightly, waving toward the letter on her friend's lap. "What are your thoughts concerning the contents? Is it not strange that he will come all the way to Lynn from Ipswich just to talk with me? That is a very long journey, and he does not like to travel; in fact, this might be the longest travel he has ever embarked upon in the whole of his life."

Sophie shifted in her chair and crossed one leg over the other, bouncing her foot that peeked out from beneath her solid blue skirt. They were allowed to wear only solid-colored dresses at school, which Sophie found irritating as she liked to dress in all manner of colors and patterns. Hazel, on the other hand, preferred plain and simple dresses and owned only one striped dress that, in comparison to the rest of her wardrobe, felt so overstated she rarely wore it even when she could.

"So, you sign your letters casually, and he continues to sign his more formally. Do you use 'Sincerely' as well?"

Hazel put her tea saucer on the table with a thump. "I do not want to debate salutations or valedictions; I want to discuss him coming all this way to talk to me."

Sophie blinked at her, then cocked her head and looked her up and down as though assessing a bolt of cloth. "I think you should wear the striped dress. What better opportunity will you have to show off the fine cut? I have always thought purple your best color, and so the striped dress is the perfect choice, I think."

"Enough," Hazel said, reaching for her cane and using it to push herself up from the chair. This was why she did not discuss her personal life—not that she had much of a personal life. Duncan's letter had been so surprising, however, that she'd obsessed over it for a full day before deciding to ask Sophie's help making sense of it.

"Don't leave. I am sorry for taking fun in your letter," Sophie said, rising to her feet with a single movement that seemed to defy gravity. She gestured to Hazel's empty chair. "Sit down, and let us discuss it in actuality."

Hazel hesitated, shifting her weight to her bad foot to relieve the increasing pain in her left hip. She *could* limp out of the teacher's parlor with her nose in the air and leave Sophie to her regrets, but then she would have no help making sense of the letter.

She sat.

Sophie gave her a grateful and apologetic smile. "What do you think of Mr. D. Penhale? Do you like him?"

"I like Duncan well enough. He is . . . unique."

Sophie raised her eyebrows but said nothing as she added enough milk and sugar to bring the tea to the rim of her cup.

Hazel shifted to her side; the pain in her left hip made sitting as uncomfortable as standing sometimes. "I have enjoyed his letters. He is very intelligent and . . . thorough."

"'Thorough'?" Sophie repeated, her tone flat. "Is that a compliment or a complaint?"

"Compliment," Hazel said, but she frowned. "I think."

Sophie smiled, then tapped her spoon on the side of the cup before placing it on the saucer. "He is a financial clerk in Ipswich? You have said very little about him to me."

Hazel wished now that she'd been more forthcoming, but she hadn't known exactly how to explain Duncan, and so she . . .

hadn't. She looked toward the pink curtains framing the window. A black horse pulled a black carriage with large yellow wheels past the window, and she wondered how Duncan planned to travel the sixty-five miles from Ipswich to King's Lynn. Mail coach? She did not imagine he could afford to hire a private carriage. She hoped the trip would not be too uncomfortable for him.

"Nothing in those paltry details explains why you would be anxious about his visit," Sophie said.

Hazel looked back at her. "I am not anxious."

"Yes, you are, dear." She took another sip. "Perhaps if I had a better understanding of how you and Duncan interacted that day in Norfolk I could better know how we should proceed with this conversation."

Hazel looked at the fraying brocade on the arm of her chair and picked at the fibers with her fingernail as she centered her thoughts. She took a breath and explained Duncan, as best she could. "He is personable, good with numbers, attentive, honest, odd."

"What do you mean by 'odd'?"

"Well, on the day we met—the only day we've ever spent in one another's company—he needed me to justify our addressing each other as cousins. He also does not look me in the eye when we speak." The memory made her smile, but she tried to suppress it so as not to give the wrong impression. "He became so excited about the ham served at breakfast that he brought me a slice to try for myself. He mentioned my foot . . . out loud."

"He did?" Sophie said, eyebrows raised again. "What exactly did he say?"

Hazel felt her cheeks warm at the memory. "I had said I had no prospects for marriage, and he said, 'Is that because of your

. . . deformed foot?' Only he did not pause as I did just now. He said it as easily as he might have commented on the weather."

Sophie choked on her tea. She put down her cup and lifted a napkin to her mouth. Her eyes were watering as she lowered the napkin. "Gracious. You were discussing marital ambitions over breakfast the first day you met? And he called your foot—"

Hazel understood why her friend could not say the word. However, she suddenly realized she hadn't explained the marriage campaign to Sophie. Hazel had not wanted to admit that her uncle wished to buy a husband for her, which was perhaps why she'd said so little about Duncan—he was tied to that entire experience at Howard House. And now she had to explain everything, a year and a half later, with Duncan's upcoming visit making every detail more uncomfortable.

"Hazel?"

Hazel opened her eyes and looked across the table at Sophie who appeared genuinely concerned. "What is it? Is there something you haven't told me that I need to know to make sense of this?"

Hazel remembered one of the Latin phrases Sophie had taught her over the years: *Audentes fortuna juvat*—fortune favors the bold. Hazel pulled together whatever boldness she possessed. "Well," she said, focusing on her friend and trying to be the person Sophie believed her to be. "My uncle had given both of us a . . . proposition."

# Chapter Six

The doorknob to the teacher's parlor turned, and Hazel swallowed. She spread the skirts of her purple-striped dress one more time, double-checking that her hideous boot was covered.

Last night, her right knee had given out on her as she'd readied herself for bed. She had been moving too fast because it was cold in her room and she was eager to get into bed. She'd fallen hard against the bedrail before crumpling to the floor. It had taken her almost an hour to get up, and then she'd slept poorly. That morning, she could hardly walk. Gretchen and Sophie had helped her down the stairs, and Cook had wrapped her knee enough for her to walk with her cane. At least she hadn't bruised her face in the fall.

As the door opened, she smiled and reminded herself that Duncan had once said she was well-featured. That long-ago compliment gave her *some* confidence now, and she desperately needed any confidence she could muster.

Gretchen entered first, curiosity prominent on her features. It was not often a teacher requested a private meeting with a male visitor.

"Mr. Duncan Penhale to see you, Miss Stillman."

"Thank you, Gretchen." Hazel gave the girl a small smile before turning her attention to the man following her into the room.

Duncan looked awkward and out of place in the faculty parlor. He did not look at her as he entered the room, gazing instead at the rose-colored curtains and the pieces of furniture as if they held particular interest for him, which she did not think they did. The furnishings were good quality, but worn and old-fashioned. Rather like herself, she thought.

Gretchen stepped aside so Duncan could come further into the room. He took two steps then stopped. Gretchen left the room, the door clicking softly behind her.

Social protocol would have Hazel ask after his journey and discuss the weather, but Duncan was not the type of man to expect, or perhaps even want, such rote behavior.

"You may sit across from me, Duncan," she said. "Do you still prefer one sugar and no milk in your tea?"

Duncan sat in the chair she'd indicated on the opposite side of the tea table between them. The school cook prepared a limited selection of sweet and savory items for teatimes, so Sophie had visited the corner bakery that morning to round out the selection with some macarons, marzipan, and sweet breads. Sophie had also changed out the usual four-inch plates used for teatime with a standard dinner plate.

Her effort was validated by the way Duncan's face lit up. He thanked her and put three of each item on his plate before picking up the bright-pink macaron located in the twelve o'clock position and lifting it almost reverently to his mouth.

"This looks delicious, Cousin Hazel. Thank you."

"You are welcome, Duncan," she said, pouring the tea.

She expected him to comment on her dropping of the "cousin" in her address, but the food seemed to have distracted him. He ate so intently she wondered if he'd forgotten she was there or why he'd come all this way.

When he'd tried one of everything, he put the plate on the table, took a sip of tea, and returned it to the saucer; only then did he lift his head enough that she knew she had his attention, even though he did not look her in the eye.

"Thank you for seeing me," he said, leaning forward to move his cup and saucer to sit directly next to the dinner plate. "My reason for coming is of great importance."

"So your letter stated," Hazel said, layering her hands in her lap. Sophie had done Hazel's hair in a softer style despite Hazel insisting that Duncan would not notice. "I have been anxiously awaiting this meeting."

He cocked his head slightly. "Anxiously awaiting or eagerly awaiting? 'Anxious' means that you are nervous, whereas 'eager' denotes excited anticipation."

"Well, then, I suppose eagerly anxious anticipation would be the best description."

He did not smile. "You said eager first, which implies that you are more excitedly anticipatory than you are nervous. Is that correct?"

It was tempting to tease him with wordplay, but she did not. "Yes, Duncan. That is correct."

"Why do you feel excited?"

"Why don't I answer that after you tell me why you came all this way for this meeting?"

"Oh, yes, that is a fair request," he said, straightening in his chair rather formally. He met her eye and smiled, but both gestures were stiff. After two seconds—he might very well have counted them out they were timed so exactly—his eyes shifted to the table between them, and his smile relaxed into one that looked more natural on his face.

He had a nice jawline, defined and cleanly shaven, though she could see the dark shadow of what would be a beard if he were less attentive. His hair was combed back with pomade, as it had been the last time she'd seen him, and there were flecks of silver in his sideburns that she had not noticed before.

"I think that you and I should marry one another and claim our inheritances from Uncle Elliott in order to secure our futures."

Hazel had expected the marriage proposal—it was what she and Sophie had concluded would be the only reason big enough to warrant his journey all the way to Lynn—and yet a shivery feeling ran through her chest and belly at the words. She took a breath to help the sensation pass, then focused on his precise words.

"What do you mean by 'secure our futures'?"

"I am unhappy with my employment situation, and in your last letter to me, you said your school is to be sold, which makes your future insecure. If we marry, I will become owner of the Burrow Building and you will receive fifty thousand pounds."

"*You* would receive fifty thousand pounds," she corrected.

"Within the legal precept, yes, your dowry will become mine, but it shall be at your disposal as I will have no need of it. You could build your life independently, as you wish. It is the perfect solution to both of our problems and gives us both what we do not have—security."

The defensiveness shifted, and she ignored the disappointment as she released the romantic fantasies—and romantic fears—she had allowed to grow the last two weeks since having received his letter. Focus was essential, and she would not allow herself to be distracted.

"You would give me full discretion over my dowry?"

"It was bestowed upon you just as the Burrow Building was bestowed upon me. You deserve to have full control of it. You could buy your school."

The air in the room froze, and Hazel blinked at him. "Buy Cordon Academy?"

"You said in your letter dated August fifth that the current owner of Cordon Academy was looking to sell. She should sell it to you, and you should continue to offer the advanced classes that girls deserve access to the same as boys—it is what you have explained is your wish and desire. You can then make any changes you feel appropriate to the curriculum and run the school yourself."

Hazel opened her mouth but could find no words.

Duncan popped up from the chair and began pacing in the space between the chair and the window. "For my part," he explained, "I shall become the owner of the Burrow Building and can work from my own accounting office that will be dedicated to proper practices of finance. I can set the office hours from nine a.m. to six p.m. and only hire competent junior clerks as my assistants. I shall make income from the rents of the building and have more control over who I rent to—for instance, I shall give Mr. Southey immediate notice. He dumps his bin in the alley and has regular altercations with Delores over any number of petty irritants that do not warrant his interference."

He continued explaining his plans for the Burrow Building for several minutes, giving Hazel adequate time to consider this idea from every possible direction. When he finished repeating himself, he stopped pacing and looked at her, direct and in the eye.

"Are you agreeable to this arrangement?"

"My school"—she blushed at having taken ownership already—"*this* school is in King's Lynn; the Burrow Building is in Ipswich. We would . . . live separately?"

"Of course," Duncan said with a nod. "As the marriage is solely for the purpose of attaining our inheritances, there is no need for cohabitation."

Hazel nodded, feeling the prick of disappointment again before arguing herself out of it. When she'd thought he was coming to propose marriage, she'd wondered how she would determine if any stated affection was genuine and not based solely on the wealth he would receive upon their marriage. She should have known he would not pretend to feel anything he did not feel. *Focus.* He did not love her, and he did not want her money.

"Separate locations are in the best interest of us and Elizabeth," he said before she'd managed to determine what to say out loud.

"Elizabeth?" Hazel said, her thoughts taking another sharp turn. "Who is Elizabeth?"

It was after dinner when Sophie knocked on Hazel's door, two knocks, a pause, and two more knocks—as was her signal. She had accompanied the girls on a day trip to the pier, and though Hazel would have liked to analyze her meeting with Duncan with Sophie before now, she appreciated having time to review it on her own.

"Come in," Hazel called.

Gretchen had already helped her into her nightdress and into bed. She could not use the maid as her personal assistant regularly, however, she appreciated the help tonight. Her knee was badly bruised from last night's fall, and though she'd rubbed it with lavender oil and wrapped it tightly, it ached something awful.

Sophie let herself in and pulled the chair from its place beside the dresser to the edge of Hazel's bed. She leaned in with bright anticipation in her eyes. "Tell me everything!"

"He wants us to marry in name only so he might gain his inheritance of the Burrow Building. He will then give the entire fifty thousand pounds of my dowry to me so I may build my own independent life."

Sophie's eyes went wide, and she remained perfectly still for several seconds. "What?"

Hazel repeated the explanation, and Sophie leaned against the chair back. "In name only? Oh, Hazel . . ."

Hazel shook her head quickly to waylay the regretful tone. "It is all right. As I told you, I was not sure I could be his wife, and I have no worry for that now. He is not the sort of man any woman could tolerate for long—he paced for the whole of his explanation, then sat down to eat a second round of refreshment, and then popped back up to pace while essentially repeating everything he'd already said. He barely let me get a word in edgewise. *But* he was not the least bit deceitful in his presentation, which I appreciate. I feel that I know exactly what to expect from him."

"You would never be able to marry anyone else," Sophie said, her eyes still wide. "Both of you would be legally committed to one another for the duration of your lives."

"I will not marry anyone else anyway, you know this."

"I know that is what you have always believed, but what if you meet a man who makes your heart skip and—"

"I am willing to take that risk," Hazel said, because it was not a true risk. "He suggested I purchase Cordon Academy with the money from my dowry and manage my own school."

Sophie froze just as Hazel had when Duncan had proposed the idea in the drawing room. Then she leaned forward and grabbed for Hazel's hand, full understanding dawning on her round face. "Oh, my goodness," she breathed.

Hazel looked Sophie in the eye. "Now, you must understand that I do not believe my uncle will allow it; he has to approve our partners, and Duncan and I marrying one another is not at all in keeping with his purpose in offering these inheritances, but . . ."

"But?" Sophie repeated.

Hazel took a breath and lowered her guard enough to let Sophie into the fantasy growing in her mind. She was a fool to even consider it, but the idea would not let go of her. "If, for some reason, this actually works and I receive fifty thousand pounds, would you help me run Cordon Academy as an advanced school for girls?"

Sophie gasped and took hold of both of Hazel's hands. Hazel remained silent, watching Sophie work through all the thoughts racing in her mind.

Tears began to fill her friend's eyes. "Do you mean it, Hazel?"

Hazel nodded and felt a lump in her own throat both from offering such an opportunity and fearing that it would never be reality. Focusing on this possibility was how she had managed her feelings about not being asked to be a real wife.

"I am only twenty-eight years old, but you and I, together, with fifty thousand pounds at our disposal . . ." Hazel smiled.

"We could create a school that we ourselves could only have dreamed of when we were girls."

"A school of your own," Sophie breathed, sitting back in her chair and releasing Hazel's hands.

"Of *our* own," Hazel said. "Partners, legal and binding. Of course, saying this is completely premature, but—"

"Our school," Sophie breathed.

Her excitement was almost too much for Hazel to bear, and she hoped she had not made a mistake in saying so much. "Assuming my uncle agrees, which I do not think he will, so we must not get our hopes up."

Sophie leaned forward, took Hazel's hands again and lowered her head. "Our most righteous Lord," she said in a soft voice. It took a moment for Hazel to realize Sophie was praying. *Oh dear . . .*

"Please hear the prayers of your daughters, who, through trial and struggle, have worked unfailingly to do good in this fallen world. Soften the heart of Hazel's uncle, sharpen the desire of her own heart, and help us to navigate whatever might lie ahead."

The words of Sophie's spontaneous prayer echoed in Hazel's room long into the night. Hazel had never said a prayer of her own, had never attended church outside of those services required at St. Mary's. She had decided long ago that she had no place for a god who would give her a deformity that made it impossible for her to be loved. Not by her parents. Not by a man. Not by the children she would never have. It was far easier to view the world simply as a place where life was created, sometimes with mutations, and then that life died into nothingness. When others talked of God, she listened to their stories the same way she listened to Greek mythology and Irish folklore.

Sophie, however, had spoken to God in her prayer as though

he were right there in the room, as though he would hear them and grant them their desires like a fairy godmother from a child's tale.

Hazel would have scoffed and pulled her hands from the supplication but for the sincerity of Sophie's intention and the . . . softening of the air in the room. The air had remained peaceful even after Sophie retired for the night, and though Hazel did not necessarily feel comfortable within . . . whatever had been left behind, she felt a peculiar energy that made her think that maybe that prayer had invited something metaphysical into their sphere.

And maybe that something would change things, and her life would not forever be limping from one school to the next to earn her daily bread. Maybe the result of that prayer would be something more than anything she'd dared hope for. She closed her eyes and filled her lungs with the soft air of the room, holding it close for a few moments.

Maybe.

Probably not.

Perhaps.

# Chapter Seven

*I*t is a reasonable solution for all of us," Duncan said to Lord Howardsford after he finished repeating the explanation he'd given to Hazel a fortnight ago in the drawing room at her school in King's Lynn where she had served him those excellent macarons. Saturday, September 13—today—had been the soonest Hazel could leave the school long enough to accommodate the travel to Howard House.

The meeting with her had gone so well that Duncan assumed it would go as well today. Things had become nearly unbearable at the office since he'd punched Mr. Ludwig in the nose.

The partners had not agreed with Duncan's justification in hitting Mr. Ludwig—even though Duncan had told them Mr. Ludwig had shoved him first—and instead of reprimanding the other man for leaving early, they had moved the lout into Mr. Cromley's office. Duncan was glad to have his office to himself again, but he was being given less new work to do and primarily proofed Mr. Ludwig's work, which had not improved in quality.

The partners interacted with him very little, even Mr. Perkins with whom Duncan had always been on friendly terms. Mr.

Ludwig acted as though Duncan were not there at all, laughed louder, left within minutes of the partners leaving each day, and, Duncan suspected, purposely did his work even more poorly than usual because he knew it irritated Duncan to have to fix it.

Duncan had chosen not to inform Lord Howardsford of the situation at the office because he did not know what the older man thought of violence, even if the violence was justified by self-defense. Also, though the proposal of he and Hazel marrying was both logical and brilliant, he needed Lord Howardsford's good favor for this pursuit to be successful and therefore did not want to share anything of a negative nature.

Lord Howardsford did not respond for seven seconds after Duncan finished his explanation, so Duncan summarized the proposal in case the lengthier explanation had created confusion. He felt quite energized, which made him talkative.

"Cousin Hazel can secure her future with the purchase of Cordon Academy, I can open my own office that keeps consistent hours and hires competent junior clerks, and you will have achieved the goal of having your niece and nephew properly married as you feel is right."

Duncan took a breath, quite satisfied with how this was going. He had arrived nearly an hour before Hazel. The travel from Ipswich had been horrible, as he'd known it would be, and he'd walked the grounds until her hired carriage had arrived, then hurried to meet her so they could enter Howard House together.

She had smelled of lavender, as she always did, which he liked very much. They'd had a delicious lunch, just the two of them due to the hour of their arrival, and Hazel had agreed to let him do the talking when they met with Lord Howardsford. Not that Hazel would have done a poor job had she served as mouthpiece—she continued to impress him with her personable disposition and quick intellect—but as the plan was his idea, it seemed fair that he be the one to present it.

When he'd said as much to Hazel, she had smiled and said, "By all means. Take the lead."

Lord Howardsford stared back at Duncan, his expression unreadable, though many expressions were difficult for Duncan to interpret. Duncan looked at Hazel, who fidgeted with the lace at the cuff of her white-and-purple-striped dress—the same dress she had worn when they met together in King's Lynn. Fidgeting with her cuff was a nervous movement, and he felt bad that she was feeling unsettled. It was much more comfortable to feel confident and optimistic.

"So," Lord Howardsford said, drawing Duncan's attention back to him.

Duncan straightened in his chair, anticipating Lord Howardsford's positive response and imagining Mr. Cromley's regretful reaction when Duncan marched into the office and told them he was now their landlord, would not work for them anymore, and would be setting up a new office in Mr. Southey's room in direct competition with their own business, which now only employed one incompetent junior clerk.

"Your plan is that you and Hazel marry each other"—he waved his hand between the two of them—"in order to collect your inheritances and . . . ?"

After six seconds of silence, Hazel said, "That is all."

Duncan looked at her and then back at Lord Howardsford, whose lips were rather pale and pinched. He looked an awful lot like Catherine had when she was angry, which made sense since they were siblings and would therefore have similar expressions but did *not* make sense because Lord Howardsford had no reason to be angry. Unless he was angry about the plan Duncan had presented.

"This proposal perfectly fulfills the terms of our contracts," Hazel said to her uncle, lifting her chin in what looked like defiance. "Therefore, I do not see how you can object."

"Actually," Duncan cut in, lifting a finger as a physical signal of his interruption for the sake of clarification. "I do not fulfill the terms of Hazel's contract in regard to her finding a husband of gentle birth. That is the one weakness of our plan, but we are hopeful that your regard for me will override your prejudice against the working class and—"

"Prejudice?" Lord Howardsford said, without any indication he was going to interrupt. He sat up straighter in his chair. "I am not prejudiced against the working class."

"I would respectfully argue that point, my Lord. You wrote into both of our contracts that our intended partners must be of gentle birth, which shows a preference for those of gentry class over those of working class."

"I am not prejudiced," Lord Howardsford said again, his neck turning red. "I only want to ensure equanimity of status and situation, as those are important elements in a happy marriage."

"If equanimity is the goal, then my terms should state I should find a wife of working class, as that is my status and situation and the class into which I was born and raised," Duncan said.

"I am also working class," Hazel added. "Which means that if it is *equanimity* you wish to achieve, I should not be required to marry a gentleman."

"Hazel," Lord Howardsford said, looking at her directly. "You are of gentle birth and—"

"Twenty-eight years old, crippled, dependent on myself for my support, and smarter than most men." She shrugged, which Duncan found perplexing, as her voice was animated and reflected intense feeling. "I was also educated in an all-girl's school and have taught in all-girl's schools for more than a decade. I can count on two hands the men I have had actual conversations with in the last five years."

She held up her two hands, palms facing Lord Howardsford. She lowered one finger at a time as she continued. "You, Duncan, and Harry top that list. Then comes Mr. Fawson, the seventy-three-year-old gardener at St. Mary's. The other six men are fathers of my students who either wanted to discuss their daughter's progress or debate some point of scholarship with a woman for the game of trying to best me, which they rarely did."

Duncan laughed at the summation of Hazel's prospects, but then stopped when both Hazel and Lord Howardsford looked at him, their expressions void of any humor.

Lord Howardsford frowned. "Fathers of students are excellent prospects for you, Hazel. Perhaps you should not dismiss them so easily."

Hazel's jaw tightened.

"He does make a point," Duncan said.

"Be quiet, Duncan," Hazel said, looking only at Lord Howardsford.

He went quiet.

"I will not be marrying anyone, Uncle Elliott, unless you approve Duncan. I have no interest in the sort of man who would marry me for money, and I have no romantic fantasies for any man to fulfill. Duncan is not just the only option for me, but the perfect one. He will have his own financial security, he will allow me full discretion to the money I would inherit, and he's comfortable living a separate life of his own."

"Marriage should not be about living separate lives," Lord Howardsford said.

"Many partners give less accommodation to their marital

status than either of us would. We have already proven to be effective communicators in regard to finances and other life changes. Should we need someone to help us sort out personal problems, we would likely turn to one another in that capacity. That is far and above what many married couples expect of one another."

"Hazel, you are willfully misunderstanding my intentions."

Hazel squared her shoulders as her expression turned rather aggressive. Why was she so much easier for him to read than other people? "As I have never fully understood your intentions, that is entirely possible."

They glared at one another across the table, then Lord Howardsford looked at Duncan. "Hazel claims you are her ideal partner, Duncan, and she would have no other man. Do you feel the same? Marrying Hazel would prevent you from ever marrying another woman. Are you certain that she is your *ideal* partner?"

Duncan said nothing.

Hazel turned to look at him too. "Duncan, tell him why I am your ideal partner."

He inferred that along with her request, he was being given permission to speak once more. He cleared his throat. "Hazel is my ideal marital partner because she fulfills the terms of your inheritance parameters."

They both watched him for several seconds.

"Is there any other reason, Duncan?" Lord Howardsford said.

"No."

"Duncan," Hazel said. Her jaw remained remarkably tight. "Are there any additional reasons why I am a good choice for you to marry?"

"Oh, well you also have an inheritance that, Lord Howardsford willing, I can be approved to fulfill."

"And . . . ?" Hazel made a winding motion with her hand.

"And?" Duncan repeated, confused by what she was asking. Perhaps he was not any better at determining her mood and emotion than he was with any other person after all.

"Is there any other reason why you are marrying *me* and not another woman with a marriage inheritance?"

"I do not know any other women with a marriage inheritance of which I could be the fulfilling partner."

Hazel made a growling sound that reminded him of the dogs on the street where he'd grown up. Duncan did not like dogs.

There was still a grumble in her tone when she spoke again. "Do we have accord with one another, Duncan?"

"Yes," Duncan said with a nod.

"Explain that accord to Uncle Elliott."

He nodded and turned to Lord Howardsford, focusing on the knot of his cravat; it was the most comfortable place to look when talking to a man. "I find Hazel an interesting conversationalist, and I admire her grasp of mathematics. She is remarkably self-possessed and honest, and she does not laugh at me or speak in ways that are confusing or out of context. I enjoy her company and feel equal to her in regard to life goals and intellect, something which I have never found with any other woman."

Hazel and Lord Howardsford's expressions changed, but he could not determine if it was favorable. Duncan looked at his knees, placing them exactly parallel to one another and imagined an angled line crossing the parallels. He began writing a linear equation in his mind to distract him from their uncomfortable staring.

After three seconds, Hazel cleared her throat and took charge of the conversation. "We have been writing back and forth since having first met here when we were told of our inheritances, Uncle Elliott," Hazel said, her voice softer, which Duncan preferred. "We have gotten to know one another and respect one another, and both of us are facing personal situations that make the inheritances you have created timely advantages for us."

"But you do not love one another. You are making this decision for increase, not desire."

"That is precisely what your inheritances support—financial increase," she said.

"You are attempting to manipulate the situation," Uncle Elliot said sharply.

"That is incorrect," Duncan said, offended by the suggestion that he would be disingenuous. "We are utilizing the opportunity you created for the betterment of both of our situations."

"Will you live together as man and wife? Will you have children together?"

"No," Hazel said. "Should I buy Cordon Academy, as is my goal, I would continue to live in King's Lynn. Duncan will remain in Ipswich. Our lives will be improved, which should bring you some satisfaction that your inheritances were put to good use. You did not dictate love or children in your inheritances, only a partner of approved situation, which we fulfill for each other. I have no other prospects, Uncle Elliott, and Duncan is thirty-seven years old."

Duncan did not understand why his age was of any consequence but said nothing as Hazel's intensity deepened. He had had women speak to him with that sort of intensity before, and he found it disagreeable, therefore he did not want to draw that intensity to himself.

"I will not agree to it," Lord Howardsford said firmly.

Duncan was stunned by the refusal and felt his chest heat up. "That is unfair, Lord Howardsford! We have presented our situations clearly."

"I agree, Uncle," Hazel said, her eyes narrowed. Her anger

did not help Duncan's attempts to remain calm. He could not go back to Perkins & Cromley on Monday morning without this plan in place!

Hazel continued, "You told me that you had created an equal opportunity for all your nieces and nephews. It's unfair for you to prevent us from collecting when you have let others. Peter and Timothy found wives and—"

"They did not try to turn my gift against me!"

"We are turning nothing against you!" Duncan said, his hands forming into fists. Da's voice came into his mind, *Anger can cloud your judgment. Leave the situation if you can.* Duncan did not want to leave, but neither did he want to lose his temper. It could be difficult to calm himself once that happened. He took another breath, but his heart was racing and his fists were tightening. This was not fair! Lord Howardsford was *not* being fair!

Hazel slapped the desktop, and the percussive sound sent a shot of temper through Duncan's chest, increasing his anger until it crackled like a fire.

"How is it turning the gift against you if we are simply enacting it according to your terms?" she asked.

"As I said," Lord Howardsford said between tight teeth. He was angry too, which fueled Duncan even more. "You are willfully misinterpreting the proposal—"

"That is an unfair accusation!" Duncan bellowed, the words reverberating in his chest. He jumped to his feet with his fists clenched at his sides.

Lord Howardsford leaned back in his chair.

"This is unfair!" Duncan yelled, then pointed to Lord Howardsford's face. "You are prejudiced, unfair, and unfeeling!"

It had been a long time—years—since he'd let anger override his control, but that was because Duncan lived a careful and structured life that prevented variables that left him feeling powerless and misunderstood. It had not been so long, however, that he did not remember the steps to calming himself down. The first step was to remove himself from the situation. He did not want to leave, but if he waited much longer he might lose the presence of mind necessary to make the decision. He turned on his heel and stomped out of the room with his fists clenched and his blood pounding in his ears.

He would have to go back to work on Monday.

The distance between him and the partners would continue.

Mr. Ludwig would continue to treat him rudely.

He would not have his own office.

Mr. Southey would continue to dump his bin in the alley and antagonize Delores.

Nothing would change.

Nothing.

Would.

Change.

Duncan had been to Howard House only a few times and had never been in Lord Howardsford's study before today, but he remembered all the correct turns to go down the hallway, stairs, through the music room, across the entry, and out the front door of the house.

He continued walking until he came upon the back garden he remembered from his visit in the spring. The plants were not in bloom now as they had been then, seeing as how it was September. He sat on the stone bench, clasped his hands together, and began counting by sixes. Each time the number ended in a six, he doubled it and continued.

*Thirty.*

*Thirty-six.*

*Seventy-two.*

*Seventy-eight.*

*Eighty-four.*

Without the marriage inheritance, he would have to continue tolerating Mr. Ludwig's inept abilities and dishonest work practices. He would continue to be ignored by the partners. He could lose his position entirely.

How would he find another position? He knew his manner made some people uncomfortable. Could he find another firm that would see past his social limitations? Lord Howardsford had arranged the original apprenticeship with Perkins & Cromley twenty years ago, but Duncan did not want to ask for Lord Howardsford's help anymore. There were three other accounting firms in Ipswich, but none of them presented as an attractive substitution for an office of his own where he answered to no one.

The application to Lord Howardsford should have worked. He hit his closed fist against the stone bench, taking strange comfort from the pain that shot up his arm. He stood and began to pace across the stone walkway.

*Ninety.*

*Ninety-six.*

*One hundred ninety-two.*

*One hundred ninety-eight.*

*Two hundred four.*

His fists clenched so tightly he could feel his fingernails digging into his palms.

*It should have worked!*

# Chapter Eight

*H*azel often wondered how she would react in certain situations if she had two good feet. Right now, she felt sure she'd have followed Duncan out of the room. She was as frustrated as he was, but she suspected she possessed a few more skills when it came to managing difficult situations.

She looked from the doorway Duncan had disappeared through to Uncle Elliott, whose expression was both irritated and frightened. She suspected he did not get yelled at with such passion very often.

Instead of fantasizing a dramatic escape, she thought of what she could do *without* two good feet. The answer was the same one she'd had most of her life when faced with this sort of decision—*use your mind and keep your focus.* She took a deep breath and consciously relaxed the muscles that had tightened over the last several minutes. She should not have let her frustration get the better of her. She also should never have let the possibility of running her own school dominate her thoughts as it had these last weeks.

She consciously kept her voice calm when she spoke, hoping

to contrast Duncan's parting words. "One of the partners in the accounting firm where Duncan works has hired his nephew. That nephew is now threatening Duncan's security there. My school is to be sold, and there is no way of knowing if the new owners will continue to employ a female mathematics teacher. We are both facing uncertainty, and Duncan saw us marrying each other as a solution to those insecurities."

Uncle Elliott looked at her. "Duncan saw this as a solution? But not you?"

"More than I should have, I'll admit. But I learned a long time ago that the only way to avoid disappointment is to not have any expectations, so I had at least kept them tempered. Duncan does not think that way; he sees ideals as possibilities and does not understand why the logical solution is not always the one that is realized."

She pushed herself up from the chair. With the help of her cane, she found her balance and limped a few steps toward the door before turning back to look at him.

"You are a good man, Uncle, and I know that your intentions for these marriage inheritances are rooted in wanting the best for us. Since Peter and Timothy have successfully attained your goals for them, your belief that Duncan and I can achieve the same result has been encouraged. However, Duncan and I have been given difficult circumstances in life that do not put us in the same situation as the others." She waved toward her foot currently hidden by her skirt. "I will never overcome my defective foot, and Duncan is not going to overcome his literal nature that makes relationships of all kinds difficult for him to manage, including those with the men for whom he works.

"If nothing else, I hope you will consider his situation and see if you can help him find a solution. I do not think he will be able to manage one on his own, and I worry for his future. I will try to help him understand. I am sure he will apologize for his behavior when he has calmed down."

Uncle Elliott said nothing as she limped out of the room with her "public" gait, then she fell into the more rocking ambulation as she continued unseen so that she could move faster and with less pain to her hips, both of which hurt all the time now.

So much for prayer and hope and soft air.

It seemed to take her forever to find Duncan in the garden. He was pacing and muttering to himself but did not seem as angry as he'd been in the study, for which she was grateful. She'd felt his rising tension as the meeting had moved away from their goal, but she had not expected the explosive anger. His anger was not *frightening* to Hazel. Perhaps because the anger was not directed at her, or perhaps because, despite his having punched Mr. Ludwig, she felt an overall gentleness about him which seemed his natural disposition.

The day was cold, and she'd have liked to have a shawl, but that would have necessitated going to her room to fetch it and that would have been more steps than she could manage. She spied a bench and gratefully headed for it; she had not done this much walking in a long time, and her hips were on fire.

He did not seem to notice that she'd joined him for a nearly a minute, and only then because she cleared her throat. "Duncan?"

"What?" he barked.

Excellent question. She took a breath and thought of her former student who reminded her so much of Duncan. She'd helped talk Audrey through her fits of temper several times; for all Audrey's intellect and ability, she seemed to reach a threshold of frustration sooner than other people. Once Audrey had reached that level, it was very difficult for her to change the course of her emotions on her own.

"Would it help to talk through your feelings?"

He stopped mid-stride and stared at her, full in the face. She felt the intensity of it, and wondered if he avoided such direct eye contact because it was always this intense to him.

"Catherine used to say that when I was upset. 'Talk to me, Duncan,' she would say. 'You can better understand your own feelings if you explain them to someone else.'"

"I suppose great minds think alike," Hazel said, smiling to hide her discomfort of being compared to the fallen woman who had filled the role of his mother. "Did it help to talk about how you felt when you were upset?"

He was still looking at her. He had very nice eyes, rich brown with a black ring on the outer rim that blended with the brown unless you looked very closely. His slicked-back hair had begun to fall out of its style, a lock hanging over part of his face. He tucked it behind his ear.

"It was helpful to talk to Catherine about my feelings when I was upset, but Catherine is dead."

She hid her surprise at his bluntness, but nodded and turned her hands out, palms up. "Then talk to me. Tell me what you are feeling. I will listen just as Catherine did and try to help you better understand yourself and the situation."

He began to pace and talk. She watched and listened.

# Chapter Nine

*E*lliott finished recounting the details of the very poor interview to Amelia, who had come in after Hazel had left. He'd wanted her there for the interview itself, but as she had met Hazel and Duncan only one time each, she'd felt uncomfortable taking a position of authority. He felt certain things would have gone better if she'd been with him.

"And what did you say after Hazel explained?" Amelia asked, eyes wide, which encouraged Elliott to share his full feelings.

"Nothing," Elliott said before letting out a heavy breath. In India, he had purchased a paperweight that looked like an Egyptian pyramid. When turned on its point, it spun like a top. He spun it on the desk now and watched it spiral in place.

When Hazel had written requesting an audience for Duncan and herself, he'd extended an invitation to both of them to come to Howard House today. He'd been prepared for them to ask him to reconsider their inheritances, but he had not considered that they would suggest marrying *each other* in order to collect. The idea made his stomach feel heavy, as though he'd done something wrong.

Had he?

Peter and Timothy were happily married to extraordinary women; he and Amelia could not be more pleased with their outcomes. Harry was doing remarkably well with his recovery, which was currently taking place in Howard House, though Amelia had thought it best he be kept ignorant of Hazel and Duncan's visit, which Elliott could now see was very wise.

Elliott had encouraged Harry to assess the immediate needs of Falconridge for a few days, starting yesterday, so that he would not be here. Upon Lady Sabrina's return in February, Harry was planning to make her an offer that, oddly enough, Amelia and Elliott both thought she would accept; they had met her in London and felt her Harry's perfect partner.

In large part because of Harry's improvements, Elliott had felt increasingly confident in his "marriage campaign" and was prepared to encourage Hazel and Duncan to not give up. He had not expected *anything* like this. How could his inheritances be so horribly misunderstood? Willfully so or not. It was a gift. A reason to seek something they were hesitant to seek. Why did they not embrace it and express their gratitude? The spinning top wobbled, and he grabbed it before it fell.

"Where is Hazel now?" Amelia said.

"She went after Duncan." One twist of his hand and the top spun and spun and spun; that was how he had envisioned his marriage inheritances happening. He would set the possibility in motion, and it would move forward with an energy of its own. "Duncan thinks that I am prejudiced toward the working class."

"Are you not?" Amelia asked, standing and moving to the north windows that overlooked the gardens of Howard House.

"Amelia!" Elliott stammered, leaning back in his chair and

staring at her incredulously. "How can you say such a thing? I have absolute respect for the working class of our country."

"But they are not as good as gentry in your mind, are they?" She raised an eyebrow and moved to the next window, pausing this time to stare at something through the glass. Probably the family of rabbits that lived in the hedge; Amelia loved those rabbits, even though they regularly decimated the foliage.

"I am not making any judgment of *goodness*, only equanimity of situation," Elliott explained. "Ask Peter and Timothy how well the inequity worked for their parents—scandal and disaster."

"That is an extreme example. Teddy was the son of a viscount and their mother was a chambermaid. Need I remind you that my Julia is of working class and you approved her."

"That was different."

"Only because you see it differently," Amelia countered. "Duncan is respectable middle class, so it *is* an unequal expectation for him to marry into the gentry; you know men do not marry up half so easily as women. Hazel has been supporting herself for more than ten years, which means she is *technically* working class as well."

Elliott slumped in his chair. "That is what she said." The pyramid wobbled again, and this time he let it fall. He stared at the fallen monument for several seconds. "My reasons for each inheritance are as different as each of these young people in my charge. I wanted Peter to consider finding love again, Timothy to not have to marry for fortune, and Harry to have reason to change his dissolute ways and settle into a responsible existence.

"For Hazel and Duncan—I knew that neither of them factored the opportunity of marriage very highly, so I tried to create a plan that would encourage them to consider the possibilities.

I wanted to give them a reason to look for it." He sighed. "I did not expect that they would act out of greed."

"Hmm," Amelia said, still looking out the window.

"Are you even listening to me?" Elliott asked, offended by her apparent distraction.

"Of course, I am, dear," she said, still not turning in his direction. "But I'm also thinking. You wanted them to consider marriage by giving them incentives that would bring that possibility to the forefronts of their minds, yes?"

Elliott huffed a breath. "That is what I just said, Amelia. You *weren't* listening."

"I would think you would see their petition today as a success, then. They are both considering marriage and seeing beyond the boundaries of their lives to this point."

"They are manipulating the intention behind the inheritances."

She turned to look at him. "Are you quite certain of that?"

"I want them to fall in love and be loved in return. I want them to have families that will serve as a foundation for the rest of their lives. I want to fortify the connection between the families of their siblings and cousins so that those bonds that were once broken in the Mayfield line might be restored. These inheritances were not meant to only provide them financial security, they were meant to provide for generational comfort and connection."

"And if they found comfort and connection in each other?"

Elliott shook his head. "Hazel was quite clear that they would marry to receive the inheritances and that was all. She wants to buy the school where she currently teaches in King's Lynn."

"Ah, darling Hazel," Amelia said with a sigh. "She has done an admirable job of making a life for herself, hasn't she?"

"Of course," Elliott said, though he did not see how that applied to this particular topic.

He greatly admired Hazel's independence and how well she had overcome her disadvantages, but she was approaching this from *that* position rather than widening her expectations. It was frustrating that of the five individual presentations of these marriage inheritances, only Timothy had grasped his intentions from the start.

Peter had found the invitation insulting, as he'd never planned to marry again, and Harry had focused only on the fact that Elliott would no longer pay his debts. Hazel had been perfectly offended. Elliott had *thought* Duncan grasped the idea; he'd been gracious when presented the plan, but he'd now proven himself ignorant of the purpose too.

Why was it so difficult for people to see the brilliance of this idea? Why did Peter and Timothy's successful arrangements not give the others hope for their own happiness? It was maddening.

Elliott had returned to England three years ago after learning of his sister Jane's death—his last living sibling. He'd come back determined to gather his remaining family around himself while setting them on paths to success their parents had not set out for them. He had not foreseen giving that gift to be this difficult.

Amelia continued to stare out the window, and Elliott made a discontented huff.

"Have you nothing else to say?" he asked sarcastically.

Instead of an answer, she beckoned him to join her at the window. She held back the sheer curtain. He scowled until she gave him a pointed look, eyebrows raised, and gestured to the portion of floor beside her at the window. "I want you to see something."

Elliott huffed again and pushed himself up from the chair. Was this any time to watch the rabbits?

He joined her at the window.

Hazel sat on the stone bench outside the arbor that led into the rose garden. Duncan paced in front of her, gesturing angrily as he spoke words Elliott could not hear. Seeing him upset humbled Elliott somewhat.

If Duncan's situation at Perkins & Cromley really was in danger, he must be feeling very unsettled. In exchange for Duncan's employment, Perkins & Cromley paid a reduced rent. Elliott wasn't sure they would actually terminate Duncan because of that agreement, but if Duncan was uncomfortable there, then the arrangement was not working.

"Look at her face," Amelia said, drawing Elliott's attention to Hazel, sitting on the bench. Her small face was calm, a contrast to Duncan's animation. She nodded slowly, seeming to be listening to his rantings, but not interrupting as he continued.

She was an attractive woman with a commanding air and sharp mind. If not for her foot, she'd have had a very different life. Her words from their earlier interview came back to him: *Duncan and I have been given difficult circumstances in life that do not put us in the same situation as the others.*

He watched as Hazel began to speak, and Duncan, though he continued pacing, put his hands into his pockets as he listened. After nearly a minute, Hazel patted the other side of the bench.

Duncan paused, looked at the bench, then sat down on the opposite end, allowing several inches of space between them. He immediately took his hands out of his pockets and began gesturing again while Hazel once again listened, her energy composed and centered.

"I wonder," Amelia said softly as she took Elliott's hand and gave it a squeeze, "if there may be more potential here than any of us realize."

# Chapter Ten

*H*azel lowered herself into the chair next to Duncan and across the desk from Uncle Elliott—the same chair she'd sat in for their first interview that had ended so badly. Duncan sat rigid and tense, reminding her of a cat ready to pounce if Uncle Elliott said the wrong thing. How Uncle Elliott could say the *right* thing at this point, she could not imagine.

She'd spent nearly an hour listening to and then talking Duncan down from his fit of temper, but he was still frustrated. During that time, she had wondered why she'd ever thought Uncle Elliott *would* agree. Though he'd made large sacrifices for the good of the Mayfield family, those sacrifices had still been choices *he'd* decided to make, balances he'd had the opportunity to weigh out. Hazel and Duncan were from an entirely differ-ent situation—their limitations were chronic and lifelong. Elliott could not be expected to understand what that was like.

Hazel was determined to remain respectful through this interview, however, which she expected would be Uncle Elliot's attempt to clarify his position and restore friendly connections. There was no point in allowing the discord to continue—she had said all she needed to say—and so she would accept his olive branch without lingering resentment. She had no power over Duncan's reaction, however. Should his anger be reignited, this very long day would be even longer, as she would once again need to talk him down.

Uncle Elliott smiled uncomfortably as he looked between them, his hands clasped on the desktop and his back nearly as rigid as Duncan's. He had just opened his mouth to speak when the door to his study opened.

"My apologies," the new Lady Howardsford said, looking first at Elliott and then between Hazel and Duncan as she entered the room. There were two blue, velvet-covered chairs set near the window, and she took hold of one as though to move it toward the desk.

Uncle Elliott jumped up and took over the task. She smiled her thanks at him in that easy sort of acknowledgment between couples that Hazel had seen only a handful of times in her life. An acceptance of the other, a joy of their company, a gratitude for the part they played in one another's life.

Hazel inhaled to chase away the envy, replacing it easily enough with renewed cynicism. Uncle Elliott had come back to England after his heroic actions of saving the family from ruin and reclaimed the love of his youth. Bully for him.

Uncle Elliott settled the chair for the countess beside his on the other side of the desk. "I have spent these last hours discussing your proposal with Amelia," he said.

"A proposal which is both appropriate and fair to all parties," Duncan added.

Uncle Elliott opened his mouth but then seemed to reconsider and closed his mouth. He turned to look at his wife, raising his eyebrows at her expectantly and betraying the choreography of this meeting.

"I have a few questions," Lady Howardsford asked, the softness of her voice changing the tension in the room just enough for Hazel to notice. "As I was not here for the original proposal, would you mind repeating it for me, Duncan, so that I am sure I understand it fully?"

"Certainly, Lady Howardsford," Duncan said.

"Please, call me Amelia."

"That would not be appropriate, but I shall explain the proposal."

Duncan then repeated, almost word for word, the proposal he'd delivered to Uncle Elliott earlier that morning, which was almost word for word what he'd said to Hazel two weeks before in King's Lynn.

"To make sure I am clear, you and Hazel are not in love with one another," Amelia asked when he'd finished.

"Being in love with one's proposed partner was not part of the criteria outlined in either of our inheritance proposals, nor is it a requirement for legal and lawful marriage in Great Britain."

"Yes," Amelia said, her voice still soft. "I just want to make sure I understand. And the two of you have no expectation of living with one another as man and wife?"

"Living together was also not stipulated in the inheritance proposal." Duncan took a breath likely meant to fuel a further explanation.

Amelia hurried to cut him off. "I know that as well. Both of those things, however, are *implied* expectations of your uncle's proposal to all of his nieces and nephews."

"Implied expectation is hardly enforceable," Duncan said, a tone of disgust in his voice that, under other circumstances, would have made Hazel smile for its sincerity. He was quite particular about certain things.

"Implied expectation *is* enforceable because I am the only one who can approve your choice," Uncle Elliott said defensively.

Duncan's already stiff posture became tighter. Hazel reached over and put her hand on his arm, meaning to calm him and remind him that they were in this together. He jerked his arm away and turned his head toward her though he looked at the wall behind her head. "Do not touch me!"

Hazel startled, and the room went quiet. The heat that rose up her neck was a stark contrast to the sense of victory she'd felt when she'd been able to calm him down in the garden.

"Duncan!" Uncle Elliott reprimanded.

"It is all right," Hazel said, though her face burned. "Please continue, Lady How—Amelia." She put her hand back into her lap and held Amelia's look, nodding that she was all right.

Amelia looked concerned, but cleared her throat. "We are only trying to clarify your expectations so we can better meet them, Duncan, that is all. At the risk of being indelicate, is there no expectation of . . . intimacy between you. No children?"

"That is not a stipulation of the—"

Uncle Elliott cut Duncan off. "Enough of this, I believe we are clear on the expectations from your side of the table. I would like to negotiate the terms of your proposal."

Silence.

"Negotiate which terms?" Duncan asked after a few seconds, leaning slightly forward, his posture curious.

Uncle Elliott and Amelia shared a look Hazel thought was meant to inspire courage. She felt her own muscles tighten, exhausted by all the emotional energy the day had required. Did Duncan feel any of that emotional tension, she wondered? Or only his own disappointment? Sometimes he seemed to exist above things like feelings and internal struggle, and yet other times, he showed great insight. He always took her arm when they walked up any steps, for instance, and did not hesitate to compliment people when he felt impressed by something they had done or said.

Uncle Elliott looked between them, and Hazel centered her focus as he spoke. "As Duncan pointed out earlier, you are asking us to accommodate the fact that Duncan's class does not fulfill the expectations of Hazel's inheritance."

Duncan tapped his finger on the desk. "Which class requirement we have already pointed out is an unfair expectation due to her deformity."

"Duncan!" Amelia said, shocked. "That was uncalled for!"

Heat flooded Hazel's cheeks that had only just cooled. "It is all right," she said. The sooner this meeting came to an end, the better. Without looking at Duncan, she said, "Please continue, Uncle Elliott."

Uncle Elliott hesitated, but when she waved him forward, he nodded and resumed his explanation. "I propose that in exchange for me approving Duncan as Hazel's choice in husband, that the two of you live together for one year's time after the wedding."

Hazel let out a breath, realizing belatedly that it had been audible to the rest of the room. Live together? Her and Duncan?

Duncan leaned forward even further. "Hazel's plan will forgo the expectation of gentry in exchange for our agreeing to one year of cohabitation?"

"Let us not call it . . . that," Uncle Elliott said. "You will be legally married and will live as such in a marital home for one year. You must not confide in anyone that you are not expecting to live that way for the rest of your lives, and therefore you will live and socialize as any other married couple would."

Hazel took a deep breath against the anxiety swirling and churning in her chest. Living with Duncan—or any man for that matter—wasn't something Hazel had considered since she had been a young girl. At the possibility, however, the youthful imaginings of what, for most people, was a normal and ordinary expectation began to play out. Breakfasting at the same table. Sharing the events of the day over dinner each night. Separate bedrooms, of course, but someone to sit beside at the fire. Not surrounded by students and teachers every hour of every day. There was something unreal about it, as though she were looking at a painting meant to symbolize a world different from her own.

Regular women—wives—had morning calls and a variety of dresses to accommodate whatever the day held. They managed a household, chose furniture, had servants. Hazel recalled a memory of her mother discussing menus with their housekeeper, Mrs. Grey, and chiding a maid who spilled a bucket of ash on the rug after cleaning out the fireplace. Hazel tried to put her own face and twisted posture into those scenes. It would not fit. She was no "Mistress of the Manor."

And Duncan? Would he go riding in the morning and dress for dinner? That was the life of a gentleman, which he was not, but she could not picture what the life of the middle class looked like since the only family life she knew was that of an estate house. She enjoyed his company but had shared it so little. Would he irritate her if they spent more time together? How did he act in public? But then again, Hazel did not socialize or go to public places like regular women did. She did not attend church, she could not dance, she did not throw dinner parties. Would she be expected to throw dinner parties?

*I am not that woman,* she thought. *Duncan is not that man. How would it work?*

"Hazel?"

She looked up from the spot of carpet where her eyes had become fixed. The conversation had continued without her, and now all three of them were looking at her. Duncan's posture had softened, and his eyes showed excitement that increased her own anxiety. Was Duncan in *favor* of this madness?

She settled her attention on Uncle Elliott even as she settled herself into the present moment. "You think that if we live in the same house as a married couple, we will find comfort in that lifestyle enough to fulfill all your expectations of family and future."

"What?" Duncan said, stiffening once more and turning to Elliott.

Duncan's offense justified her discomfort and spurred her boldness.

"The reason for this stipulation, Duncan, is that Uncle Elliott believes living as man and wife will lead us to develop an emotional connection to one another, and we would therefore want to remain living as a traditional married couple after the year has passed—thus fulfilling the implied expectations of his original proposal."

"Love is not a *requirement*, however," Elliott said. "How could it be?"

Hazel held his eyes and tried to swallow the lump in her throat. It was ridiculous that she should feel emotional, but this new proposal was yet one more reflection of Uncle Elliott's inability to face the truth of their situations.

"It is a good thing you do not require that as an additional stipulation," Duncan said, nodding and relaxed again. "Because emotional connection between two people cannot be guaranteed in such a way."

Duncan's insight distracted her, and she stared at him. Who was this man? Why did he think the way that he did? How did he feel? What was important to him in his life? Living with him for one year's time would likely show her the answers to all of these questions. However, the two of them as a married couple would be like a carnival sideshow. Her twisted foot and his awkward demeanor would be gossiped about and laughed at behind the hands of their neighbors.

Hazel could feel Amelia watching her and was glad she knew how to hide her feelings.

"Exactly right, Duncan. I cannot guarantee anything of the sort," Uncle Elliott said. "So, what have you? Do we all agree to the terms?"

"Yes," Duncan said with a sharp nod.

"We need more information," Hazel said, putting out her hand as though to stop Uncle Elliott's words. "How would it work? Where would we live? I cannot manage a school I cannot live in, and Duncan cannot leave his work in Ipswich." *Unless he could,* she found herself thinking. Uncle Elliott managed the Burrow Building from afar, and Duncan did not like his work. But what would he do in King's Lynn? And why was her mind trying to solve this equation that had no rational basis?

"Oh, yes, excellent question," Duncan said, nodding. "The terms of our inheritances specify that we are to be in receipt immediately upon marriage."

"I will honor that term," Elliott said. "The dowry will be fulfilled, and Duncan shall become the title holder for the Burrow Building based on good faith that you will live as man and wife for one year's time. If you do not fulfill the terms, I shall be in my rights to demand a return."

"That is fair," Duncan said. He grinned. "How soon could we be married?"

"Wait," Hazel said, a bit panicked. She turned to Duncan. "Where would we live?"

"In Ipswich, of course. That is where the Burrow Building is located, and I shall need to open my own accounting office and evict Mr. Southey."

"What about my school? I need to be on-site if I am to manage it."

"Did you not say Sophie was to help you with the management?" Duncan asked, then moved forward seamlessly. "She can manage for the time being, and you can join her after the year is finished. Her efforts can be counted as equity toward the partnership, since she has no financial resources to offer."

Hazel opened her mouth to protest, but it was an adequate solution . . . wasn't it?

"Ipswich is the more convenient location for the length of our cohabitation," Duncan added with a sharp nod.

"For the love of all that is good, do not call it that, Duncan," Elliott said, placing his palm on the desk and spreading his fingers as though that gave him some additional balance.

Duncan's excitement was running high. "I have a flat above the pub in the Burrow Building. We can live there quite comfortably. There is a bedroom and a common room and a stove that works well for both heating and cooking. There are three windows on the—"

"I shall help you find a suitable house," Amelia cut in, directing an understanding smile toward Hazel. Hazel was too shocked to respond.

"There is no need," Duncan said, cutting his hand through the air. "The flat is perfectly accommodating. There are three windows on the south wall and two on the north wall that afford excellent lighting."

"Lord Howardsford will also cover the expenses of the house," Amelia said, ignoring Duncan's commentary.

Uncle Elliott straightened in his chair. "What?"

"It is your stipulation, after all," Amelia said, her tone sweet enough to stick to the walls. "And the house and the servants must be suitable to their purposes, of course."

"My flat is very suitable," Duncan said, his tone excited. "I have lived there for eighteen years and keep it shipshape at all times. There is the brown sofa and the green chair, as well as—"

"The stairs to your flat will be difficult for me to manage, Duncan," Hazel said. The room spun. She would have her own household. She would be expected to manage it like any other woman.

"But I like my rooms and my furniture. I am comfortable there, and it is convenient to live and work in the same building."

Hazel looked at him directly, realizing he was the hurdle in resolving her concerns, not Uncle Elliott. "Duncan," she said, then waited for him to face her. "Because of my foot, I cannot live somewhere that necessitates so many stairs. There are other accommodations that must also be seen to. The house would need to be close enough to your office building for you to walk, for instance, and have separate bedrooms."

"Separate bedrooms are unnecessary," Duncan said, shaking his head. "It is fully appropriate for a married couple living as such to share a bedroom, though we shall need a bed that can better accommodate two people."

The room went silent again, and Hazel blinked. He expected to share a *bed*?

"How soon can we be married?" Duncan asked again.

The room was pressing down on her like the time Harry had tackled her with a pillow because she had said she would tell Mother that he'd been smoking Father's pipe. Hazel cleared her throat and looked between her aunt and uncle, not bothering to fake a smile. "Might Duncan and I have a few minutes to converse about this in private?"

Duncan looked at her, his expression filled with delight. "What is there to discuss?"

Amelia pushed to her feet. "Why don't you take the afternoon?" she said. "We'll have dinner at eight o'clock and can continue the discussion then. Elliott?" She gave him a pointed look. He nodded and rose to his feet.

Hazel stared at the floor until they had left, then took a breath, let it out, and wondered how on earth all of this had become so complicated.

# Chapter Eleven

As soon as Lord and Lady Howardsford had exited the room, Duncan jumped to his feet and began pacing between his chair and the south window. Fourteen steps away. Turn. Fourteen steps back.

"This is a most excellent resolution," he said, thinking excitedly about owning the building. Being a landlord. Of course, the acquisition of the building would mean additional duties, but as he would also be running his own office, he could better adjust his workload to accommodate the time the increased responsibility would demand.

There were five shops and three offices on the ground level of the Burrow Building and six top-floor apartments, four of which were occupied by persons who worked in the ground-level shops. He would evict Mr. Southey and take that office for himself, which would be perfect as it was located two doors away from Perkins & Cromley. It was also right next to Ye Old Pub, which would make picking up his dinner every night even more convenient. Except he wouldn't be living in his rooms anymore and likely wouldn't be picking up dinner from Delores.

He swallowed and counted his steps for two sequences as the anxiety began to build. After Catherine had died, he'd gone to school in Bury St. Edmunds for three years, and when he'd returned, there had been a new family living in his rooms.

A smaller apartment had been set aside for him, which were the rooms he lived in now. He'd found the changes uncomfortable, and the new apartment had not felt or smelled the way he liked. It had taken several weeks before he felt at ease there. Though that experience suggested he would be able to settle into this new house just as he'd once settled into his new rooms, he did not look forward to the transition. This house would not smell the way his rooms smelled.

And other people would live there with him. Hazel, of course, though he felt they would adapt well to one another, but there had been mention of servants. Strangers who were meant to help manage the house. Elizabeth would not like that, he was certain. She liked things a very specific way. What if she would not leave the Burrow Building? What if the servants did not like her?

Sweat prickled along his hairline as his anxiety overtook his excitement. He did not actually know how to be a landlord. He knew all the tenants, of course, but not his exact responsibilities. At least he knew how to manage the financial aspects. If he had pursued a different occupation, like butchering, for instance, it would be a much more difficult transition.

What would he do if someone could not pay their rent on the rooms? What if the Garrises fell on hard times? They had four children. Would he evict them? What was the legal process of eviction? Maybe he would not evict them since he did not necessarily need the income from every tenant, but what if the other tenants learned he had not charged the Garrises rent? They would find that unfair, and they would be right.

He would need to pay taxes on the building every year. And pay for regular maintenance. How much would that cost?

"I know you are excited about this," Hazel said. "But we must discuss some factors before we agree."

"Which factors?" Duncan asked. *Twelve, thirteen, fourteen, turn.* He thought better when he was moving. He wished Catherine were there to help him sort out the details, then realized Hazel could help him like she had in the garden. He felt much better. She spoke again.

"Living together was never part of our plan and—"

"Prior to the inheritances, I had never planned to own a building," Duncan pointed out. "And you never imagined you could own your own school and teach your own curriculum."

"You are not the least bit concerned about us living in the same house for one year?"

"I am not excited to live in a house—I like my rooms—but I think it an exciting prospect to live with you."

"You do?"

"Certainly." *Turn, one, two, three . . .* It was good to talk about his feelings with Hazel; it helped clarify them in his own mind. "I have only ever lived with my father and Catherine, and Elizabeth, of course, but she is not the same as the relationship between us is very simple and she cannot talk. I enjoyed Da and Catherine's company and found it comfortable to live with them the majority of the time. I find your company equally enjoyable, and you possess a high intellect, which will likely contribute to more engaging conversation. You also seem, to the best of my knowledge, to not have a penchant for excessive drinking, which was my only complaint against my former roommates."

Duncan imagined coming home from work—as both a landlord and a clerk—to discuss with Hazel Humphry Davy's new understanding of elemental interactions. There were only a few people in Duncan's life with whom he could have such discussions, but Hazel would be living in the same house, which would make it convenient for him. What fun this would be! It would be more fun in his own rooms, of course.

What would the new house look like? Would there be a window he could adjust to allow Elizabeth the freedom she'd come to appreciate in the Burrow Building? How would it smell? Would it be damp?

"I am glad to hear you have such high expectations of my company, Duncan, but just how far do you expect this accord to develop between us?"

"As far as we are both comfortable."

"And how far is that?"

"I may want to go to sleep either before or after you, which would bring any conversation to an end as a discussion would require both of us. We may need to take turns sitting at the head of the table if we both like that particular place. I may be more tolerant of cold temperatures indoors than yourself since I am used to coming home to a cold apartment, so we may have to make adjustments. I think we should create a schedule of discussions for the evenings, so that it is fair between us and we both have an opportunity to introduce the topic."

He took the fourteenth step and turned.

"Duncan," Hazel said.

He could never pace fourteen steps in his apartment; the rooms were too small. The most he could manage was eleven, and that necessitated the eleventh step be half as long as the others. Perhaps the new house would accommodate enough space for pacing; that would be a positive improvement. Catherine had taught him to focus on the positive aspects of life, and he had made it a daily practice. Mr. Ludwig, Mr. Southey, and dogs were among the things that were not improved by optimism, however.

"Duncan," Hazel said again, alerting him to the fact that he was not properly focused on their conversation.

"Yes."

"Are you expecting marital relations between us?"

"Certainly."

He continued pacing, thinking of the books he ought to have her read so they would both be in possession of the same basic knowledge on a topic before a discussion ensued. It would be uncomfortable, for instance, if he introduced Davy's theories and Hazel was not familiar with them. Certainly Dr. Randall would let Duncan borrow from his extensive library so that Hazel could study. She was well-skilled in mathematics and had read at least the first four volumes of *Euclid's Elements*, but not the fifth, sixth, or seventh. Perhaps he would use his rental profits to purchase his own set of the Elements!

"I am talking about . . . intimacy," she said.

"I know."

"*Physical* intimacy," she said. "Sexual relations. Do you know what I am talking about?"

He stopped pacing so as to better appreciate the lovely pink shading of her face and further consider the words she was saying in such a pointed way. "You are speaking of lovemaking."

The color in her cheeks darkened, which was not quite as becoming as the pink shade had been on her olive skin but still quite flattering. "I like it when you blush. It is very pretty."

"Um, thank you, but, are you expecting . . . *that* between us?"

"Lovemaking?"

"Yes," she said.

He nodded. "I understand it to be both enjoyable and expected between husbands and wives."

"Except that our arrangement is based on the security of our individual inheritances, not procreation or physical attraction."

"I find you very physically attractive."

Her eyebrows jumped up her forehead, which he found humorous as it made her eyes go very wide. "You do?"

"Certainly," he said. "Your features are highly symmetrical, though your left ear is slightly lower than your right and your left eyebrow extends nearly a quarter of an inch further than the other. The chestnut color of your hair is well-balanced with your hazel eyes and dark brows, and you have an engaging smile and fine teeth, though you do not smile excessively. Your figure is feminine, but strong as I believe your deformity has required you to develop your upper-body strength more than a typical woman of your age and class, but I find it emphasizes the narrowness of your waist in a way that is very becoming. Additionally, you do not tease me or slight me in any way, which puts me at ease and increases my desire to be in your company." He looked at her a moment. "Are you crying?"

She blinked quickly and looked away. He hoped he had not said something out of place.

"Thank you for that, Duncan."

He pulled his eyebrows together. "I've upset you?"

She shook her head and wiped quickly at her eyes. Obviously he *had* upset her, but if she would not acknowledge how he'd done it, he was unsure how to remedy it.

She shifted in her seat, inadvertently moving her skirts so the toe of the specialty boot for her deformed foot showed. He could not help but stare at the thick sole that showed extreme wear on one side. The leather was thick and stiff, like a military boot, scuffed on the toe and the sides. It looked heavy and cumbersome. He tilted his head to look at it from a different angle, trying to determine how it worked. What must the shape of her foot be for this boot to accommodate walking in it? Did the worn places explain the lumbering cadence of her walk?

"I sense that I must be very direct on this topic, Duncan, as nuance might lead to further difficulty. I am unwilling to accept this agreement if it requires intimate physical relations."

His eyes snapped from the awkward footwear to her face. "You do not find me physically attractive?"

"It's not that," Hazel said, shaking her head. Her cheeks were still pink, but her face looked tight with either anger or irritation, he couldn't tell. "For me, such interactions would require love and desire in order for them to be appropriate."

Duncan furrowed his eyebrows. Many marriages were based on security and convenience on the part of either or both partners. Love, as he understood it, was built over time, and while he could see that such feelings would make intimacy more desirable between partners, it was certainly not a prerequisite.

When he'd begun having questions about human anatomy and reproduction, Mr. Marcum had introduced Duncan to Dr. Randall, who had given Duncan a book that explained things from a physiological perspective. Duncan was allowed to keep the book and read it as many times as he liked so long as he promised never to ask questions or discuss his feelings about the contents to anyone other than Dr. Randall. He'd read the book eighteen times but, having never had the opportunity to apply what he'd learned, he—

"It would also risk a pregnancy," Hazel said, stopping Duncan's thoughts.

Duncan sat down on the blue-velvet chair Amelia had occupied earlier. "I had not considered that," he said, disappointed in himself for not realizing that possibility. Catherine would say that was because he was only thinking of the man's side. It was something she'd accused him of quite often, which was how he'd learned that men and women thought about things very differently.

"A child deserves to have the continuity of a family circumstance," Hazel continued.

"Conception can be avoided through methods of timing and—"

"No, Duncan," Hazel interrupted. "If we agree to Uncle Elliott's terms, it will not include sharing a martial bed or risking us having a child together that we will not raise in a traditional household. I am afraid I must insist on this. If that changes your willingness to agree to Uncle Elliott's terms, then so be it."

"But—"

"I do not love you, Duncan, and I will not submit to such intimacies without both a connection and a belief that the relationship would be a permanent one. We are agreeing to share a home for one year and live as a married couple in every other way, but the arrangement will not include physical intimacy."

Duncan considered her words for several seconds, disappointed, but understanding it was her right to make such stipulations. They would be partners in this arrangement, and she had equal right to insist on comfortable terms. Duncan understood right and wrong and tried very hard to do right.

"Are you opposed to Elizabeth?"

Hazel paused, then let out a breath that seemed to communicate relief. "I would like her to be kept out of the main areas of the house, but it is acceptable for her to have access to your room and the kitchens, so long as it does not annoy the cook."

That reminded him of the discomfort of having servants. "I have never had a cook."

Hazel smiled, and when she spoke, her voice was different, lighter. "You will like having a cook to make all your favorite dishes, Duncan, and most cooks like having a cat in the kitchen to catch any mice that might make their way inside."

"The cook will be skilled?" Duncan asked.

"You can interview her yourself to make sure of it."

Duncan liked the idea of vetting the cook himself. "Are you opposed to discussions in the evenings and shared meals?"

"No, I am looking forward to the discussions and benefitting from your detailed knowledge. It will be nice to share meals with you."

That was a relief to hear, and his excitement began to grow once more. "I am very excited to teach you the proper history of mathematics."

"And I am eager to learn it," Hazel said, inclining her head slightly.

Duncan relaxed even further. "I will like having you there when I come home from work every day."

Hazel cleared her throat, and her cheeks turned pink again. "Everything that goes into a marriage is agreeable to me, except . . . lovemaking. Does it change your mind about wanting to accept Uncle Elliott's terms?"

"No," Duncan said. "But I *am* disappointed."

"As disappointment is not fatal, then I suppose we shall survive it." She sighed and lifted a hand to her forehead.

"Do you have a headache?" Duncan asked. "I can fetch you some powders—or tea? Catherine liked good strong tea when she experienced her headaches. She also said whiskey helped, but that also made her drunk, which I think contributed to further head-aches."

Hazel watched him for a moment, then smiled. "I am fine, but thank you for the offer of help. There are just so many details to make sense of. I think I would like to lie down before dinner and think all of this through."

She pushed herself up from the chair, leaning toward her good side as she did so. She'd forgotten to pick up her cane while she was still sitting down, and he retrieved it for her.

"Thank you, Duncan." She centered the cane on her right side and looked at him.

They were standing very close, but it was not unpleasant.

*Hazel's hazel eyes. A lavender dress that smelled like lavender.* The symmetry of her face renewed the attraction he felt toward her, which reminded him of his disappointment that she was not attracted to him and did not want to participate in marital relations. They were quiet for several seconds, then she looked away, and he took a step back to let her pass, realizing he'd broken social protocol by standing so close to her and looking at her so directly.

She limped a few steps, then turned back toward him. "Do we agree to the terms, then?"

"Cohabitate for one year as man and wife, but without marital relations."

Her cheeks turned pink again, and he remembered that was a sign of embarrassment in some people. Was she embarrassed by the topic?

She looked toward the south window and nodded. "Yes. If we agree to the terms, we can tell Uncle Elliott at dinner, and things will move forward. If we are not agreed, then we shall need to tell him that this will not work."

"If we are not agreed, we shall not receive our inheritances."

"Yes."

Duncan let out a breath. "Then I shall agree to the terms. The disappointment does not overshadow the benefits. I will work very hard to be a good husband, Hazel."

"I will work equally hard to be a good wife."

She smiled, and he smiled back. They held one another's eyes a moment more before she turned to leave the study. He did not mind looking her in the eye the way he minded with other people.

The bedchambers were on the second floor of Howard House, which meant she had to go up the central stairs to reach her room, which was called "The Gold Room" because it was decorated with gold. Duncan did not like the Gold Room—it was overwhelming. He was glad that, when he came to Howard House, he stayed in the Lake Room, which was decorated more simply and incorporated the colors of green and blue that he preferred over gold.

Duncan hurried to catch up with Hazel so he could help her navigate the stairs.

"Thank you," Hazel said, taking his arm.

He held himself very tightly, expecting the uncomfortable burning sensation he often felt when he made physical contact with another person, such as when Hazel had unexpectedly touched his arm during the first meeting with Uncle Elliott. The burning sensation, however, did not come. In fact, he rather liked being so close to Hazel.

Interesting.

He made a note to offer his help with the stairs on any occasion possible so as to see if this sensation, of not being uncomfortable touching her, would be a lasting one.

# Chapter Twelve

Two weeks later, Uncle Elliott came to King's Lynn and, with him and Sophie beside her, Hazel presented Mrs. Cordon with an offer to purchase Cordon Academy at the end of the spring term, 1824, some seven months from now.

Mrs. Cordon gaped like a fish, but later that afternoon, Hazel was beside Uncle Elliott in a solicitor's office laying out the terms of the contract.

She would leave the school on November first, a little more than a month from now, but Sophie would retain her teaching position through the spring term. Then she would become the acting headmistress until winter of 1824. Hazel had explained what she could to Sophie without breaking her promise not to share the exact details of the arrangement.

Sophie seemed to infer the basics, however, and agreed to fulfill the responsibilities Hazel had asked of her. They would correspond weekly, but Hazel could not even visit the school unless Duncan came with her, as she and Duncan had to spend every night of the year in the same house.

Mrs. Cordon would tell none of the faculty who the new

owner was until the end of spring term, though they would be informed of the sale.

Hazel and Sophie discussed at length which of the teachers they would keep, which they would replace, and which new subjects they would introduce to the curriculum. Sophie wanted to begin teaching German. Hazel was particularly keen on finding a female teacher for physics and astronomy.

Hazel put in her official notice at the school and fielded the curious questions from her fellow teachers who, like her, had long ago given up thoughts of marriage.

During the weeks that the banns were read in both her and Duncan's local parishes, Hazel corresponded with Amelia regarding the house Amelia had found in Ipswich. It would be furnished and staffed on Hazel's behalf, though Hazel and Duncan would marry at Howard House.

Duncan had chosen the cook but continued to struggle with the idea of leaving his rooms. The idea of furnishing his upstairs bedroom with the furniture from his apartment helped ease his anxiety but did not remedy it completely. Hazel was able to override her irritation at his fixation on the topic by acknowledging that he had lived in the Burrow Building most of his life. Everything was changing for him, which would be very difficult for a man who relied on routine and structure.

Everything was changing for Hazel, too, and she felt she was making the greater sacrifice by leaving King's Lynn. But she was looking forward to having a house—a space—of her own. The management of it felt overwhelming, but it would be for only one year. She hadn't had a home for such a long time, and it was rather exciting to live a version of the life she'd given up on years ago.

On November first, her fellow teachers held a special tea in her honor. Hazel felt guilty both for keeping the details of her ownership from them and for leaving the school without an advanced maths teacher to replace her, but she comforted herself with visions of what this school would become after significant renovations and a revised curriculum.

At eleven o'clock, Gretchen announced that the Howardsford carriage had arrived. Hazel pushed herself to her feet and limped to the door where her trunk was being loaded beneath the carriage. Duncan had taken it upon himself to find a cobbler in Ipswich who could make her a new boot; she would meet with him as soon as she was settled. It was enough for now to know there was relief in sight.

Hazel had been expecting a solitary ride from Lynn to Ipswich, and so was surprised when she heard a familiar voice behind her in the entry.

"Good afternoon, Hazel."

Hazel turned, surprised to see Lady Howardsford standing next to Sophie. "Amelia?"

"You were expecting someone else?" Amelia said with eyebrows raised. "I had meant to wait in the carriage but needed a comfort break. We have not stopped for hours and will travel straight to East Ashlam so as to avoid traveling in the dark."

Hazel blinked. "You came all this way to accompany me?"

"Well, certainly, dear," Amelia said with a smile, putting her hand on Hazel's arm and giving it a squeeze. "I did not want you to travel on your own, and we can use the time to go over the details of the wedding."

The wedding.

Through letters, they had agreed on Thursday, November 20, for the ceremony. Hazel had asked Amelia to manage all the details because she had no idea how to approach it herself. Plus she was overwhelmed by trying to finish her teaching and plan for such a different life.

Hazel shared a final goodbye with Sophie, who held the embrace a few seconds longer than usual.

"I will miss you," Sophie whispered into Hazel's ear, "but wish you every happiness. Write to me as soon as you arrive and tell me everything."

Hazel nodded and blinked back tears. "I will miss you too."

She limped to the carriage and let the footman help her inside. She would not see Sophie until the year-long arrangement was up, and by then, the school would have already begun its first fall term under Sophie's management. Hazel wished she could be there for the beginning, but had she not agreed to this year away, she would not have the school at all.

She and Amelia had only just moved through the barest of small talk in the jostling carriage before Amelia produced a notebook filled with pages of notes regarding Hazel and Duncan's wedding. Hazel could not capture her vision, however, and felt her anxiety mounting as the details continued to pour from Amelia's mouth. She had planned aspects Hazel had never thought about: a luncheon and flowers and a wedding gown—the final fitting for which was scheduled this coming Monday. When she began talking of guests, Hazel could take no more.

"I know I asked you to manage the wedding, Aunt Amelia, but I had no expectation of all of . . . this. I have a dress that will serve the purpose."

"Wearing an ordinary dress does not diminish the importance of these covenants."

"Wearing a *formal* dress does not empower such covenants either," Hazel said in a soft but firm tone. "I am not accustomed to being the center of attention and do not want any of the typical pomp and ceremony. I am sorry I did not realize until now what you were planning. I did not fully appreciate the details, but I am not comfortable with this." She waved toward the papers in Amelia's hands.

Amelia looked at her for a few moments before she spoke, the feather of her bonnet bouncing in time with the road. "It should be a special day, Hazel."

"It is a business arrangement, Amelia."

Amelia pursed her lips.

"I understand you want to pretend this is a real marriage, but it is not. Duncan and I are fulfilling the terms of a business contract, and while I am willing to go through the basic expectations of the wedding, I would prefer to wear my own dress to shore up my comfort in an uncomfortable circumstance. And I only want you and Uncle there to witness."

The carriage hit a rut in the road, and Amelia reached for the fabric loop fastened to the ceiling. "No guests?" she said, surprise and dismay in her tone. "What of Harry and Hannah? Of your cousins? I've already written out the invitations."

"Especially not them," Hazel said, looking out the window. "They know of the inheritances and will see through all of it. If for nothing else than Uncle Elliott's insistence that no one know the details of our arrangement, those most likely to solve the puzzle of it should be kept as far away as possible."

The only thing worse than her family discovering the truth of the arrangement would be the pity that would follow.

Hannah—the daughter their parents had always wanted—would make a pouty face and call Hazel "poor dear" as she fussed over her the way their mother had fussed over Hannah herself on her wedding day. Harry would slap her on the back and congratulate her on taking advantage of the situation.

Her cousins were little more than strangers to her, but she did not want their judgment. Besides, what would Harry or Hannah think of Duncan? Harry would identify Duncan's peculiarities in a glance and taunt him into saying ridiculous things. Hannah would feel sorrier for Hazel than she already did to be marrying such an unusual man.

Amelia did not say anything, but merely folded her notes back into the leather cover and placed it beside her on the bench on the far side of the carriage.

"Are you sure about this marriage, Hazel?" Amelia asked softly, but loudly enough to be heard over the carriage wheels rattling beneath them. "If it does not feel right to you, do not push ahead. Find another way."

"There is no other way," Hazel said, continuing to look out the window and avoid eye contact. "And I feel right about the marriage. I simply do not want to pretend the vows we make to one another are more than the essentials."

"All right," Amelia said.

Hazel gave her a sidelong look, primed to continue her defense. But Amelia had her hands in her lap, the picture of accommodation.

The plan had been to go to Howard House and stay there for the next three weeks, but without a wedding party to plan, was that wait necessary?

"Thank you for preparing the Ipswich house."

Amelia smiled, which helped Hazel set aside her fear that her position had damaged their friendship. "It is called Lavender House, and it is on land that was once a friary. Preparing the house was quite enjoyable for me, and Duncan helped with a great deal of the details. He is moved in and settled, though Elizabeth has been a bit of a trial."

Hazel laughed. "Yes, he wrote to me saying she keeps returning to the Burrow Building."

Amelia nodded. "He finally sealed shut the window she'd been using at his old apartment and revised the window to his new bedroom to allow her access, but she'll stay out on the roof and complain at him." She laughed, and Hazel laughed with her.

"He is already living there, then?"

"Yes, as of Wednesday," Amelia said. "Elliott's solicitor has spent a great deal of time teaching him the management of the building. I think it's been rather overwhelming, but he has risen to the responsibility. Mr. Southey should be gone as of today, which means, come Monday, Duncan will have his own office." She shook her head. "I've enjoyed getting to know him. He can be . . . intimidating, but he is good-hearted."

"Yes," Hazel agreed, paused, and then spoke before she lost her nerve. "What if we got married . . . sooner?"

Amelia blinked. "How much sooner?"

"If the house is ready, and if the wedding doesn't require the time we thought, and if Duncan is finished with his responsibility to Perkins & Cromley, I see no reason to wait."

"Well . . ." Amelia shifted on her seat. "The banns have been read, and if there are no invitations to send out, I suppose it can take place whenever you and Duncan decide."

"I shall write to him as soon as we arrive at Howard House. Thank you for understanding."

"I am not sure I understand any of this," Amelia said, putting out her hands, palms up, before she folded them back into her lap. "But I nearly ruined my relationship with my own daughter when she wanted to marry Peter, and I am determined to have learned from that." She waved one hand through the air and looked out the window. "That is a story for another time," she said with a smile. "However, there are other things we should discuss if you truly want to move up the date of the wedding."

The road had smoothed some, but the feather in her bonnet continued to dance above her head. "You shall need a new wardrobe, for example—dresses, underthings, gloves, and hats."

Hazel's tension returned, erasing her small moment of peace. She opened her mouth to protest, but Amelia hurried on.

"You will be the married woman of a respectable man and must command respect about town. There will be social calls and dinner parties that require the appropriate costume."

Hazel immediately felt like a fish flopping back and forth on the bottom of a boat. "H-how will I go about that? I have never had to order a . . . wardrobe."

"Duncan has already found a dressmaker with a good reputation in Ipswich." She retrieved the papers she'd set aside and began sorting through them. "I've made up a list. Here it is."

Hazel swallowed as she scanned the list of items she'd never owned before—sleeves to wear under her cap-sleeved dresses when it was cold, morning dresses, and evening dresses.

"Duncan found a dressmaker?" Hazel asked as that detail finally registered in her mind.

"He's very resourceful, your husband."

*My husband.* Heat burst forth on Hazel's cheeks.

Amelia laughed, but Hazel was too disconcerted to be offended. "You shall need to get used to that term, Hazel. He *will* be your husband, never mind that this is a *business transaction.* You shall be Mrs. Penhale."

Hazel leaned back against the bouncing cushion and only just resisted putting her hands over her face. She took a deep breath while trying to formulate a response.

Amelia saved her by continuing to speak. "I believe he made

appointments for the week after you were to be married, but I am sure that can be changed if you marry sooner."

"I shall need to draw from my inheritance to cover the costs."

"Fiddlesticks," Amelia said, waving a blue-gloved hand. "It is my wedding gift to you. Have you anything set aside for your trousseau? Harry is staying at Falconridge now and can send anything you need."

"A trousseau," Hazel repeated with enough bitterness to change Amelia's expression. The day had been too heady, and her manners were suffering.

Hazel looked out the window at the trees sliding by the moving frame. "The first school I was sent to was Williamson Academy, a small school in Essex. My parents chose it because it would board girls as young as six years old."

"Six?" Hazel did not hear the word as much as see it on Amelia's lips as her expression fell.

"The school was shabby and poorly heated. They gave physical demerits, which terrified me but kept me well-behaved. I used a set of forearm crutches to walk back then and was terrified of being injured to a point that I might not be able to walk on my own. At the age of nine, I had proved myself intellectually proficient enough to go to St. Mary's—that was when Uncle Elliott began to subsidize my education, and I had my first customized boot that allowed me to walk without crutches."

She smiled at the memory of limping into St. Mary's and knowing that, while she drew the attention of everyone there, none of them knew she'd ever used crutches. She had felt remarkably self-sufficient and proud of all she'd done to earn her place.

"St. Mary's was superior to Williamson in every way; I plan to utilize a great deal of their structure at my school, in fact. When I was, I think, eleven years old, I came home on a mandatory holiday—I stayed at the school for holidays unless required to return home, which was only twice a year.

"Hannah was working on the third of a set of pillowcases, embroidering the same garland upon each one. It was beautiful work, especially for an eight-year-old child, but I could not determine why she would need three of the same design. As it turned out, it was the third of what would be ten matching pillowcases for her trousseau."

Hazel shrugged, as though to say she was unaffected by this, which, of course, was not true. "After I went back to school, I asked a friend what a trousseau was, and she explained it was a collection of articles a girl made as she prepared for marriage. My friend was surprised that not only did I not know what it was but had made no additions to my own.

"I still did not realize the significance of all of this until months later, when I next returned home. I asked my mother if there was something I could work on for my trousseau while I was there. She became very uncomfortable and said she would find something for me to work on, but she never did. It was Harry who told me that I was not to have a trousseau because everyone knew I would never marry and therefore would never need items meant to make a new bride feel at home in her new place."

"Oh, Hazel," Amelia said.

"Do not pity me," Hazel replied, shaking her head and smiling slightly to take the edge off her words. "I share this only to help you understand what my life has been like and how the expectations of my future have shaped me. I did not build a trousseau. I did not learn how to flirt or embroider in a drawing room—though I am a fairly good stitch. I was not raised to plan a menu or interview staff or be a wife and mother the way my sister was raised.

"Quite frankly, I was not *raised* at all. Rather, I was educated and kept far away so as not to disrupt the lives of my family or cause them embarrassment." She was saying too much, being too open—something she rarely did. She looked at her hands in her lap and took a breath. "Forgive me for making you uncomfortable, Amelia."

"You did not make me uncomfortable," Amelia said. "I am glad to have a fuller picture of what your life has been."

They both fell silent long enough that Hazel startled slightly when Amelia spoke again. "My daughter, Julia—she married your cousin Peter—was raised a banker's daughter until her father died, then she was raised only by me, a rather hardheaded widow who managed her own household with as little help as possible." She smiled at her self-reference. "When Julia fell in love with Peter, she was completely overwhelmed by the responsibility of managing staff. I moved into the house for a few months before they married so as to help train her in the expected responsibilities since, while I had never managed such a lifestyle for myself, I was raised amid the noble class and grew up in a grand estate house." She paused. "I would be happy to offer you the same assistance, though I understand if you would rather find your own way."

Hazel looked at Amelia, this woman with graying hair and an aging smile that showed wisdom and sincere concern. Hazel had met Julia last Christmas. She had been quiet, but the affection she and Peter shared had been obvious. In them, Hazel had seen an ideal situation of two people perfectly situated for the places they fell into as easily as sinking into sofa cushions. She had not considered that they might have had their own struggles in blending their lives.

"You would move in with Duncan and me for three months to train me?"

Amelia laughed and grabbed the strap again as the carriage hit another series of ruts in the road. With her other hand, she pressed the papers onto her lap so they would not fall to the floor. Hazel grabbed for her strap as well.

"I hardly think that will be necessary," Amelia said. "But I would be happy to come to Ipswich for a week or so and help you find your way until you feel capable. The house only has two bedrooms, however, so I can stay at an inn in town."

"Thank you," Hazel said, unable to remember the last time she'd felt such genuine care from another person. "I do not even know enough to know what I do not know," she admitted with a shrug. "I am extremely intimidated by the tasks ahead. This arrangement is only for a year, but I do not wish to live in discomfort and angst."

"Then I should be happy to guide you, if you'll have me."

Hazel shared a shaky smile across the shaky carriage. "That would be most welcome, thank you." She paused. "Forgive me my sharp edges today, Amelia. You have been nothing but kind to me, and I am acting the part of a spoiled child."

"Oh, Hazel, there is nothing to forgive. I have my own share of sharp edges, but I do hope you will see me as the friend and ally I wish to be."

Hazel nodded, grateful and humbled. She'd never had enough connection with her own mother to truly know what a normal mother-daughter relationship should feel like, but she thought it might feel like this. "Thank you, Amelia."

"You're welcome, Hazel. Shall I tell you about the staff that's been hired for the house? You'll be glad to know that the cook Duncan approved quite likes cats."

# Chapter Thirteen

Though Hazel had voiced her decision to be married in one of her teaching dresses, in the week between the carriage discussion with Amelia and the actual day of her wedding, she changed her mind.

Amelia had taken her to a dressmaker friend of hers, who fitted a few already made dresses to Hazel so she would have some things a step above her teaching gowns to take with her to Ipswich. Among those dresses was a lavender-sprig muslin that Hazel had loved as soon as she'd put it on. The wide neckline showed off her collarbone, and the sleeves came to just above her elbows. There was no lace, no ruffles, no beading, or frippery, just clean lines that defined Hazel's shape in ways her teacher dresses never had. When she wore it, she felt beautiful, and even though the marriage was not a love match, she found herself wanting to *feel* beautiful on her wedding day.

On the morning of November 7, Amelia's ladies' maid twisted Hazel's chestnut hair into an elaborate style woven with tiny white flowers. Hazel studied her reflection in the looking glass and swallowed the emotion that rose up in response. She looked so much like Hannah had on her wedding day, and it gave her a connection she rarely felt to her sister. It was too late to invite Hannah or Harry, but the fact that she wanted to, even for a moment, was something she tucked away to be looked at later.

She had declined a bouquet and refused to walk down the aisle of the church—the last thing she wanted was to have anyone watch her walk. Instead, she followed Uncle Elliott, Aunt Amelia, and Duncan into the church, stepping forward to greet the vicar, Mr. Tottenshod, when he arrived.

She sensed the vicar's confusion as she hurried through the introductions and thanked him for making the time. She caught Amelia's tight expression from the corner of her eye and realized that her desire to treat this event like a business transaction was coming across as rude. She pulled back, stilled her tongue, and pasted a smile. She went along with things from that point on, silently willing things to move quickly.

Without her prodding, the entire process slowed, and she lowered herself into the front pew and waited to be called forward. While she waited, she looked around the church—a lovely light-gray stone with a stained-glass window depicting a bearded man in a white robe—Jesus, she assumed—touching the eyes of a man who knelt at his feet. The colors were bright, and the morning sun made them seem almost alive.

Glass was made of nothing but sand. Stained glass, as she understood it, was colored by adding different minerals to the sand before the heating process that liquified the elements, allowing them to be shaped and formed. Chemistry. Focus. Creation.

She was so engrossed in the details of the window that she startled when Duncan appeared in front of her. He put out his hand, and she looked at it—the hand of the man who was soon to be her husband. Her gaze traveled up to his face. Were they doing the right thing? Would the sand and minerals of their lives melt down properly to form something useful to them both?

Strangely enough, she thought that they would, and she glanced at the window, remembering the soft air of the room the night Sophie had prayed. If marrying Duncan was the right thing to do, what did that mean? What constituted right or wrong in their situation? She did not think that the God Sophie believed in would smile upon Hazel and Duncan marrying one another for the worldly gain it brought to both of them. But was He not also the God who created sand and heat and oxidizing minerals?

"I can stand on my own, Duncan," she said as she pushed herself to her feet. "But, thank you."

He lowered his hand and stepped back, then put out his arm. He tensed when she put her arm through his, but then he relaxed, and they walked to the pulpit together. Almost a wedding march except for her staccato gait. Aunt Amelia and Uncle Elliott were serving as witnesses and came to stand beside them, Amelia on Hazel's side and Elliott on Duncan's.

"Dearly beloved," the vicar intoned.

Hazel took a breath in anticipation of the rather lengthy service. Her hip already hurt.

"We are gathered together here in the sight of God, and in the face of this . . . congregation, to join together this man and this woman in holy matrimony; which is an honorable estate, instituted of God in the time of man's innocency . . ."

The vicar droned on and on, and Hazel struggled to be attentive despite the butterflies in her stomach. This was truly happening, and even though she'd had two months to prepare, she did not feel ready for the changes these words were going to create for her.

One year. Twelve months. She could playact this role for twelve months, couldn't she?

"Therefore, if any man can show any just cause," the vicar said, his tone signaling he was nearing the end, "why these two may not lawfully be joined together, let him now speak, or else hereafter forever hold his peace."

Silence filled the church.

The vicar took a step back and closed his Book of Common Prayer. "Now, though it is not an official portion of the Church of England ceremony, it is a tradition growing in popularity, and I find it particularly fitting, so much that I believe in time it shall become a standard practice." He smiled at both of them and then seemed to realize that he hadn't actually said what this additional portion was. "You may share a kiss as a physical symbol of your commitment to one another, body and soul."

Hazel blinked. *A kiss!* She looked at Duncan, expecting him to be equally taken aback, but his bright eyes and eager expression reminded her immediately of their awkward discussion regarding marital intimacy. For the space of a moment, she considered putting her hand up to stop him moving toward her.

But she did not, and Duncan closed the space between them. He put his hands on her shoulders as though preventing her from fleeing, and then lowered his mouth to hers. He pressed his lips against her own and, although every muscle in her body was rigid, she felt her lips yielding. Something happened, though she could not identify exactly what it was. A softening. A joining. A momentary wish for more of whatever it was.

And then he pulled back and released her shoulders. He stared at her, the room still and silent, and she stared back wondering if he had felt it too but knowing she would never ask.

"Congratulations, Mr. and Mrs. Penhale," the vicar said. "You are now officially husband and wife."

Amelia sighed as she came forward to embrace Hazel. Uncle

Elliott patted Duncan on the back, but upon contact, Duncan jumped and turned sharply. "Do not touch me!"

"My apologies," Uncle Elliott said immediately, his face flushed. He put his hands behind his back and stepped away. "I forgot."

An awkward silence fell for three seconds before Hazel found words of remedy. "I believe a luncheon is awaiting us in the dining room at Howard House." She looked to Amelia, who eagerly nodded to confirm. "Would you like to join us, Mr. Tottenshod?"

Amelia, as mistress of the house, should be the one offering the invitation, but Hazel needed to get used to taking the lead. It felt awkward, and she expected it would remain so for the next year.

"I, uh, would enjoy that very much," Mr. Tottenshod said, looking markedly uncomfortable.

"Wonderful," Hazel said in a very Duncan-esque way. She slipped her arm through the vicar's as a way to further put him at ease and took a hobbled step toward the doorway of the church. She thought of the lessons Amelia had given her on how to make small talk at parties and turned her newly acquired skills on the man who clearly did not know quite what to make of the ceremony he'd just officiated.

"How long have you lived in East Ashlam, Mr. Tottenshod?" Hazel asked as they made the reverse wedding march out of the church and into the carriage. She was aware of Uncle Elliott and Amelia behind them, and Duncan at the rear. She hoped he wasn't upset that she'd let another man escort her; should she try to explain herself later? Would he understand her reasons?

"Um, all of my life," Mr. Tottenshod said. "My father was the vicar before me."

"Really?" Hazel said with feigned interest, grateful to see the footman already holding the carriage door open. "Did you always know you wanted to be a clergyman? Raised to it, so to speak?"

A recounting of Mr. Tottenshod's childhood and schooling filled the carriage ride and accompanied the party into the dining room. The three-course luncheon was first-rate, and Mr. Tottenshod proved an excellent conversationalist. Duncan focused on his meal until Mr. Tottenshod mentioned his interest in bird-watching.

"What are your feelings regarding woodpeckers?" Duncan asked, his head coming up as he engaged in the conversation for the first time.

Mr. Tottenshod paused, and Hazel held her breath, willing him to answer kindly. When he did, she relaxed. "Well, I do not think highly of them when they go to work before the sun is up, but I find them rather fascinating—their beaks are incredibly strong."

"Do you feel that they cause fatal damage to already sick trees by puncturing the bark, or do you feel the trees become diseased due to the damage created by the woodpeckers?"

"Um, well, as I understand it, the woodpeckers target trees that are already infested with insects, which is an indication that internal damage is already being done."

"Do you believe the damage caused by the woodpeckers hastens the demise of the tree?"

Hazel noticed Amelia and Uncle Elliott tensing, yet she did not feel the same discomfort. Duncan's engagement was far more comfortable than his silence, which she feared reflected a poor mood on his part.

Mr. Tottenshod seemed unsure exactly how to interpret Duncan's tone, however, prompting Hazel to join the conversation. "It seems to me the woodpecker's efforts would make a difference in the tree's demise, but I wonder how much? Does it take the years of decline from six years to three, for instance? Or is the variable of demise closer to a three-to-two increase?"

"And *should* the damage necessarily be prevented?" Duncan

asked. "A dying tree will die one way or another, and perhaps it is for the overall improvement of the natural world, of which the tree has been a participant, for the tree to weaken at a faster rate so that the nutrients might be added to the soil sooner for the continued propagation of future vegetation."

Hazel and Duncan looked at Mr. Tottenshod for his reaction. She'd meant to diffuse the intensity of Duncan's attention to the man, not encourage it, but now it was up to the vicar how he would engage.

The vicar looked at both of them in turn, and Hazel gave him an encouraging smile. After a few seconds, he cleared his throat. "There is an extensive wooded area behind the parsonage with a variety of aging trees, which helps to facilitate my bird-watching—I am quite fortunate in that sense. When I find a particular tree is drawing the attention of a woodpecker, I know that it is already infested, often beyond the ability for any remedy.

"However, I had success saving a young oak a few years ago because a woodpecker had alerted me to a beetle I would likely not have found otherwise; oaks tend to be quite resistant to beetle infestations. I was able to utilize the holes the woodpecker had drilled into the tree to treat the infestation, and now, half a dozen years later, that oak is strong and robust. I see every indication that it will outlive both myself and my children, and all because a friendly woodpecker alerted me to the trouble."

"Fascinating," Duncan said. "How exactly did you treat the diseased tree?"

The vicar went on to explain the concoction he had created to treat the tree, and Duncan returned to his meal as he listened to the man's account of household chemistry in action.

Hazel shared a look with Amelia and Uncle Elliott, who relaxed once they saw the vicar had not been offended. Yes, this husband of hers was quizzical, but when seen from the right point of view, that was not a negative aspect. A woman could certainly do worse for herself in life than to be paired with a man interested in increasing his knowledge.

Hazel caught that thought, her fork halfway to her mouth, and revised it in her mind: a woman could certainly do worse for herself for *one year*.

*It is not a real marriage,* she reminded herself. But she was eating real food and drinking real wine at a real wedding luncheon beside a real vicar. And the kiss Duncan had given her had certainly been real. She thought back to the something she had felt when Duncan's lips had pressed against hers.

Surely it was a biological reaction that stemmed from the instinct all creatures had regarding propagation of their species. If one simple kiss in the presence of other people could feel like that, however, what would a kiss in private feel like?

She took another bite of the braised pork and allowed herself to ponder the thought for the amount of time it took to properly chew and swallow. Then she took a longer drink of wine and pushed the pondering from her mind completely. It did not serve her to fantasize.

Upon finishing the meal, she and Duncan would step into the carriage that would take them to Ipswich, where they would sleep in separate rooms for the first of three hundred and sixty-five nights.

Tomorrow morning, she would awaken in her own home with a husband and begin a life that, for one year, she would live like any other woman.

What a remarkable thing a single day could be.

# Chapter Fourteen

*A*melia arrived in Ipswich on Tuesday and took rooms at the Ipswich Inn for the next week, spending her days at Lavender House teaching Hazel how to properly run it. The small house was lovely, but nearly half a mile from the Burrow Building. Duncan complained every single day about how much more convenient it had been to live in the same building where he worked. After a few attempts to talk it through with the goal of improving his understanding, Hazel stopped defending their decisions and simply agreed, moving on to a new topic each time he renewed his dissatisfaction.

Thursday morning, Amelia stayed at the house to write a letter to Uncle Elliott, while Duncan escorted Hazel to the cobbler. Hazel was looking forward to the new boot almost as much as she was dreading the appointment. When Uncle Elliott's carriage pulled up in front of the squat building with the shoe-shaped sign that simply read "Cobbler," Duncan jumped down from carriage and put up his hand to help Hazel descend—always a tricky action for her.

"Thank you," she said when she reached street level. "I shall manage the rest on my own."

"I will go with you," he said, dropping her hand, but then extending his arm for her to take.

Hazel did not move. "I prefer to do this alone. In fact, the Burrow Building is only a few blocks away—you can go to work if you like."

"I planned to take the morning off in order to accompany you to your appointments as you are unfamiliar with Ipswich."

Hazel took a breath. That he'd arranged this appointment, and the dressmaker's appointment for later in the day was very thoughtful, but she did not want him hovering, especially here. "But I do not need your attendance, though I thank you for coming with me in the carriage and having arranged the appointment."

He furrowed his brow. "You do not want me to come?"

*You appreciate his honesty and directness,* she told herself, *you should trust him enough to give him the same.* "No."

"Why?"

It required another fortifying breath to remain honest. "Because I do not want you to see my foot."

His shoulders slumped, betraying his intrigue about her foot, which annoyed her. "I am only curious, Hazel, not in judgment of a deformity that was no fault of your own. In the Bible, Christ teaches that physical defects are not the punishment for sin on the part of the person who suffers or their parents, as was a prior belief, but rather an opportunity for growth and personal development of virtue."

Christ again. They had argued religion Sunday morning when Duncan was surprised she did not want to attend church. It had ended with her flat-out refusal and his mood dour as he left for church alone. By the time he'd returned from church, she had read up on Pythagoras and his wife, Theano, enough to begin an engaging conversation that had left the religious discussion in the past. She had no interest in revisiting the topic.

"Your curiosity does not overcome my right to privacy, Duncan. Thank you, again, for your assistance with this appointment. Please either return to work or wait here."

"Very well," he said with a sigh. He looked around the particular block of shops and buildings. "I shall go see Dr. Randall." He turned west.

"Dr. Randall?" Hazel repeated, suddenly worried. "Are you unwell?"

"No, I just enjoy talking to him about his work," he said, pointing to the end of the block. "His office is on the corner of Westgate and Elm Street."

She cocked her head to the side. "You talk to the doctor about his work?"

He put his hands into the pockets of his knee-length wool coat with patched elbows. Amelia had been encouraging him to purchase a new wardrobe that would better reflect his position as a landowner and married man, but he was resistant, claiming he had made enough changes and could not tolerate uncomfortable clothing in addition to everything else.

"If he is not too busy, he will let me practice with his instruments and review his more curious cases. He once let me help him set a broken leg where the bone had come apart. It was quite fascinating."

Hazel made a face; that did not sound fascinating at all. "Do you visit Dr. Randall often?"

"Not often. It has been some months since I have stopped in."

"So, Dr. Randall is a friend, then?" She'd wondered if he had friends, aside from Elizabeth and Delores, a friend of Catherine's he talked of a fair amount.

"We do not socialize, other than my visits and when we greet one another at church, so I do not know that I would call him a friend. I consider him more of an associate, like the blacksmith or Mr. Talmage, the butcher."

"Do you visit with them as well, observe their work?"

"When I can," Duncan said. "Before deciding upon accounting for my occupation, I made it a goal to observe as many men at their work as possible. I was quick to determine my aptitude, but still felt a great deal of appreciation for the work some of them perform as their occupation. Some men found my attention irritating, but there are some who invited me to return and I have continued my associations with them."

"That is very good, then," Hazel said, finding this information odd but encouraging. It was good that he had some sort of relationship with other men in town. "Enjoy your visit. I imagine I shall be finished in about half an hour."

"I shall meet you at the carriage and accompany you back to the house until it is time for the dressmaker appointment."

Hazel watched him walk a few steps before she turned back to the cobbler shop and the uncomfortable appointment ahead.

A bell sounded when she entered. The shop smelled of leather and polish. There were a few finished shoes on display in the window, but as most shoes were custom-made, there was not much variety. The interior of the shop itself was more workshop than store.

"Good day," a voice said from behind the counter set in the middle of the room.

Hazel approached and looked over the counter at the small man hunched over a boot upended on a metal shoe form. He finished pulling at a thick thread at the top of the boot, then looked up at her over the spectacles perched on the end of his nose.

"Mrs. Penhale?" he asked.

"Yes," she said with a smile while trying to keep from blushing. She was still not used to her married name.

"Mr. Leavitt," he said by way of introduction. "Let me finish this seam, and I'll be right with you. Mind you take a look at that basket of samples and choose the leather you prefer."

She looked around until she saw a basket the size of a cooking pot on the far side of the counter. She limped over and shuffled through the irregularly shaped scraps. She'd only ever worn a black boot, and the leather needed to be quite stiff in order to give her foot the proper bracing. She chose the blackest and stiffest leather in the basket before returning to the counter.

The cobbler stood from his task, bringing him to his full height, which was only a few inches taller than she was. He had tufts of gray-white hair above each of his ears and a shiny pate that reflected the light from the oil lamp burning in the corner. He wiped his hands on his thick canvas apron that was smudged and smeared with a variety of polishes.

"Come around to the back," he said as he turned, waving his hand to indicate she follow him through a doorway. "We'll get started on the fitting."

He gestured her toward a low chair as he sat on an even lower chair on the other side of a small bench between them. He took the leather sample she handed him.

He rubbed it between his fingers and then tucked it into the front pocket of his apron. "Put your foot up here on the bench so I can see what you have been using until now."

Hazel hesitated, pushed away the shame she always felt about her foot, and then lifted her leg so the heel of her atrocious boot rested on the bench.

He turned her foot this way and that, then pulled a knotted string from his apron pocket and took some measurements. He did not write down any of the measurements. "You've put this boot to good use, I see."

"Yes," Hazel said simply.

He ran his finger on the portion of sole that was worn almost to the leather along the inside edge. "Does your left hip give you trouble when you have to walk a fair distance?"

"It gives me trouble all the time," she said with hesitation, as though admitting a shameful secret. She was not used to talking about her body.

"That does not surprise me. This boot is not properly balanced."

"I have worn it more than three years, which accounts for the state it is in. The cobbler I have always used is in Northampton, you see, and I have been in King's Lynn a year and a half, and I have put off finding a new cobbler to make a new boot."

"It was *never* properly balanced, I'm afraid," the cobbler said, looking at her over his glasses again. "If it had been, the wear would be evenly distributed." He rested the boot on the bench again and began to undo the laces.

Hazel tensed. She could count on one hand the people outside of her immediate family who had ever seen her foot—two cobblers and two physicians.

When the laces were loose, he carefully slid the boot from her foot, revealing a thick sock meant to help cushion the points of pressure caused by the boot. Without asking her permission, he slid off the sock, then turned her twisted foot this way and that as he'd done with the boot a minute earlier. He made a tsking noise, then pressed against a deep bruise on the outside of her ankle.

She hissed slightly at the pain that shot up her foot.

"My apologies," he said, but then turned her foot and pressed against another area that was nearly black with bruising. She'd had the bruises for months now.

She winced again.

"Oh, my dear, I am so very sorry that you have had such a poor device. You have suffered with this boot three years you said?"

"Nearly four," Hazel admitted. "But it was sufficient up until just this last year."

"We can do better than sufficient," he said, looking up at her and smiling. "I can only suppose that this boot, nor any others you might have had previously, was not made from a mold of your foot."

"A mold, sir?"

"I mix a quantity of plaster which I put into a tray in order to preserve imprints of your foot. It allows me to create perfectly shaped interior."

He must have seen the fear in her expression because he smiled calmly. "Making a mold is a painless process, I assure you. Having the exact shape of your foot allows me to add cushions and braces into the structure that will support your foot in the best alignment possible. I cannot promise that you will not still have some discomfort when you walk, but I do believe I can create a device that will offer better support than what you have had.

"The boot I design will not be as bulky as what you are used to, and I shall make the leg portion of the boot longer, partway up your calf, so as to better brace your ankle, and therefore re-place the need for such stiff leather as what you chose."

He patted the pocket where he'd deposited the sample of leather she hadn't chosen as much as believed was her only op-tion. He turned her foot again, tsking as he rubbed his thumb over a callous that had formed on the top of her foot. "I can see you take proper care of your foot, which is excellent and will allow quicker healing of the injuries caused by your current boot." He looked at her again. "Shall I mix the plaster, then?"

"You—you seem quite experienced at this," Hazel said, still feeling awkward despite his ease.

"Started my work in the King's army," he said, getting to his feet. He stretched out his back, and she heard two distinct cracks that he did not react to in the slightest. "I made boots for the most part and, in time, had to learn to adapt existing boots when there was a soldier missing a few toes or even an entire foot."

"You made boots for men without a foot."

The cobbler nodded. "After I returned to Ipswich, soldiers still managed to find me. I chiefly make the same shoes every other cobbler does, but I also make any number of specialty shoes now—prosthetics, weighted shoes, built-up soles, crafted things like what you need. Mr. Penhale found me through one of my clients who works with Perkins & Cromley. He gave me a fair enough interview before granting me the work."

He smiled, which helped ease Hazel's embarrassment at the imagined interview or, rather, interrogation, Duncan likely administered.

"You did not know Mr. Penhale previously?" Hazel asked.

"Not personally, no. Though he's the sort of man everyone in town knows of, I suppose."

She needed no clarification of what he meant, Duncan certainly stood out, but she was relieved that there was no animosity in the cobbler's voice.

The cobbler lifted a bulky paper bag off one shelf and a metal bowl off another. "If you can afford the expense, I would suggest having two sets of boots made from this mold, perhaps two different leathers for the sake of variety and matching them to their pair. If you can alternate which pair you wear every other day, it will allow the leather to rest between wearings and extend the life of both boots.

"As soon as you feel any new sensation, after the first few weeks of acclimation, of course, come for a new pair. I do new molds each time I design a new boot, but there's no reason for you to be in pain like I suspect you've come to accept as your lot. These boots should last a solid year or two."

Hazel nodded, a bit stunned and . . . excited? Was that what she felt? If this man could be believed, she would not feel the chronic ache in her hips and the twinge in her knee. She would have two pairs of shoes in *soft* leather. Did she dare believe it?

He poured some white powder from the bag into the bowl, added water from a ceramic jug, mixed, added a bit more powder, mixed again, then a bit more still. After a few minutes, he poured what looked like gray cake batter into three wooden trays already set on the floor but unnoticed by Hazel until now. As he worked, he asked her about her life and schooling, how she knew Duncan, what she thought of Ipswich. Such easy conversations were uncommon for her, but she felt herself relaxing into this man's company.

When the mixture was ready, he moved the trays to the area beside the bench where her foot had rested all this time and moved one tray beneath her foot. He gave her an encouraging smile.

"All right, Mrs. Penhale, lower your foot into the mixture slowly . . . try to bring it straight down—there you go. Let's rest it there a bit to make sure we get the impression. Good. Now lift it straight up, yep, just like that. Excellent. The second impression will be of the right side of your foot so the angle will be a bit awkward for a moment . . . Perfect. You are a quick study. Very good. Now, just one more from the left side."

# Chapter Fifteen

r. Randall was in the exam room with a patient who seemed to be suffering from a bad cough. Duncan could not hear the conversation, which was only right since one's health was a personal matter, but he could hear the murmur of voices and could tell when they began to come closer to the door that divided the exam room from the waiting room.

In addition to these two front rooms, a surgical room was located at the back of the building. It was used for procedures like the removal of external growths or cleaning an infected wound. Duncan had not been into that room very often.

Dr. Randall was an oddly clean man. He used a chlorine solution to wipe down surfaces after treating a patient, and he was particularly attentive to the cleanliness of his surgical room, which more often involved bodily fluids. Dr. Randall believed that the bad air known to be the cause of all disease could be transferred from one patient to another through these bodily fluids. Because of this, he preferred to treat patients in his office rather than at a patient's home, which could not be cleaned as easily.

Duncan had heard people whispering behind Dr. Randall's

back about his strange theories, but Duncan considered himself a man of scientific study and felt there might be some value to Dr. Randall's beliefs. Dr. Randall himself claimed that he lost fewer women in childbirth and that fewer of his patients developed additional infections after being treated for the initial illnesses that had brought them to his care. Duncan thought that suggested better proof of his hypothesis than a layperson with no medical knowledge who could present no case study to the contrary.

The door to the exam room opened and a slightly bent man, one hand to his chest, proceeded Dr. Randall out of the office. "What if me wife won't allow me the brandy?"

"You tell her that I recommended it. Make sure you strike the center of your chest three times after each swallow, however. This will help break the bad patches of air inside of your lungs so you can better expel it from your body. Spit anything you cough up into the fireplace and then take another swallow of brandy to ensure it is properly expelled."

Dr. Randall caught Duncan's eye and nodded, which Duncan returned. Hearing this instruction confirmed that Dr. Randall was a very good doctor. Duncan felt proud to be his associate.

"I'll be glad to tell me wife I'm to have all the brandy I can drink."

"Come see me next week if you haven't seen improvement."

The man shook Dr. Randall's hand and exited the office. Dr. Randall turned his attention to Duncan but did not put out his hand to shake Duncan's because he knew Duncan preferred to avoid physical contact when possible.

"Good day, Mr. Penhale. Congratulations on your marriage."

"Thank you," Duncan said, which is what Hazel had told him was all he should say when people asked him about their marriage. He was not, under any circumstances, to share that the marriage was only for the duration of one year or that its purpose was independent financial security for both of them.

"What brings you here today?" Dr. Randall said as he moved behind his wooden desk set on one side of the room. He raised his eyebrows. "Questions about, um, marital relations? Such things can be a bit tricky in the beginning."

"I have no questions. Hazel has disallowed marital relations, so the knowledge from your excellent book is useless to me."

"Oh, well, I am sorry to hear that."

"Not as sorry as I, but I did agree to the terms, and I still find marriage an agreeable arrangement."

"I am glad. Is there something else on your mind?"

"I was curious as to what new advances you have employed in your treatment of disease since we last talked. It has been several months since I was last able to visit."

"Yes, I think you are right," Dr. Randall said, standing and moving toward his exam room. He beckoned for Duncan to follow. "I do have some new literature you are welcome to read as well as a new device that allows me to more clearly hear a person's heartbeat. Would you like me to show you how it works?"

"I would like that very much," Duncan said.

Dr. Randall showed Duncan the device he called a stethoscope and let Duncan press one end of the tube against Dr. Randall's chest and listen to his heart and his breathing before explaining why it worked and why its utilization was an improvement in medical science. Duncan found it all very fascinating, and they had a wonderful discussion about its uses. When they finished, Dr. Randall stood as though to usher Duncan from the room, but Duncan remained in the chair as he had completed only one of his purposes in coming to visit Dr. Randall.

"Is there anything else, Duncan?" Dr. Randall said. "I am expecting another patient in a few minutes."

"I would like to hear your medical opinion on a situation I am having."

"Does it have to do with Mrs. Penhale?"

"Yes."

Dr. Randall returned to his own chair—the one padded in leather—and laced his fingers. "What is the situation?"

"You know that I do not like to be touched," Duncan said. "And I do not typically like to touch other people."

"But you don't mind touching your wife?"

Duncan looked at him, surprised that he'd guessed correctly. "Yes. Is it normal for a man like me to have such a change in behavior when he marries?"

Dr. Randall smiled, which was a reaction that sometimes made Duncan nervous as a smile often meant Duncan had said something out of place and the smiling person would soon be laughing at him. But Dr. Randall had never laughed at Duncan before.

"I think it is perfectly normal for any man to enjoy touching his wife. But you said she has disallowed marital relations. Is that upsetting for you?"

"It is not upsetting. I understand that she does not love me or find me physically attractive and she does not want to risk becoming pregnant, but it is disappointing. That is not the focus of my question, however. My wife . . ." He paused, finding it strange to use that phrase—*My wife*. "She has a clubbed foot and so walking is sometimes difficult for her, especially when she encounters stairs. When I realized this, I offered to help her up the stairs without thinking she would need to touch me. Then she took my arm, and it did not . . . startle me."

"If you offered to help that means you were prepared for the touch. We have talked about how helpful it is in regard to your reactions if you are expecting to be touched."

"Yes," Duncan acknowledged. "But I still do not *like* to touch or be touched, even when it is expected. However, I have found that I genuinely like to have her hold my arm, and so I find myself offering my assistance even when it is not precisely necessary. When we were married, the vicar asked us to kiss one another, it is a tradition he finds symbolic, and I felt very excited to kiss Hazel, and when I did kiss her, I liked it very much."

Dr. Randall chuckled, and Duncan turned sharply to him. "Why are you laughing?"

"Because I am happy to know that you enjoyed kissing your wife. Is that the only time you have kissed her?"

"Yes." He would like to kiss her again, but without being invited to do so, it would be inappropriate.

"Are there other instances of pleasurable touch you have shared with your wife?"

"Yes. I have touched her accidentally and felt pleasure from the sensation, which I have never felt before. I thought perhaps it was because she is a woman, and men and women are supposed to touch for reasons of procreation, though Hazel and I have agreed not to have such relations." He thought for a moment. "I still startle each time Delores touches me, and she is a woman."

"I see. So, you think there is something particular about your wife in this reaction on your part, or rather, lack of reaction?"

"Yes, I want to understand why touch is different with Hazel than with other women."

"Do you have affectionate feelings for her?"

"Yes, but I have affectionate feelings for Delores too."

"Perhaps different types of affection."

"Perhaps," Duncan acknowledged. "I want to understand

why, and I want to explore this change of reaction without making Hazel uncomfortable."

"It sounds to me that an experiment is in order, then."

"What sort of experiment?"

"Practice different types of touch with your wife and keep a record of which ones are pleasurable, which ones create no sensation, and which ones create a negative sensation, such as the burning or bruising sensation you have described to me before when people touch you."

Duncan nodded; this was a very good idea.

Dr. Randall continued. "It sounds as though you have already determined that walking arm-in-arm with her is pleasurable. What about sitting beside her, close enough that your knees touch, or your shoulders? Have you noticed any sensation in that sort of touch?"

"I have not been attentive to that sort of touch, though we do not often sit next to one another."

"Look for opportunities to touch her without her notice. If any sort of touch is uncomfortable, then do not initiate it again until you feel prepared to be uncomfortable again. It might take a certain number of exposures before you feel comfort, or even pleasure, from different types of touches."

"That is good advice. What other sorts of touches could I add as the experiment continues?"

"Perhaps brushing your fingers across her arm as though on accident would be a good sort of touch. Placing your hand on her back as she enters a room."

Duncan began to feel nervous, but he was curious enough about the results to continue listening to Dr. Randall's suggestion.

"In time, you might want to try holding her hand."

Duncan felt a prickle of sweat at his hairline. "I do not like to hold hands. My mother would try to hold my hand when I was very small, and I felt as though my fingers would break off—like her fingers were knives and would cut though my bones if she squeezed too tight." Remembering the sensation of having his hand grabbed and squeezed made his stomach churn.

"Perhaps do not intertwine the fingers, then. Simply hold like this." He mimicked an arrangement similar to a handshake, fingers closed, wrapping around the back of the other hand.

Social protocols required handshakes sometimes, and so Duncan had learned how to execute one without showing an adverse reaction as a matter of professional conduct. Duncan used his own hands to practice and looked at his clasped hands. The fingers did not feel like knives, but then his own touch had never bothered him, only touch from other people.

The front door of the office opened. Dr. Randall smiled at Duncan, creating creases that fanned out from the edges of his eyes. "Let me know how the experiment progresses. I am curious to hear the results."

Duncan agreed to share his results and thought over everything Dr. Randall had said as he made his way back to the cobbler shop where he was to meet Hazel. Sitting side by side so that their hips or shoulders touched, brushing fingers across her skin as though on accident, a hand on her back, possibly holding hands with the fingers closed. Just thinking of these actions made his heart pound.

What Duncan could not tell for sure, however, was whether the racing heart was anxiety at doing something that had previously been so uncomfortable or excitement for the possible pleasurable sensations that might result from this experiment.

# Chapter Sixteen

By the time the impressions of her foot were finished, the new, soft leathers were chosen, and her foot was cleaned and roped back into the boot that now felt like a torture device compared to her expectations of the new and improved boot, Hazel was nearly giddy with excitement. Would her gait improve? Would she no longer need to sleep with a hot-water bottle against her hip to manage the pain every night? Mr. Leavitt said he would have one pair for her in a week and the other a week after that.

As soon as she opened the door to the street, she saw Duncan approaching. He put out his arm for her to take, and then led her to the carriage. She thought that, in this moment, they likely looked like a perfectly ordinary couple. She felt a surge of pride at the thought.

He helped her into the carriage, his hand resting on her back a moment to help her keep her balance on the step, and the sensation made her blush—this blushing was getting out of hand. Once inside, she fell into the seat—there were no rails to ease a smoother transition—and Duncan slid in across from her. Beside him on the seat was a stack of periodicals he must have put there before she'd finished her appointment.

"Was the cobbler proficient enough to meet your needs?" Duncan asked as the carriage lurched forward.

"He was excellent," Hazel said. "Thank you, again, for arranging the appointment."

"It was no trouble," Duncan said. "I am glad you are satisfied."

"I am looking forward to the new boot. He found this one almost offensive."

"As do I."

Hazel startled. "What?"

"The uneven wear shows that it was not properly crafted," Duncan said, waving toward her hem and prompting her to pull her boot back beneath the curtain of her skirt. "Whatever cobbler made it for you did not do an adequate job. That is offensive to any man who takes pride in his work."

"Of course," Hazel said, keeping to herself that she'd thought he was offended by her foot, not the construction of the boot. "How was your visit with Dr. Randall?"

"Wonderful," he said, growing animated. "Dr. Randall has purchased a medical device called a stethoscope, the name of which I believe has roots in Greek. It is quite fascinating. It is a brass tube which condenses sound when placed against any surface, specifically a person's chest. He let me listen, and I could hear the actual beats of his heart, which are not only percussive but also have whooshing tonations as the blood moves from one portion of the heart to another. I also listened to the inhalation and exhalation of air through his lungs. Perfectly fascinating."

"It does sound fascinating. Did the discussion occupy the whole of the visit?"

Duncan looked out the window and cleared his throat, which made her wonder if there was something he did not want to tell her.

He suddenly looked directly at her with that unblinking stare he sometimes used. "What do you know about vaccinations?"

The sharpness of his words startled her, but she was learning to simply go with what he said and not expect clarity as she might from someone else. "Do you mean the theory of inoculation against disease by giving the patient a reduced version? I find it a bit frightening as disease is something I believe we should avoid at all costs."

Duncan's face lit up. "You have read about vaccinations, then?"

"I have read about Dr. Jenner and his cowpox."

Duncan smiled and relaxed, nodding his head with excitement. "Wonderful. Let us discuss."

The conversation followed them from the carriage to the study where Amelia was finishing her correspondence. Duncan brought up the theory that bloodletting was a sound practice to remove tainted blood; Hazel disagreed, and the conversation grew rather heated

Duncan finally said he needed to return to the office even though he had no appointments and no work.

After he left, Hazel took a breath and let her energy settle back to normal levels.

"That was a very . . . intense discussion," Amelia said after a minute of silence. She had moved onto her needlework.

"Indeed, it was," Hazel said, pushing herself up from the chair and walking to the bookcase. Lavender House had been mostly furnished, and Hazel particularly appreciated the collection of books that, while not extensive, covered a variety of topics.

She pulled *The Canterbury Tales* from the shelf. It had only been three days since she'd arrived in Ipswich, and each day had been packed with lessons from Amelia on how to manage this new life. An hour or two of reading before the appointment with the dressmaker would feel like a holiday.

"Was that conversation uncomfortable for you?" Amelia asked.

Hazel turned, putting too much weight on her bad foot. Pain shot up her hip. She caught her breath but spoke as soon as she could so as not to draw attention to her discomfort. "Not at all."

"Even when he said you were ignorant of the facts? I was offended on your behalf."

Hazel laughed. "I *am* ignorant of the facts, or at least those facts. Duncan is very well read and has an incredible memory. I always come away from our discussions more knowledgeable than I began."

Amelia made a gesture somewhere between a shrug and a shake of her head. " I suppose every relationship is unique in one way or another. I could never tolerate such insulting comments."

"From someone else, such things *would* be insulting, but it is different with Duncan. He is not trying to . . . win or keep me in my place. He is simply passionate and eager to share his point of view. If you notice, he also listens to what I have to say."

"Does he?"

Hazel smiled, thinking of Duncan's expression when he was listening, tight and ready to speak as soon as his turn came again. "Well, sometimes."

"You truly do not mind it, though? His . . . manner."

Hazel gave the question adequate consideration before

formulating a reply. "I have not spent much time in his company until these last few days, and though there are times when I am annoyed or uncomfortable, I am learning that I can be as direct with him as he is with me, and he is responsive to that."

Amelia seemed to consider that. "During the meeting at Howard House, you told him to be quiet and he was."

"Exactly," Hazel said. "There is something to be said for obedience and honesty."

"Enough to make up for his lack of tact?"

Hazel limped back to the chair. She put the book on the side table, then grasped the arms of the chair to lower herself into the seat. She picked up the book again. "Perhaps because I have trusted so few people in my life, I am willing to choose honesty over tact without much hesitation at all."

Amelia watched her closely for a few seconds. "Hmm," she said simply before returning to her needlework.

Hazel opened her book, but she worried she'd been too positive in her replies to Amelia's questions. She did not want to give Amelia the wrong idea, and yet hadn't she just proclaimed honesty to be an essential virtue? It would be hypocritical for her to then be dishonest in her feelings regarding Duncan's manner.

She turned the page and began to read about how "the droghte of March hath perced to the roote."

# Chapter Seventeen

*H*azel's new boot was incredible. The inside truly was molded to her foot, and the internal supports braced her ankle on three sides, holding it straight and better distributing the weight throughout her foot, rather than leaving the pressure concentrated on the jutting parts.

She still limped, but she no longer adjusted her gait based on whether or not anyone could see her, nor did she have to rely on the momentum of her body to start walking. And though there were a few blisters to contend with at the start, and her foot still ached at the end of the day, the improvement was enough to bring tears of gratitude. After only two weeks, her hip pain was nearly nonexistent.

Their marital routines quickly fell into place. Monday and Friday evenings, Hazel and Duncan engaged in discussions based on predetermined topics chosen by Duncan. On Tuesdays and Saturdays, they discussed topics of Hazel's choosing. On Wednesdays and Sundays, they played chess, gin, or worked on a puzzle of some sort: physical or intellectual. On Thursday evenings, they responded to correspondences and did their own individual reading.

Hazel had initially found the idea of the routine a bit severe but had agreed to try it for a few weeks. To her surprise, she found it nice to know exactly what to expect. Thus, on the fourth Thursday of her married life, Hazel reread Amelia's latest letter, which had come two days earlier and contained an invitation for Duncan and Hazel to come to Howard House for Christmas in two weeks.

It seemed that the Mayfield family was on a trajectory toward repaired relationships and new connections. She was glad for that for all their sakes, but did she want to travel the fifty-five miles to Howard House and playact her marriage in front of Harry and her cousins?

Peter was the only cousin Duncan had met, at Eastertime last spring, which meant the rest of them would have to make their own decisions about him. Did Hazel want to witness the awkwardness? Beyond that, the cooling temperatures of winter and comfortable routine they had established in their cozy house felt more comfortable than traveling to Howard House.

She turned in her chair at the writing desk to face Duncan, who was reading one of the medical journals Dr. Randall had given him earlier in the month.

"Duncan," she said.

He did not look up from his reading. "Yes."

"Aunt Amelia has invited us to Howard House for Christmas. Do you want to go?"

"We promised one another last year that we would attend this year together." He continued reading, and she wondered if his amazing brain allowed him to focus on two mental tasks at once.

"Yes, but do you *want* to go?"

He did not look up as he responded. "I do not like to travel, but we promised."

"I must confess that I am not looking forward to the long journey either, and I am less inclined to see my other cousins or Harry, for that matter. So much has happened these last few months, and I'm finding our life here in Ipswich comfortable enough that I do not want to leave it even for a week or two."

"I should like to meet your brother," Duncan said, finally lowering his periodical and looking in her direction. "He did not attend Easter weekend."

Hazel was *especially* reticent about Duncan meeting Harry. Her attempts at subtle introduction of the idea not to attend had not worked, but then subtlety never worked with Duncan. "Would you be terribly opposed to celebrating the holiday here in Ipswich?"

"We promised we would attend Christmas at Howard House this year," Duncan repeated.

"We promised that when we had not seen each other in over a year. Now we see each other every day, so the reason of the promise is no longer valid. We *could* forgive each other the broken promise and celebrate here, in Lavender House, instead."

"How, exactly, do you expect to celebrate?" Duncan placed the periodical upside down on his lap and looked at a place past Hazel's shoulder.

Hazel had not thought through the details, but did so quickly now that she had his full attention. "Well, when I was home at Christmas, our family would have a nice breakfast and there would be a small gift for each child at the table. On Boxing Day, we gave gifts to the staff." Hazel's family had not had elaborate celebrations, and the years she'd spent Christmas at school had been rather dismal. She feared her ideas could not compete with

Amelia's. "Did you celebrate Christmas with Catherine and your father?"

"I mostly remember putting up greenery on Christmas Eve and singing carols, which was enjoyable because Catherine was a very good singer. Since Catherine's death, I go to Christmas services in the morning and then have supper with Delores at the pub on Christmas Day. There are not a great many patrons that day, so the pub is not too loud and they cook a goose for the Christmas meal, which I eat with Delores at the pub. I usually work on Boxing Day as there is a great deal to be done before the end of the year."

"We could, um, make our own traditions."

"Tradition implies repetition, but this will be the only holiday we shall share as man and wife."

The comment made Hazel unexpectedly sad. "Still," she said with a shrug, "we could enjoy a nice meal and avoid the requisite travel to Howard House."

"Could we attend Christmas services?" Duncan said, sounding more excited. "It would be excellent to attend services together. Many of my fellow parishioners are curious about the woman who would marry me."

Hazel cringed, wondering if that was exactly how the comment had been said. "I'm not much of a churchgoer, Duncan, as we have already discussed."

"But surely you attend *Christmas* services. It is all about the birth of the Savior and helps to better focus our lives on the messages of His gospel. Even the non-religious should attend Christmas services." He jumped up and began pacing.

"We could attend services on Christmas morning together, then have brunch upon our return as is your tradition. We could read about the birth of Christ in the book of Luke, his account is the most inclusive of that event, though Mark is my favorite gospel to read. Then we could go to the pub and enjoy roast goose with Delores. Celebrating in that way would be an acceptable exchange for not traveling to Howard House and meeting your brother." He nodded in a way that made Hazel wish she'd not made the suggestion. He looked at her face suddenly. "That is acceptable to me, Hazel. Do you agree?"

To argue would risk ending up at Howard House. An hour of church was worth the trade, but Christmas dinner in a pub?

"Would you be willing to attend the dinner at the pub without me? It would be difficult for me to walk the distance, especially if I am to walk to church that day. And if the weather is poor, it may not even be possible."

"Go alone?" Duncan said as though he had not eaten alone at the pub for years.

"Or perhaps Delores would like to join us for our Christmas brunch."

"She is always at the pub on Christmas. She makes a roast goose."

They continued discussing until they had sorted the details—church, brunch, Luke, and then Duncan would go to Christmas dinner at the pub alone.

"I would still like to meet Delores, however. Perhaps we could invite her to tea."

"I do not think Delores has the same respect for teatime as you do."

"Well, maybe she will like teatime here at Lavender House. Cook can make some biscuits and scones, and then Delores and I can get to know one another. I would offer to go to the pub, but it is a fair distance for me to walk and perhaps she would like to see the cottage too. It is customary to invite one's friends over to visit after one moves into a new house."

Duncan kept watching his feet as he paced. Hazel was curious about this woman who seemed to have taken over as Duncan's mother figure after Catherine's death yet had not called on Hazel during this month of marriage. Some women from the neighborhood had stopped in for short visits, and the conversations were not as awkward as Hazel had feared they would be.

"Issue her an invitation," Hazel told Duncan. "Let her choose the day and the time, and I shall make sure to have a fine tea available for all of us to share."

Duncan paced two more lengths of the room before he seemed to have sorted through Hazel's suggestion. "All right, I will invite Delores to tea and inform the vicar that we are to attend Christmas services. I need to go check on Elizabeth."

Hazel looked after her odd husband and returned to her letter, relieved to have found an alternative to Christmas at Howard House and grateful to see how well she and Duncan were managing to communicate.

Against all odds, this marriage was *working*. Imagine that.

# Chapter Eighteen

 uncan helped Hazel create her own set of ledgers, a business one that tracked her expenses and interest from the inheritance, now managed at Gurney's Bank in Norwich, and a personal ledger where she accounted for everything she spent aside from that of the school. He had taught her how to use the different columns and how to properly separate expenses, which she reviewed and updated every morning. It was a heady experience to see the numbers on the page that reflected her personal wealth.

Wealth.

Hazel Stillman . . . Penhale, had lived a life that had been paid for and managed by other people, namely Uncle Elliott, until she reached the age where she could care for herself. She'd never had more than sixty pounds at one time in all the years she'd taught, and she had grit her teeth when she had to buy a new dress or stockings. Having so much money at her disposal now should give her a sense of freedom and extravagance; perhaps she should buy a collection of hats and parasols and face creams from France guaranteed to give her a glowing complexion.

The idea of spending the money, however, made her heart rate speed up and her palms sweat. Face creams from France seemed as frivolous now as they had when she could not afford them. Having the means to buy an entire collection of hats invited a fear that she would buy *all* the hats and never be satisfied. What if one day she turned from admiring her extensive hat collection to find that she had no money left? What if it all became a case of easy come, easy go?

All she'd had to do was speak a few vows in a church to earn the money in the first place. Could a few misspoken sentences make it disappear again?

What if she were more like Harry than she thought and she became reckless and hedonistic?

She could not imagine herself in what she suspected the London gaming hells to be—dark, smoky rooms filled with leering men, grasping at her purse—but she had not been able to imagine herself as the mistress of a house a few months ago. She was still unable to imagine herself in the scene of her mother giving instructions to the housekeeper. Yet she had met with the cook just that morning, following the pattern of the meeting she'd learned from Amelia. The weekly meetings still felt awkward, as if she were grasping at a place above what she deserved. She didn't imagine it had felt like that for her mother.

Perhaps because her mother had always expected one day to fill that place and Hazel never had. That she was filling that position now still felt false because there were only forty-seven weeks left in the one-year arrangement in which she was the kind of woman who gave instructions to housekeepers. Then she would instead be a headmistress who instructed staff, teachers, and students. The thought pushed her back in her chair, and she found herself as unable to picture herself as Mrs. Cordon any more than she could picture herself as her mother.

A knock on the parlor door startled Hazel. She closed the ledger on the writing desk and looked up as Corinne, the house-keeper and maid, entered the room wearing a charcoal-colored dress and a crisp white apron.

"Mr. and Mrs. Marcum to see you, ma'am."

Hazel searched her memory for recognition of the names but recalled nothing. "Who are Mr. and Mrs. Marcum?" she asked.

Corinne lowered her voice. "The parish vicar and his wife, ma'am."

Hazel stood from the writing desk and surveyed the grouping of chairs near the fireplace that was the best spot for visiting. Her bad foot tingled as it often did when she'd been sitting for a long time, and she shook it out as best she could as she moved toward the chair furthest to the right of the fireplace. Between the new dresses and better boot, she felt like a new woman. Unfortunately, that new woman had to entertain uninvited visitors and pretend to be happy about the interruption.

"Please show them in. And will you make up a tea tray?"

"Certainly, ma'am."

Hazel reached the chair just as an elderly couple entered the room.

Mrs. Marcum was apple-cheeked and bright-eyed, the lace of her mobcap framing the smooth gray curls surrounding her face. Mr. Marcum was a few inches taller than his wife, a bit more nar-row, and not as easy to read, though Hazel sensed he was reading her without any trouble. She could not cross to them without drawing attention to her limp, so she stayed where she was, hands clasped in front of her and a polite smile tacked to her face as they crossed to her instead.

Mrs. Marcum reached her first and took both of Hazel's hands in hers. The smile on her face did not seem the least bit forced, but morning visits were likely something this woman did every day amid the parish.

"Oh, it is so wonderful to meet you, Mrs. Penhale," Mrs. Marcum said, not releasing Hazel's hands. "I have been simply athirst for the chance to meet you, haven't I, Mr. Marcum?"

*Athirst?*

Mrs. Marcum did not look at her husband when she addressed him, nor did Mr. Marcum attempt a response from where he stood in front of one of the chairs.

"I told him 'she must be exceptional' and look at you." Mrs. Marcum took a step backward, still holding Hazel's hands, and then spread her arms, forcing Hazel's arms up and away from her sides. "Yes, beautiful, of course, that's what I told Mr. Marcum, didn't I, dear?"

Once again, her husband did not attempt to answer, and she did not allow him the time to do so.

"And poised, just as a granddaughter of a viscount would be. Accomplished too, aren't you? Duncan said you have been teaching these last years. It takes more than a pretty face to teach anything, now doesn't it?" She was still holding Hazel's arms out, as though the two of them were frozen in place within a dance.

Hazel's thoughts were swirling. Accomplished? Beautiful? Who was this woman talking about? The reference to Hazel's grandfather caught her attention most of all. The nobility contingent of her pedigree was often seen by others as a golden thread of value sewn into her human fiber. Never mind that Hazel had been treated like an embarrassment to those noble people, all except Uncle Elliott, who was, in fact, the only person of official rank.

Did Mrs. Marcum know Hazel was a cripple? Perhaps she

should have limped across the floor to meet them after all. She forced her smile a little bigger and brought her arms down, gently pulling them out of Mrs. Marcum's grip.

"Lovely to meet you, Mrs. Marcum," she said as she lowered herself into her chair. She looked past the woman in front of her to the vicar who was still on his feet, watching. "And you, Mr. Marcum. To what do I owe this visit?"

Mrs. Marcum bustled to the chair between Hazel and the vicar, and her husband finally sat when she did. "Oh, we visit all the new members of the parish, especially those of rank—don't we, Mr. Marcum?"

Rank again. Fabulous.

"We have great affection for Mr. Penhale," the vicar said, his voice steady and resonating, a stark contrast to his wife's twittering tones that seemed to still be bouncing around the parlor walls. "And were very glad to hear that he had married. We're grateful you have agreed to attend our Christmas service."

Hazel felt a tremor of discomfort shudder through her. The vicar held her eyes in such a way as to make her feel as though he could see her thoughts, a frightening prospect. She looked at his wife, suddenly the safer place to turn her attention.

Mrs. Marcum lifted her shoulders excitedly. "We do wish the ceremony could have been performed here in the church—didn't we, Mr. Marcum?—but we understood it took place in your uncle's parish."

Hazel considered telling her that the best part of the day had been a discussion about woodpeckers, but she knew better than to make such a jest. Thinking back on that day also brought to mind the kiss she had shared with Duncan. Why that had popped into her mind, she could not say, but it seemed to be happening with increasing frequency.

"Yes," she said simply, then looked at Mr. Marcum. "Have you known Dun—Mr. Penhale long?"

The vicar's wife answered. "He attended our school for, what, eight years? Isn't that right, Mr. Marcum? An excellent student, of course, if perhaps . . . unique."

"It was *your* school he attended here in Ipswich?" Duncan had said he started school for the first time when he was six and attended until he transferred to a more advanced school in Bury St. Edmunds.

"Yes," Mr. Marcum said, inclining his head.

"Usually we are a three-year school, aren't we, Mr. Marcum?" Mrs. Marcum said. "But Duncan was a special consideration." She laughed as though she'd made a joke, which caused Hazel's chest to tighten. Was she making fun of Duncan?

Mr. Marcum cleared his throat at the same time he touched his wife's arm. Her mouth was open to say something more, but she paused instead. A signal they had worked out ahead of time when her husband wanted her to stop talking?

"We generally do not take boys under the age of eight," Mr. Marcum explained. "But Miss Mayfield had asked if we would give him special consideration. I recognized his keen intellect and understood that a more traditional education would likely not work for him. By the time he was twelve, he had moved past my teaching abilities and spent the next two years teaching himself until he went on to Resins in Bury St. Edmunds."

"Teaching himself?" Hazel questioned.

Mr. Marcum smiled broadly, even proudly, Hazel thought. "There is not a personal library in the parish that Duncan has not read through, so long as the topic interested him, and likely not a professional he has not at some point asked to explain their trade. By the time he returned from Resins at age seventeen, he'd settled on accounting. He began his apprenticeship with Perkins & Cromley shortly after his return."

"He has told me a bit about that—the visits to other working men in the city. He still visits with some of them when he can."

"Yes, he is very engaging and rather insatiable in regard to learning and debate."

Hazel smiled, liking how Mr. Marcum spoke of Duncan with affection and even admiration. "Yes, I have noticed that." She paused a moment, her thoughts going to something else he'd said. "You knew Catherine too, then?"

"Yes," Mr. Marcum said with a nod. "She was a good woman."

*Was she?* Hazel wanted to ask. She hadn't married Duncan's father and drank more than was decent, yet the local vicar admired her enough for him to take her lover's son on as a student? "I'm afraid I never met her, but Duncan is quite complimentary."

"Oh, well, Duncan is complimentary about everyone, isn't he, Mr. Marcum?" Mrs. Marcum laughed nervously. Hazel suspected she did not like talking about Catherine.

"I do not think anyone knew Catherine *well*, but I found her to be kind and personable on the occasions she came to the school."

"Did she not come to church with Duncan?"

"Oh, no," Mrs. Marcum said, shaking her head though her curls did not move.

"She was welcome, of course," Mr. Marcum amended. "But being welcome and feeling welcome are often opposing ideas."

"That was nothing to do with us, of course, was it, Mr. Marcum? We welcome all, saints and sinners and all between." She laughed again.

Hazel wanted to ask more questions but sensed that Mrs. Marcum would prevent the kind of conversation Hazel might have with Mr. Marcum if they could speak without interruption.

Hazel attempted to turn the topic. "Did you ever meet my uncle, Lord Howardsford?"

"Only once, I'm afraid," Mrs. Marcum said. "Didn't we, Mr. Marcum? When Duncan returned from Resins. Such a gracious man. Duncan was lucky to have such a benefactor, I should say so. And for you, Mrs. Penhale"—she smiled wider, though that hardly seemed possible—"to have such a man as an uncle? What an advantage."

There was no malice in her voice, but her admiration hit Hazel wrong. Even though Uncle Elliott was all the things a nobleman ought to be—intelligent, generous, gracious, and kind—Mrs. Marcum did not know him enough to know these things about his character. For her, his title seemed enough reason to admire him, which was both shallow and unwise as there were a great many men of noble birth without any of the traits that made Uncle Elliott worthy of admiration.

"Lord Howardsford *has* been a great advantage for me, to be sure," Hazel said. "He paid for my schooling as well, which allowed me to pursue my teaching career."

"Yes," Mr. Marcum said, his voice showing curiosity. "I had heard you were a teacher. Arithmetic?"

"Mathematics," Hazel clarified. "Mathematics involves theory and formula-based equations, whereas arithmetic is primarily the study of numbers."

Mrs. Marcum blinked, but Mr. Marcum nodded. "That is an unusual emphasis for a female teacher, if you do not mind my saying so."

"I do not mind your saying so, and I quite agree." Hazel smiled more honestly now. "I feel a great deal of pride regarding my education. A fair amount of it was left upon my shoulders when I outmeasured my own teachers. I have been teaching advanced maths for nearly a decade and will be opening my own school for the advanced education of young women in a year . . . or so." She realized too late that she'd said too much.

"Open an advanced school for girls?" Mrs. Marcum repeated. Before she could ask the looming question "why?" Mr. Marcum spoke instead.

"That is remarkable, Mrs. Penhale. Here in Ipswich?"

Did she dare lie to a vicar? Having no use for religion did not mean she did not respect his place. "A bit north," she said, which was still a lie but more comfortable for the context of the conversation.

"I cannot see the need for an advanced school for girls here in Ipswich, or even in the whole of Suffolk really, can you, Mr. Marcum? There are a handful of girl's schools, of course, but an advanced school? Why I cannot see how that would—"

"Well, we have taken enough of your time this morning, Mrs. Penhale," Mr. Marcum said, coming to his feet. "It was delightful to meet you. Duncan is well-respected, and we are very glad of his marriage. I hope you will enjoy Christmas services. I think you will find this community interested in knowing you better, and I know that God would like the same opportunity."

"God can only know me if I attend services?" she asked without filtering it for something more appropriate and respectful.

Mrs. Marcum tittered.

Instead of taking offense, the vicar smiled deeper. "He knows all of His children, of course, but He does not force Himself upon them. A willing heart is what makes room for Him to dwell, and a life lived with His influence is a more peaceful one than that lived without."

Hazel held his eyes, looking for the judgment there but not finding it—much to her disappointment. She wanted to dislike this man; it would be one more reason to strengthen her pedestal of agnosticism.

Mrs. Marcum spoke as she rose to her feet. "It will be such a boon to our congregation to have such a fine lady in our midst."

Hazel almost laughed at the silly comment from the silly woman, but Mrs. Marcum was as sincere as her husband, which made it difficult to mock her. She truly found Hazel's genteel connections as something worthy of reverent celebration. It was all ridiculous, of course, and yet, as Hazel looked between them, she wondered when she had last felt so genuinely . . . wanted. Even if it was for her soul and her rank.

"I shall look forward to the Christmas service," she said, careful not to make any additional commitments.

"You will love it!" Mrs. Marcum said, bringing her hands together. "Won't she love the service, Mr. Marcum? Duncan has always sat in the back pews," Mrs. Marcum added, leaning in slightly as though there was some risk of being overheard. "But as a married man, and with your family associations, you are entitled to accommodations closer to the pulpit, of course. I shall watch for you myself and introduce you to the other women of influence in the congregation. They will be excited to meet you."

"Well, thank you," Hazel said, her smile getting tighter on her face. She stood and walked toward the entryway, not bothering to hide her limp.

Mrs. Marcum's smile fell as Hazel limped past her, going around the back of the chairs so as to take the lead position and forcing them to follow. If Mrs. Marcum was determined to know Hazel only by what she saw on the surface, she might as well see everything.

# Chapter Nineteen

*D*uncan would sit for a few moments, eat a sweet from the tray, then jump to his feet and begin pacing again. Hazel watched him—up and down, back and forth, up and down—while she sipped her tea and tried not to absorb his anxiety.

"She's late," he said at five minutes past the hour. He sat back down, knees parallel while bouncing his feet. "Ten o'clock sharp, she said. It is excessively rude to waste other people's time."

"Delores has never been to this house, Duncan, and it's a fair distance from the pub, so we mustn't hold her tardiness against her."

Duncan had talked to Delores, and she had agreed to come to tea today. She needed to come early because she was expected at the pub by eleven o'clock. Hazel wondered if Duncan recognized that he was nervous about the two women in his life meeting for the first time or if he thought he was upset solely due to Delores's late arrival.

"Excessively rude," he said again, then jumped to his feet and began pacing again.

He was still pacing when there was a knock at the door, and

though they had already arranged for Corinne to show their guest to the parlor, Duncan shot out of the room to answer the door himself.

"You are late, Delores." Hazel heard him speak from the entryway. She sighed and shook her head, putting her cup of tea on the table beside her chair. As she pushed herself to her feet in anticipation of greeting their guest, she heard Duncan say, "Excessively rude. Corinne, take her coat and hat and give this fish to Elizabeth. Delores, follow me." Thank goodness Delores was well-versed in Duncan.

Hazel was standing and smiling when Duncan marched back into the room. He crossed to her, then turned so he was standing beside her like a military man in a portrait. Hazel widened her smile and kept it in place as the weathered woman crossed to her.

Delores was in her fifties at least, with as much gray as walnut-brown in her slightly frizzed hair that she had pinned up in a falling chignon. Her dress was the color of faded coffee and fit tight across her ample bosom, the skirt ending a good six inches higher than Hazel wore her skirts. Her everyday lace-up boots were scuffed and worn. The closer she got to Hazel, the stronger the smell grew of pipe smoke, fried fish, and cheap floral perfume, likely meant to cover the odor of smoke and fried fish.

When Delores was close enough, Hazel extended her hand. Delores took it, and Hazel wrapped both of her hands around it. "It is such a pleasure to meet you, Mrs. Belaney, though I hope you'll let me call you Delores as Duncan does. Please call me Hazel."

"Pleasure to meet you as well," Delores said, but her smile did not reach her eyes. She pulled her hand away and turned her attention to Duncan, who was still standing ramrod straight and looking at a point above the parlor door. "Where do I sit, Duncan?"

He snapped out of his rigidity and ushered her to the settee before going about pouring her tea, even though it was Hazel's responsibility as mistress of the house to perform the task. Duncan handed Delores the cup and saucer and began making her a plate, though it should be up to Delores to choose what she wanted from the service.

Hazel lowered into her chair. When Delores had her cup and her plate piled high with biscuits and scones, she turned a much softer look to Duncan and thanked him. He nodded in acknowledgment and began filling his own plate.

Delores met Hazel's eyes again with a sharp look. "This is a very fine house." There was a touch of derision in her voice.

"Thank you," Hazel said. "We are quite comfortable here."

"Must have cost a pretty penny."

"Forty-five pounds for the year," Duncan said. He had taken a seat on the opposite end of the settee so that Hazel faced them both. "The price included the cook and the housemaid. She covers the usual duties of housekeeper, chambermaid, and butler. There is a manservant who comes twice a week for repairs and to manage the garden."

Hazel kept her smile in place, determined not to apologize for Duncan's lack of manners in discussing money and servants. She was suddenly very grateful she had been alone when the Marcums had visited.

"My, my, that is fancy," Delores said before taking a sip of her tea. "I suppose even I would marry if it earned me this kind of livin'."

Hazel paused in reaching for her tea and looked at Delores, who was staring her down. Of course. She knew about Duncan's inheritance and thought Hazel had married him for his wealth. As much as Hazel wanted to protest her innocence, she couldn't tell her the truth. She reached for her teacup again and filled her plate with a few of the sweets the cook had included on the tray.

An awkward silence grew in the room, so Hazel fell back on the universal remedy of small talk, though she felt inadequate to the task.

"So, Delores, have you always lived here in Ipswich?"

"No," Delores said, her attention on her plate much like Duncan's was. In fact, they held their plates in the same way, balanced on the palm of their left hands while they picked up the finger foods with the other. Was it her imagination or did they have similar noses: long, straight, but with a slight upturn at the end?

"Where did you grow up, Delores?"

"South Suffolk."

Again, Hazel waited for additional details. None were offered.

"What village?"

Delores and Duncan picked up a shortbread at the same time and took a bite. The movement was eerie in its symmetry, but then maybe anyone sitting beside Duncan would give the impression of synchronized movement.

"I understand you were a friend of Catherine's?" Hazel tried another topic.

Delores looked at her over the remaining shortbread in her hand and nodded.

"She was my aunt, you know," Hazel said, keeping her voice light. "I never met her, but I understand that she and my mother looked a great deal alike."

"She dinna talk much of her family to me."

That did not surprise Hazel. None of the Mayfields seemed to count their family as a priority, except maybe Uncle Elliott.

"What *did* she talk about?" Hazel asked.

"Pardon?"

"What did you and Catherine talk about? What brought you together as friends?"

"Catherine and I lived in the Burrow Building, and Delores worked in the pub on the street level. They became friends," Duncan explained oh-so-unhelpfully. Hazel had wanted Delores to answer the question.

"Then you must have had things in common," Hazel said, still trying to get through whatever walls Delores had built up against her.

"We was of an age with one another," Delores said before eating her last cookie. Duncan took her empty plate and made as though to fill it up, but Delores waved him off. "Much more of such rich food and I'll be bent over with stomach pains half the night," she said.

How could Hazel point out that Catherine was the daughter of a viscount and Delores was a barmaid and therefore the large chasm between their stations made their friendship unusual, at best? And yet, hadn't Catherine given up her station? Did that equalize them somehow? Hazel would need to build a great deal more trust between them before she could ask such questions.

"Did you also know Duncan's father?"

Delores hesitated again, her lips pursed as she stared across the tea service at Hazel. She nodded slowly. "I knew Leon."

Had Hazel ever heard Duncan's father's name before? Leon Penhale, her father-in-law.

"You knew my father?" Duncan said, sitting up straighter.

"A bit," Delores said, leaning forward to put her cup and saucer back on the tray. "I best be goin'."

"So soon?" Hazel asked in surprise.

"I got work to do." She looked at Hazel, her expression still hard. "Thank you for the tea."

Hazel inclined her head. "It was nice to meet you, Delores."

"I shall show you to the door," Duncan said, springing to his feet.

Hazel watched them go, Duncan leading the way and Delores following. She listened to all the goodbye noises, and then Duncan returned to the room.

"Yes, well, now you have met Delores."

"She did not stay very long."

"She is not one for tea, as I explained before I invited her."

"I know you used to see her every day when you picked up your dinners. When do you see her now?"

"I have no need of dinners. I saw her on Monday when I invited her for tea."

Was that the reason for Delores's cold reception? Was it the *only* reason?

"Perhaps you should create a new routine of stopping in at the pub a few days a week after finishing your office hours."

"But there is no reason to stop at the pub since we do not get dinner from the pub any longer."

"You do not have to have dinner as the reason to see her. You can just stop to visit her like you do your associates about town."

"I am not interested in the work that takes place in the pub, and I do not like it when there are a great deal of patrons."

He was so difficult to talk to sometimes, and Hazel felt herself losing patience. "Just stop in to say hello sometimes. That is what friends do."

"It is loud inside the pub and smells bad."

Hazel gave up; he would have to sort it out for himself. "Never mind."

"I am going to see if Elizabeth liked the fish that Delores brought for her."

He turned to leave, but she called him back. "Duncan," she asked. He stopped and turned back. "What do you know about the study done regarding traits passed on from parents to off-spring?"

"Physical traits or habitual ones?"

Hazel considered that. The held plates. The long noses. "Perhaps both."

"Well, there is the work of Jean-Baptiste Lamarck. There has been additional study, of course, but I think Lamarck to be the most comprehensively published naturalist of distinction to have explained his theory of perpetuation of characteristics in species."

"Yes," Hazel said, settling into her chair and then leaning forward to pull her yarn basket closer to her. Knitting had become a useful occupation for her hands when she engaged Duncan in a lecture rather than a discussion in which she was an active partici-pant. He seemed to enjoy both types of discourse, and sometimes it was nice to simply listen and make something useful at the same time. So far, all she'd made were scarves to give to the staff on Boxing Day, but it was something all the same.

"I remember only the most basic of his hypothesis, but I would like to understand his work in greater detail," she said, drawing him in.

Duncan began pacing. "Jean-Baptist Lamarck was primarily a botanist, though he had always had an interest in medicine, and it was his first published works on plants that gained him admis-sion into the French Academy of the Sciences. It was only after securing this place among other scientists of the age that he was able to fully explore his theories regarding inherited characteristics between parent and offspring . . ."

# *Chapter Twenty*

On Christmas Eve, Duncan left early and returned with an armful of evergreen boughs he then dumped on the parlor floor.

"Duncan!" Hazel said. "What a dreadful mess!"

"It is the greenery for Christmas, and it is bad luck to bring it into the house before Christmas Eve."

Falconridge had never held to the tradition of decorating, but there had been a fair amount of greenery at Howard House last year when Hazel had visited at Christmastide. The bows and sprigs had been perfectly fastened and spread along mantels and banisters along with ribbon and rose hips. Not dumped into a pile in the middle of the room.

"I have never put up greenery," she said.

"Nor have I," Duncan said, digging through the pile, sending pine needles and bits of twig and bark further into the room. After a few moments, he stood with a large evergreen branch in each hand. "Delores explained that it is a traditional practice, however, and told me where in the woods I might find a good supply."

He moved to the mantel and stuck one bough into a vase and another behind it. He did not pause to assess his work but instead returned to the pile and extracted two more branches.

Hazel pressed her lips together to keep from laughing as she looked from the haphazard display on the mantel to Duncan, who had shoved one branch into the middle of the small wood-pile beside the fireplace and now laid another on top of the writing desk like a Holland cover.

"I believe there is more to decorating than simply placing boughs around the room."

"It is one and the same." He propped a large branch next to the door and put a smaller one flat on the windowsill.

Hazel moved to the bellpull and summoned Corinne, who surveyed the room with barely hidden dismay.

"Corinne, have you ever, um, decked the hall with boughs of holly?"

"Of course, ma'am."

"I did not cut any holly, as I do not like the scratchy leaves," Duncan said as he balanced a branch on the other windowsill.

Hazel ignored him but smiled at housekeeper. "Corinne, you are the expert. Would you mind giving us a lesson?"

"Of course, ma'am. Let me fetch some twine and wire."

"What would we need twine and wire for?" Duncan asked.

It took approximately two hours to fashion Duncan's well-intentioned heap of evergreens into a pleasing addition to the room. A symmetrical garland now graced the mantel, woven with red ribbon Corinne had found in a storage closet. The vase now served as the center of the design. Additional garlands graced each windowsill with an unlit candle in the center, and a wreath hung on the front door. Duncan had grown tired of the action and cleaned up the messy remains while the women worked.

Hazel took a wide look around the room and smiled. "This is perfect, Corinne, thank you."

"You're welcome, ma'am." She stood and displayed a circle of wire wrapped with some of the smaller and more flexible evergreens. "All it needs is a bit of mistletoe before it's hung over the door."

Hazel blinked. "Mistletoe?"

"Well, you have to have mistletoe for a proper kissing bough." She walked to the doorway and held the sphere as high up as she could, which was not high enough to clear the casing. "Mr. Penhale will need to secure it; let me fetch a nail."

She left the room, leaving Hazel and Duncan alone. They were usually alone in this room, so Hazel did not understand why it should feel different now.

"Mistletoe is an invitation for kissing at Christmas," Duncan said.

Hazel limped to the mantel and tucked a stray sprig of pine into the garland. She said nothing, though her cheeks were on fire as she remembered the one kiss they had shared.

"I enjoyed our kiss on our wedding day," Duncan said from somewhere behind her. "Did you enjoy it?"

Hazel stared at the garland, keeping her back to Duncan and hiding her red face. "I do not want to talk about that," Hazel said softly. "It was simply part of the ceremony. A necessary rote."

"But did you enjoy it?"

Corinne saved her. "Here it is!"

Hazel turned and looked at the housekeeper standing in the doorway with a hammer in one hand and a nail in another. She handed off the items to Duncan. "After luncheon, I could fetch some mistletoe. There is a vendor in the square who is always selling some sprigs, and since I still need to fetch a few things for tomorrow, it would be no trouble."

"Wonderful," Duncan said. "Thank you."

"You are welcome, Mr. Penhale." Corinne smiled and looked to Hazel. "Luncheon shall be ready in another quarter of an hour."

Sometime between luncheon and dinner, mistletoe was added to the kissing bough. Hazel noticed it when she lowered herself into her favorite chair in the parlor after the evening meal. She stared at the small sprig of green that included a few white berries. Duncan had adopted the routine of staying in the dining room to enjoy a glass of port before joining Hazel in the drawing room each evening, and so she had a few minutes to prepare herself before he joined her. As it was Tuesday, she would be leading the evening's discussion.

When Duncan entered the room, he immediately looked up at the kissing bough hanging above the door. He turned back to her, looked her directly in the eye, and smiled. It was disarming in its normality, but Hazel had already made her decision.

"For tonight's discussion," Hazel said, "I would like to talk about poisonous plants, specifically those which are toxic to animals and, most specifically, toxic to cats."

Duncan's expression fell.

"Case in point," she said, pointing above his head. "Mistletoe is a parasitic plant that feeds off its host and is adorned with berries that can be fatal if ingested. For example, if a cat mistakes it for some other bit of food fallen to the floor . . ."

The discussion ended rather abruptly when Duncan tore the kissing bough from above the door, threw it into the fire, and then spent an hour tracing how the mistletoe had been brought into the house so as to ensure that none of the fatal berries had fallen to the floor and rolled into a corner.

Hazel smiled to herself as she finished knitting her last scarf.

# Chapter Twenty-One

Church services were at ten o'clock, so after a simple breakfast, Hazel focused on getting ready, though it was not as simple as she'd thought it would be. She wanted to look her best but did not want to appear as though she were playing to rank the way Mrs. Marcum thought she should. Duncan had not purchased any new items of clothing despite Amelia's encouragement, so he would be dressed in the same black pants and gray coat he wore to church every Sunday. Though not shabby, it was not fine, and if Hazel overdid her presentation, they would look mismatched.

Finally, she decided on the peach muslin with the ruffled hem. It was rather plain in design, and she did not think it her best color, but it seemed the right one for the occasion. She braided her hair into a crown around her head, then curled a few tendrils around her face. The hairstyle made up for the plainness of the dress, but she wondered why it mattered when she put on her bonnet, white straw trimmed in blue and yellow. The hat—one of only three hats she had purchased as part of Amelia's wedding-gift wardrobe—covered the entire creation.

At nine thirty, Hazel was waiting in the entry, her gray wool cape over her shoulders. Because they had to walk several blocks to the church, she had retrieved her cane from her trunk. She could not remember the last time she'd walked such a distance.

When she heard Duncan's boots on the stairs, she turned to face him.

He stopped halfway down, all his attention focused on her. "You look beautiful, Hazel."

"Thank you," she said, swallowing her embarrassment.

He continued to study her. "Other than the dress, everything about your presentation is exceptional."

"What is wrong with my dress?" She looked down at herself.

"It is orange." Duncan moved to the coatrack and removed his gray coat before pushing his arms into the sleeves.

"It is not orange; it is peach."

"Peach is a light orange, and it has too much yellow for your skin tones. You look better in colors with blue tones, specifically purple." He put his hat on his head. "Are you ready?"

Hazel felt rather flummoxed. Did she really look poor in this color? Was there time to change? She knew as soon as she thought it that there was not, nor would she change for anyone's sake but her own.

He opened the door, put out his arm, and looked at her expectantly.

She took his arm, and they made their way onto the street. Because she spent most, if not all, of her time in the heated rooms inside the house, she was unused to the cold. After three steps, her nose was already tingling. She blew out a breath specifically to see the cloud it made in front of her face. Why had she ever agreed to go to church? Oh, yes, to avoid making small talk with her cousins and seeing Harry, so she had better make the best of this.

"You know a great deal about color," Hazel said after a few more steps, her cane improving her gait more than she'd expected it would now that she had her new boots. Hopefully her hand would not be frozen solid around the cane by the time they reached the church. Her gloves were already proving to be less protection than she'd expected. She definitely should have worn a scarf. And wool underthings.

"Yes." The cold did not seem to affect Duncan in the least.

She gave him adequate time to expound on his knowledge of color, which he did not do. "Most men cannot tell what looks good on a woman and what doesn't."

"Catherine was fussy about clothing."

Hazel was intrigued. Though Duncan often mentioned Catherine, it was usually within a larger discussion where Catherine was not the focus. "What exactly was she fussy about that translated into you determining what does and does not look good on a woman?"

"Not a woman—you."

She looked sideways at him, noting that the tip of his nose was red, which reminded her of the similarities between his nose and Delores's nose. This increased her eagerness to learn more about him. "You are only attentive to what colors look good on *me*?"

"Yes."

"Why not be attentive to what looks well on other women?"

"I do not care about other women."

*But he cares about me.* Hazel swallowed, and they walked in silence for a few steps. The topic of Catherine was still wide open, however.

"Did Catherine ever attend church with you?" The vicar had said she had not, but Duncan did not know that Hazel knew, and it seemed the most natural segue.

"No. She said the church might be struck by lightning if she attended, which I found quite frightening until Mr. Marcum explained that sometimes people use lightning as a symbol of God's judgment, which is not based on fact or biblical example. Typically, God exercises his judgment through more widespread natural catastrophes such as floods and famine that, should the people follow His counsel, they could survive. There is not a single instance of the God of Abraham using lightning as a judgment.

"However, the Greek gods often utilized lightning, which makes Catherine's commentary an example of how paganism and modern Christianity share many of the same roots. For instance, in ancient Rome, December twenty-fifth was the traditional feast of Saturnalia in honor of the sun deity. Replacing an existing celebration with a celebration of Christ's birth made it easier for the populace to embrace Christianity once it was decided that its growing strength could be utilized for the propagation of Rome's political goals, which were—"

"Why did Catherine, and not your father, enroll you in the vicar's school?" Hazel interrupted. She found his information about Christmas interesting, as she did most of Duncan's lectures, but she was more curious about his personal history just now.

"My father never attended school himself and did not properly appreciate the value of education, though he supported me in pursuing my own."

"Catherine appreciated education?"

"Yes," Duncan said, nodding as the breath clouded the air before him. His nose was full red now, and Hazel suspected hers was as well. "She was very well educated for a woman. I only decided to talk to her because she would read stories out loud and I realized she said the same words each time she turned the page, which meant the black marks on the page must be the words she was saying. It was quite a discovery for me."

"What do you mean you *decided* to talk to her?"

"I did not like her at first because she was a fancy lady."

"A fancy lady?" Hazel said, not laughing, though she wanted to.

"The sort of woman who wears big hats and bright colors, like the squire's wife. The type of woman who yelled at you if you didn't wear shoes or stood too close to their carriage. I did not talk to her for the first month in hopes she would go away."

Hazel turned to look at his profile as they walked along the sidewalk. "A full month? Did she live in the same house?"

"Not a house. The apartment in Manningtree."

"Manningtree?" It was a village to the south, but Hazel had never heard of any connection Duncan had there. "Haven't you lived in Ipswich all your life?"

"No, but it feels as though I have because most of my childhood memories are centered here. I was six years and one month old when we moved to Ipswich.

"You and your da?"

"And Catherine."

"How old were you when your mother died?"

"Four years and eight or nine months, I think. She died in the spring. I remember because we had looked at the tulips the day before when we'd gone to the bakery, and the dog bit my leg."

A dog bite? Hazel was losing her place in the story. "Wait, how did your mother die?"

"She was run over by a carriage when she went out to get some bread the day after I was bit by the dog."

Hazel shuddered. "That's awful."

"Yes. It must have been very frightening. I do not remember much about it because the dog had bit my leg the day before, and I was upset about that for a very long time. I do not like dogs, and sometimes I think I do not like carriages either because a carriage killed my mother, but then I did not see that happen so I did not experience the fear and shock of it and so I should not have that same association with carriages that I have with dogs. I think I dislike carriages because they smell bad and they take me far from the surroundings that are familiar and comfortable."

Hazel needed to refocus this conversation or she would never make sense of any part of it.

"Do you know how old you were exactly when Catherine moved in with you and your da?"

"Five years and ten months."

"A year after your mother's death. How do you know that for sure?"

"A few days after she came—and before I had started talking to her—we went to a May Day celebration and she bought a book from a vendor, which was the book she read over and over until I asked her how she knew the words the black marks represented. I had never seen a book before."

"And you moved to Ipswich when you were six years and one month old." That meant Catherine had been with them for only a few months. "Did you move into the Burrow Building when you came to Ipswich?"

"Yes."

Uncle Elliott had offered free rent because Catherine had promised she and Leon would marry; Harry had told Hazel about the unfulfilled promise of marriage when he'd first told her of their illegitimate cousin.

"So then, when did you begin attending the parish school?"

"When I was six and two months old. I had learned to read the book myself by then."

"She taught you how to read a book on your own between May Day and September? Four months?"

"I am a very fast learner and have an excellent memory."

"That is remarkable," Hazel said.

"Mr. Marcum says I have a brilliant mind, but Mr. Shopledge, my literature teacher at Resins, said my brain was broken."

"It is not broken." Hazel was offended on his behalf, yet he shared the information without the least bit of malice.

"It is broken," Duncan said evenly. "I am intelligent and capable in many ways, but in other ways I do not understand what everyone else seems to already know."

That was actually a rather astute description. They turned a corner and were now walking into the wind. Because Hazel had her cane in one hand, and Duncan's arm in the other, she could not hold onto her hat, which meant the brim flipped backward. At least she'd used enough pins to secure it so there was no fear of it being blown off. And her face was nearly numb now, so the cold was not so bracing.

"Did you ever *not* talk to Catherine again? The way you did when she first came?"

"Sometimes, but never for a month—that was the longest I had ever not spoken."

"I cannot imagine not talking for such a long time," Hazel said. "How would you communicate?"

"I would not communicate," he said, shaking his head and kicking at a rock on the sidewalk. "I would pretend that I was the only person in the whole world and all the other people were statues, and since statues cannot talk, I would not hear them when they spoke to me. Catherine called it my 'going-inside time.'"

"Did you do this often?"

"Not as often after I went to school. It does not work well to treat a teacher as a statue."

Hazel quirked a smile and thought of how Audrey would sometimes turn her chair to face the corner when class became too loud. Had she been shutting out the voices like Duncan did when he'd pretended other people were statues? Was it a way to regulate anxiety? It would take a great deal of determination and a great lack of empathy for those on the receiving end of such behavior.

They walked in silence for a bit, then Duncan pointed. "There is the church."

Hazel followed his direction and could see the top of the church on the next block, thank goodness—had she ever walked this far before? Without the new boot, she'd have never been able to do it.

Duncan pulled his watch from his vest and frowned. "I did not properly anticipate how slowly you walked; we are nearly late. Can you walk faster?"

So much for feeling proud of the accomplishment. "I am going as fast as I can."

"All right." But his anxiety about being late was obvious.

Hazel increased her pace as much as she could, but doubted Duncan even noticed. Her hip ached. Not like it had every day when she'd had the old boot, but more than it had in the weeks since getting her new one. There was still the walk home when this was over, too. Learning more about Duncan's past had made the effort worthwhile, however.

The chapel was nearly full when they arrived, the room decorated with pine boughs and bright bows in red and gold and green. Duncan headed to the second row from the back, and the people sitting there moved closer together to make room. People gave her curious looks over their shoulders. Duncan sat beside her, very close in fact, and stared straight ahead. It was comforting to have him there, and she leaned toward him to feel his shoulder against hers, which made her feel even more secure in this unfamiliar church full of unfamiliar people.

She stretched and flexed her frozen hands and endured the tingling as her face warmed up. Hazel was grateful to have arrived without time for Mrs. Marcum to notice or make a fuss. A Christmas gift if ever there was one.

The vicar smiled at her from his place at the pulpit, however, and she smiled back, though sheepishly as she did not want to be noticed. He began to recount the story of the Nativity and talked about Mary being visited by an angel and told she would be the mother of the Messiah. He relayed how Mary pondered what she'd been told in her heart, and Hazel glanced at Duncan beside her.

They had been married not quite two months, and her curiosity about his life before now and how his mind worked had only grown. There was the mystery of Delores, who shared some of Duncan's features. There was the mystery of Catherine, who had given up her position in society to live in scandal with Duncan's father, and who had treated Duncan so well even after his father's death. There was the mystery of Duncan himself, who could show so much consideration in some ways yet could easily pretend people were statues.

They sang "Hark, the Herald Angels Sing!" as the final hymn, which Hazel had always liked, and then Hazel immediately stood, ready to go home. Duncan, however, seemed to say hello to everyone as they made their way from the church. Hazel tried to hang back, finding so many strangers overwhelming, but Duncan never failed to introduce her.

"This is my wife, Hazel Penhale. Hazel, this is Mrs. Sylvia Cardamom. She is the sister of the vicar's wife." Or "Hazel, this is Mr. Peter Burbidge. He is the sexton for the cemetery."

She must have been introduced to twenty different people before they even made it to the churchyard, where people were knotted together in small clusters, the sound of their chatter rising like birdsong in the trees on a summer morning even though it was absolutely freezing. Hazel held tightly to Duncan's arm as they moved slowly down the steps. When Duncan began moving toward one of the groups of people, Hazel pulled back on his arm.

"Can we go home?" she whispered.

"You do not want to meet the rest of the parishioners?"

Hazel shook her head while scanning the yard. Several curious glances were directed her way, which reminded her to paste a polite smile on her face to hide her discomfort.

"I know many of them are looking forward to meeting you."

"I have met plenty," Hazel said. She could not limp away without him, and she wanted him with her. She felt safer that way. "I am very cold, and we have a long walk to get home. Please."

"Very well," Duncan said. They turned away from the pockets of conversation and began making their way toward the street.

"Duncan."

Hazel had noticed that nearly everyone called him Duncan, which she found rather odd considering how opposed he had been to calling her Hazel when they first met. In fact, she'd never

seen him act so formally since coming to Ipswich. Was that because he was comfortable here? They turned together, since she
had clamped herself onto his arm, and she watched an older man
with a gray goatee come toward them. He wore a long charcoal
coat and a beaver-skin hat.

"Good morning, Dr. Randall," Duncan said.

Hazel recognized the name as the "associate" Duncan had
visited several weeks ago when she'd met with the cobbler. The
man who had given Duncan several medical journals to read on
their Thursday evenings. Surely a doctor would not visit too long
in such cold weather.

"Good morning." Dr. Randall drew close, but he did not put
his hand out to be shaken. In fact, no one had initiated a handshake with Duncan. Hazel looked around at these people once
more; they had known Duncan for years, decades. It was sensible
that in that time they would come to understand his peculiarities.
That they had adjusted to them and were so welcoming that softened some of her hard feelings against church in general.

"So, this is the Mrs. Penhale I have heard so much about."

She looked back to Dr. Randall. She had to let go of Duncan's
arm in order to let the doctor bow over her hand. She noticed
him glance at the cane in her other hand. "It's wonderful to meet
you, Dr. Randall."

"As it is to meet you. Congratulations on your marriage. We
are very happy to see Duncan settle down."

Hazel shifted her weight. *Settle down for ten more months.*
Sometimes that felt like an impossibly long time—like right now,
for instance. Her face was going numb again. "Ipswich is a lovely
city."

"I agree, though it is more lovely in fair weather." He smiled
but made no move to let them begin their walk home. He turned

his attention back to Duncan. "I have another periodical I am finished with if you would like to come around this week. I shall be keeping office hours on Tuesday and Wednesday."

"Wonderful," Duncan said. "I shall come Tuesday at one thirty."

"Very good, I shall look forward to that. In light of your marriage, would you and Mrs. Penhale like to come to dinner some evening?"

"Dinner?" Duncan sounded as though he did not know what the word meant. "A dinner party?"

"Well, a dinner party for four, I suppose. I'm sure Mrs. Randall would love to meet your wife."

"I am not a traditional attendee at dinner parties because of my limited social skills," Duncan said.

Hazel refused to show the embarrassment she felt.

Dr. Randall just smiled, however. "I quite enjoy your limited social skills, Duncan, and it would allow us the chance to become familiar with your new wife. I shall have Mrs. Randall pay you a visit after she returns home in a few weeks. Is that all right, Mrs. Penhale?"

"Certainly. I will look forward to meeting her." Her teeth were beginning to chatter.

Hazel noted a couple break away from one of the clusters and begin toward them. *Dear heavens!* She put her arm back through Duncan's and leaned into him. Dr. Randall seemed to watch them closely, and she realized that Duncan had not showed any tension when she'd taken his arm today. In fact, he had not showed tension when she'd been close to him at all in the last several weeks. She thought back to his words from that morning: *"I do not care about other women."* She swallowed and forced her smile higher on her cheeks.

"We really do need to be going, Duncan," she said softly.

"Yes, Hazel is not familiar with the ritual of visiting after church and does not like the cold," he said to Dr. Randall. "She is eager to return home."

Her cheeks flamed, but Hazel did not try to amend what he'd said, she only wanted to leave before this other couple reached them and this entire conversation played itself out all over again.

"Would you like a ride home in my carriage?" Dr. Randall asked, pointing toward a row of carriages lined up on the far side of the yard. Some of them had already begun to leave.

She looked from the carriages to the approaching couple to Dr. Randall. "Sir, I would pay any price you asked for a ride home in your carriage."

Dr. Randall laughed. "A promise to plan that dinner is all I ask." He spied the approaching couple and looked back at her. "I cannot spare you the Harringtons, but I shall bring the carriage around to the street as quickly as possible so you will at least have a reason to excuse yourself."

"Thank you," she breathed.

He nodded and turned toward the carriage as Hazel kept smiling, counting the seconds until she could make her escape.

# Chapter Twenty-Two

*L*ife resumed its routine in the weeks following Christmas. Duncan had not tried to retain any of the Perkins & Cromley clients, despite Hazel's encouragement to do so since he had been the clerk managing their accounts for years. He did not feel it would be right. While a few had brought their business to him without his request, and Dr. Randall had come on as a client, Duncan did not have enough work to keep him busy all day. The situation might have frustrated another man, but Duncan was not dissuaded.

He did what work there was in the mornings and then visited his associates around town or checked on the tenants of the Burrow Building to fill the remaining time. Then he would go back to the office in the late afternoon and not leave until five thirty. Because Uncle Elliott was paying the expenses of the house, all the income Duncan was making from his tenants and his accounting was being saved, which Duncan liked very much.

Hazel corresponded with Sophie every week, worked on curriculum and schedule ideas, balanced her ledgers—though she was not spending much money—and read from the books in the parlor, now expanded to include Duncan's small but prized col-lection of books on history and mathematics.

She took to sleeping late for the first time in her life, which meant she had her breakfast after Duncan had already left for the office at 8:50 each morning. He returned at approximately 5:50, and they enjoyed an early dinner and a discussion on whatever topic was dictated by the day of the week. It was a struggle to keep up with his vast knowledge of so many topics, but Hazel felt she held her own due to the study she would engage in each afternoon.

It was a good life, very different from what she'd ever imag-ined, and Hazel was grateful every day for such comfort, but by mid-January, she admitted she was growing bored. She had been used to interacting with students and other teachers every day. She had always prized her time alone but now realized that her enjoyment was at least in part because it had been such a rare occasion. Now she was alone for the vast majority of her day, and she missed . . . people.

There had been a few visitors since the vicar and his wife, including Mrs. Meyers, the wife of the local squire. She had come to acquaint herself with another "noblewoman" who fit Duncan's definition of a "Fancy Lady." Hazel did not take to the woman in her ruffled satin and her critical eye passing over the parlor that clearly did not meet her standards.

Mrs. Timoth had also come for a second visit, which was slightly more comfortable than the first. She was the wife of a carpenter and lived only a few houses away; she talked mostly of her five children.

Hazel knew it was typical to return a visit after being called upon, but the idea of limping into another person's home and making small talk as a guest made her incredibly anxious. She told herself that because of her foot, no one would expect her to return the visit. Never mind that she did not feel particularly drawn to developing a closer relationship with any of the women who had come to call. She had sent notes of thanks for the visits instead of making the returns and hoped that would not come across as too ill-mannered.

And then she had three visits in a single day! Mrs. Lester, a widow in the parish who brought a jar of honey from her bees, Mrs. Timoth again—she brought three of her children; what an exercise in patience that turned out to be—and Mrs. Randall, who was newly returned from her sister's estate in the lake district and seemed a bit rushed through their visit. She and Hazel chose a night to have dinner together with their husbands—Friday next at Lavender House, since Hazel and Duncan did not have a carriage, and it was difficult for her to make the trip across town.

Over dinner with Duncan that evening, Hazel complained about so many visits in one day. "I was nearly sick from eating so many shortbreads in a single morning, and not one of my guests had written me ahead to warn me of their visit."

"Was it not a good distraction from the boredom you spoke of the other evening?"

"Well," Hazel said, feeling sheepish because of course she *had* complained about her boredom a few nights earlier. "I think three visits in a single morning is a bit excessive, and the visits are so . . . dull. They talk about their families or their bees but nothing of real substance."

"I believe female relationships typically revolve around more domestic interests. What else would you want to talk about?"

"The world," Hazel said, her annoyance growing the more Duncan dismissed it. "Politics. Science. Women's rights, perhaps."

"But then what would you and I talk about if you discussed all those topics with the women who come visit?"

"I can talk about such topics with more people than just you, Duncan. And women's perspectives might be different, not that I would ever know since they do not seem to know anything about such topics."

"You did not ask them what they know on those topics, however, so you cannot be sure."

"Never mind," Hazel said, her irritation rising at the limitations of Duncan to truly understand her. She went back to her meal of ham and new potatoes.

"You seem to be in an irritable mood tonight, Hazel. Have I upset you?"

She stabbed a bite of potato with her fork. "You have not upset me, but I *am* irritable."

"If I am not the cause of your irritation, it seems unfair that I should be the recipient of your black mood."

Hazel growled and put down her fork before excusing herself and limping out of the room. Duncan followed, and they continued to argue until she told him to leave her alone and closed the door to her room.

She listened for his boots to retreat and then tensed up every muscle in her body, a sort of silent scream she had perfected as a child when unable to express the emotions pent up inside of her. This was all so ridiculous! She wished she could pace like Duncan did when he was anxious. Or run through the fields the way Harry would when they were young and he was in a temper.

Her stupid foot made such physical expressions impossible, and so she limped to her bed, threw herself onto the coverlet and screamed into the tick over and over again until she felt she had exorcised some portion of the demon that had followed her around all day. Then she flopped onto her back and covered her eyes with one arm.

Yes, it was lovely to have so much time on her hands, to read anything she wanted, to wear nicer clothes, and her new boot was a marvel. But having to be nice to people who would have no bearing on her future and to try to navigate Duncan's odd thinking patterns was exhausting. He was so literal, and there were things he would never understand about her. Like her feelings tonight. He felt that unless he was the cause of the irritation she was feeling, he should not have to suffer through it. As though she could just correct her mood for his sake. He did not understand what it felt like to have to socialize and pretend they were in a real marriage. He had no compassion for the fact that she was in a strange city, essentially floating through the next year without purpose.

She sighed as her protest began to lose integrity in her mind, dissolving away like snowflakes on an open palm. She was acting like a spoiled child who wanted everything just so and if she could not have it would make sure everyone suffered alongside her.

Suffered. Is that how she felt? That she was *suffering*? In this fine house with a husband who was kind and demanded nothing of her except evening discussions and a puzzle once a week?

She moved her arm off her eyes only to replace the barrier with both of her hands. Was this mood some delay of temper from childhood that she could finally express? It was ridiculous and pointless, and Duncan was right—it was unfair for her to spat with him when he had done nothing to earn it. Especially since this was not a real marriage but merely an arrangement she needed to find a way through for the next nine months. She would only make it worse if she allowed discord to grow between them.

It still took nearly an hour for Hazel to emerge from her room, and when she limped into the parlor, Duncan looked up from the book he was reading with a wary expression and his eyes on the floor to her immediate right.

"I am sorry for acting like such a child, Duncan," she said, using the words she had practiced. "I am feeling rather over-whelmed by all the changes in my life and took my frustration out on you, even though you were only attempting to help me sort through it. I hope you will forgive me. I will try very hard not to react in such a way in the future."

"I have been thinking about your dissatisfaction, and perhaps you would not be feeling so unsettled if you could bring in some aspects of daily life that are more comfortable for you, and thus invite familiarity into this life, which is so different than the one you have lived to this point."

Though determined to be humble, she was not in the mood to be lectured. "I will consider that, thank you. I think I will go to bed."

"I think you should start a school for girls."

She turned back to face him but did not cross the room. "I *am* starting a school for girls."

"I mean here, in Ipswich." He put the book he'd been reading aside and stood. He didn't move to cross the room to her. "Not a formal school like Cordon Academy, but something small and simple that will allow you to use your teaching skills and fill your time with constructive actions."

"Even a small and simple school would take a great deal of work, and by the time the structure would be in place, I would be moving back to King's Lynn."

He began to pace, and she pushed away her annoyance by reminding herself there was nothing inherently wrong with his pacing. "You do not understand what I am saying, Hazel."

Her defenses prickled, and the whining tantrum she'd recently talked herself out of begin to build again.

"I have told you of the vicar's school I attended for several years before I was sent away."

*Nine months,* she reminded herself. *Only nine more months and I will never have to watch him pace back and forth again.*

"What is your point, Duncan?"

"My point is that the vicar's school offered a basic education, but only to boys. Many girls from our parish have very little education. Most will go into service, which is why education is not emphasized. You told me once that you dream of a country where girls and boys are educated equally and that part of your motivation in purchasing Cordon Academy is to help that goal be realized.

"You are feeling off-center here because what you have worked your whole life to do—teach—is out of your reach until our contract is finished. You do not need an income as most schools do, so why not offer to educate the girls in the parish for the time that you are here? It would occupy you with work that is familiar to you, while also moving toward the overall goal of equal education for girls.

"Even basic writing and counting skills can help these girls attain better positions in service, and as our country continues to industrialize, which I believe will expand opportunities for all persons, male and female, they will be a step ahead of where they would be without those skills. You could purchase a few slates and . . ."

Despite her earlier mood, Hazel became completely captured by Duncan's idea to the point that they stayed up until nearly ten o'clock working out details and making notes.

# Chapter Twenty-Three

Hazel's ideas regarding a simple parlor school continued to grow throughout the next week. She wrote to Sophie, who agreed it was a great idea. She chatted more with Duncan, then had to set the plans aside so she could manage the dinner with Mr. and Mrs. Randall.

She had never thrown a dinner party, and though she realized it was not much different than a dinner with just Duncan and herself, she became increasingly nervous as the evening came closer. To her relief, the Randalls were personable and warm. Duncan was quite stiff at the start, but once Dr. Randall brought up an article about Halley's diving bell, which was recently used to recover goods from a sunken ship off the coast of Greece, Duncan relaxed. Mrs. Randall chimed in enough that Hazel felt comfortable adding her thoughts, even though she was the least informed about the modern process of hunting for treasure at the bottom of the sea.

When the meal was finished, Mrs. Randall and Hazel retired to the drawing room so the men might enjoy their port.

"I am very glad we have the chance to speak alone, Mrs. Penhale. I'm afraid I owe you an apology."

"Me?" Hazel said as she lowered into her chair.

"For my rudeness, when I visited you last week."

"You were not—"

Mrs. Randall put up her hand, and Hazel stopped talking.

"I had recently returned from a visit to my sister, who is . . . rather beastly. My husband reminded me last night that I have brought too much of her home with me. We rather had a row about the fact that I visited you and learned absolutely nothing."

Hazel remembered Mrs. Randall seeming to be in a hurry that day, but it had not bothered her.

"Please do not worry about that. I did not—"

"I did not want to come," Mrs. Randall interrupted.

Hazel felt her cheeks pink up.

"Not because of you, dear, just . . ." She sighed. "I had been home only two days, which meant I was still reviewing with rage all the ridiculous conversations I'd had with my sister. Also, I had not yet adjusted back to sleeping in the same bed as Peter—he snores something awful. He was so eager for me to make the visit, but as it was not my idea or priority, I did not put my heart in it.

"Patrick asked me about the visit yesterday evening, and after I recounted it, he told me it sounded as though I had been rude. I snapped at him instead of admitting he was right, and he took offense and so it went. Thus, my apology."

Hazel suddenly missed having a tea tray to offer up some distraction for the conversation that felt very awkward in the empty parlor. "Mrs. Randall, you do not owe me anything. Morning visits are new to me, and I had no expectation. Please do not worry over it; I assure you that I have not."

Mrs. Randall took a deep breath and let it out. "Thank you." She smiled. "You held your own in the dinner conversation tonight, which is impressive. Patrick told me you are a former teacher. If I'd been the least bit gracious, I'd have heard as much from you, but now I have the chance to remedy everything I missed. Begin with where you were born and tell me your story."

Hazel hesitated, but then told her "story" as directed. Mrs. Randall asked thought-provoking questions, and somehow the conversation easily turned to the idea for the parlor school.

"And what will you teach them exactly?" Mrs. Randall asked.

"Letters and numbers to start. I understand many of the girls are destined to service but—"

"The ability to read could put them in reach of a position as a lady's maid or even a housekeeper one day," Mrs. Randall interrupted, her eyes brightening.

"Exactly what Duncan said," Hazel said.

Mrs. Randall nodded, thoughtful. "What age will you teach?"

"Well, I think eight should be the youngest. I do not have much room for behavior modification."

"And the oldest end of the spectrum?"

"As old as they come to me, I suppose," Hazel said. "I understand many girls enter service before they are sixteen, so I imagine I will not have many who are older than that, but if there are some who are available and willing, I shall teach them all."

"And what of grown women?"

"I had not considered that," Hazel said slowly. Education was for young minds, or so she had always believed, but teaching grown women was an intriguing proposition. "I shall need to determine how many students I can accommodate before I begin to seek them out, but I am not opposed to teaching grown women, so long as they can make the commitment to come regularly and are willing to be taught alongside girls and younger women." She paused, feeling conspicuous with her theories and ideas. "That is assuming I find any students at all. Mrs. Marcum visited before

Christmas and seemed to think educating girls was a rather silly goal."

"Mrs. Marcum is not the sort of woman who will support an endeavor like this."

Hazel looked at Mrs. Randall, a woman at least thirty years her senior. "And you are?"

Mrs. Randall smiled widely. "I grew up a farmer's daughter. I knew my numbers and measures and enough letters to get by, but I married far above myself. A *physician*. Patrick was educated and confident in ways I had never seen. I shall ever be grateful to have had the chance to rise with his station as I did.

"We raised three children—two boys and a girl. The boys went to the parish school, attending with Duncan for a time, and then Jeffery went to university like his father, and Lindon chose to go into the church. We could not afford to send Regina to a private school. She was our eldest child and still young when Patrick began his profession. I tried to do the teaching, but I knew I could not give her the quality education I had hoped to.

"She married a merchant and is quite happy in her life, but I am frustrated by the limits it passed on to her. Her eldest daughter is nearly four, and I am watching the same patterns play out with her that played out with me. So, yes, I am the sort of woman who will support an endeavor like this. How can I help?"

"I did not expect such an answer as that." This was the first real conversation she'd had with another woman since coming to Ipswich.

Mrs. Randall smiled. "I like the idea of surprising you, but truly, what do you need?"

"Students, I suppose. I am unsure how to find them. I only want to teach those who want to be taught."

Mrs. Randall nodded, then stood and walked to the bellpull. "Finding students will not be difficult."

Corinne entered the room so quickly Hazel suspected she may have been listening in the hallway.

"Ma'am?"

"How many nieces do you have now?" Mrs. Randall asked.

Corinne hesitated, looking between Hazel and Mrs. Randall before answering. "Four, ma'am."

"And do any of them read?"

Corinne lifted her eyebrows as though she'd never heard the question. "Read?"

"Or write?"

"No, ma'am."

"And your sister?"

"Diane cannot write either, ma'am. Our father was a fisherman, and our ma died when we were very small."

"And you, Corinne?"

Corinne's cheeks turned pink, and Hazel held her breath.

"I have no desire to embarrass you, Corinne, forgive me, but Mrs. Penhale is considering the idea of teaching women and girls to read and write and factor numbers."

Corinne glanced at Hazel before looking down. The glance was enough, however. It had been filled with desire and hope.

"I think you have found your first student, Mrs. Penhale," Mrs. Randall said as she returned to her place and lifted her cup and saucer. "And a connection to the very girls you want to serve. In parishes such as this, a girl's education is usually dependent on her mother; if the mother has limited learning, the girls follow. Change that pattern, and you change everything. Now, how else might I help, and when do you think you can start?"

# Chapter Twenty-Four

*B*y the following Monday, Hazel had three students: Corinne and two of her nieces, twelve-year-old Bonnie and fifteen-year-old Rachel. By the first of February, she'd added two of the girls' friends, and by March, Corinne's sister and two more girls from the parish had joined the class. Lessons were held for just one hour each morning as it was all the time they could spare from their responsibilities at home.

Each student was assessed to see what they already knew, and then Hazel and Mrs. Randall worked together to create an individual course of study. Mrs. Randall came every morning and read with the younger girls, while Hazel focused on factoring and recitation. Corinne could read, and her grasp of numbers was excellent, but she had almost no writing skills—something that shocked Hazel due to how competent Corinne was in her work. That she had risen to the service level of managing a home, even a small one, without the ability to write was rather astounding.

By April, all the students of her "parlor school" knew their letters and numbers as well as basic addition and subtraction. They were at different levels of reading and writing, but all of them were moving forward and were excited about what they had learned. Though Hazel had taught for many years, not all of the students in her classes had wanted the education she offered them. Every one of her students in Ipswich were hungry for it. Starved.

For payment, each student was expected to bring something each week for either Hazel or Mrs. Randall. It had been Mrs. Randall's idea because she believed the students would better appreciate what they were given if they had to think of how to repay it.

Diane was an excellent cook and brought a pie each Monday. Corinne, who knew that Duncan and Hazel engaged in all manner of discussions in the evenings, found obscure articles and periodicals Hazel could use as the basis for discussions that Duncan was unprepared for. It was nice to know more about a subject than he did, and he was always eager to learn. The younger girls brought things like drawings or pieces of stitching.

Hazel graciously received each item and kept them in her writing desk as a reminder of the widow's mite, a Bible story Duncan had chosen as his discussion topic a few weeks before.

On an afternoon during the first week of April, Hazel was reading in preparation for the evening's discussion about the fall of the Assyrians. She'd taught for four hours that morning, and then had held an extra reading session with Diane's girls. Hazel was ready to enjoy her own time when there was a knock at the front door.

Hazel listened for an indication of who the visitor might be and was surprised to hear a male voice at the door. A male visitor was enough of an anomaly in and of itself, but for a man to visit in the afternoon when Duncan was still at the office was simply not done. Not once in the five months of living in Lavender House had such a thing happened. Even the vicar—who felt driven to drop by every few weeks—came with his wife if he visited during the day.

Corinne's voice rose in pitch, like a younger girl's, and Hazel suddenly knew *exactly* who was at the door. She put aside the book, straightened her spine, and took a deep cleansing breath as his voice got closer. A rather glowing Corinne entered the room first, but Hazel looked past her until her eyes—hazel like their father's—connected with eyes almost as familiar, though they were blue like the Mayfield side of their family.

Hazel forced a polite smile and put out a resigned hand to her brother, whom she had not seen since their mother's funeral. She kept her tone even. "Harry, what a surprise."

His eyes twinkled as he crossed the room. He bowed over her hand the way he used to when they played pretend as children—before she'd been sent away and play had disappeared from her life entirely. It was nice to be reminded that they had once been playmates and friends before she'd gone to school. How long had it been since she'd thought of that?

"A good surprise, I hope," he said as he straightened.

Corinne left the room, reluctantly, Hazel thought. Harry made women ridiculous.

"Of course it is not a good surprise," Hazel said evenly, putting her hand back in her lap, unwilling to give her softer side power in this moment. There was still so much ugliness in their relationship. So much disappointment and disapproval and discarding. "I had not time to fix my hair and change my dress."

Harry laughed. "As though I would expect such flippant preparation." He sat on the settee and crossed one long, lean leg over the other knee. "I am on my way to London and thought I would stop in to say hello to the sister who does not return my letters."

There had been three letters over the last few months. One congratulating her on her marriage, one asking her to attend his, and one asking why she had not responded to the other two. She was not entirely sure why she had not responded, other than the fact that she did not want to, and she found a sense of control in knowing she did not owe Harry anything.

"I have been very busy."

He held her eyes. "Apparently." They fell silent. "I think you also wanted to avoid me because you are angry with me and believe me a nitwit."

Hazel rolled her eyes even though he was exactly right. She felt unprepared for a face-to-face confrontation. "If you pull the cord, Corinne will bring a tea tray."

"I already asked if she would bring one, and she said she would. I'm starving."

"Of course you asked, and of course she agreed."

He stared at her, and his smile changed from teasing—his usual expression when they sparred—to . . . what?

He leaned back on the settee, waving a hand about the room. "Look at you, Hazel. Mistress of your castle."

She brushed at some invisible flaw on her skirt to avoid his eyes. "I would hardly call it a castle. There were not so many choices that—"

"Stop resisting my compliment," Harry said, his tone serious. "It is a beautiful home, and *you* manage it. I am impressed and trying to share that with you. You've done well for yourself."

Hazel was so unused to compliments, especially from him, that she could not think how to respond. Finally, she said, "Thank you."

"I would have liked to have attended the wedding."

She squirmed and brushed at her skirt again. Harry's

company had always changed her into a person she did not like but felt driven to play out. Cold, judgmental, impossible to please or impress. Here she was, twenty-nine years old, and she still reverted to this childish persona. Why did she do that?

"And had you in the audience at mine," Harry continued.

This was her opportunity, and she could not help but fall back on what she knew best when talking to Harry—pointed sparring. "Where is Mrs. Stillman?"

"Lady Sabrina Stillman," Harry said with a touch of pride in his voice, "is in London for the Season, which is why I am going, though I will only stay a few weeks."

He went on to explain that his new wife had been hostess for her brother, heir to a dukedom, for several years and was helping teach the new duchess the ways of entertaining for a man of his rank.

"You did not go with her from the start? Has she already seen through you, then, and run off?" Hazel finished with a smirk, expecting him to banter back, but he held her eyes without even a smile, which caused her own expression to fall.

"I would very much like for you and me to have a different sort of relationship than we have had in the past, Hazel, but that will be impossible if we cannot speak kindly to one another."

"Ah, so because *you* have decided we shall relate to one another differently, it will be so? Thank you for putting me on notice."

He still did not rise to the bait and instead turned his head and let out an audible breath. Of resignation? Irritation?

Corinne came into the room, and Harry put his smile back on like a coat he'd only taken off for a few moments. He thanked her but did not flirt as he used to do with every woman he met. Hazel distracted herself with pouring the tea until Corinne had left, and they were alone again. She should apologize for her petty mood. She wouldn't—this was still Harry, and she would keep up her guard—but she could be less acidic.

"How have you liked being back at Falconridge?" she asked without adding anything sharp to the question.

He told her about the improvements he'd made and the others he planned to do over the next few years. He'd hired a new steward last month; he'd been without one since letting the old one go in January. It was all so very . . . conversational.

"I am impressed, Harry," she said, hating that the compliment was hard for her to say. She didn't want to be petty, and yet this man had made significant impacts on her life due to his dissolute behavior in the past.

*In the past.*

Hazel was not who she had been either. Not who she'd been as an angry child brought home because the school would not keep her for the mandatory holidays. Not who she had been as a scared seventeen-year-old who had to prove herself capable of teaching students near her own age or else find herself with no means of support. Not who she had been seven months ago when Duncan had presented her an opportunity she had never imagined.

Was it so impossible to believe that Harry, too, could be changed by the circumstances of his life? Yet how changed was *she* if she insisted on reverting to childish behavior that had once kept her protected? What exactly did she believe she needed protection from?

"Thank you," Harry said, holding her eyes. He'd always had an intense stare, and she usually returned it with equal determination. It felt different now, however. Softer. Wanting. He'd mentioned in his letter last year that he'd faced who he was and had determined to be better. It seemed he was proving that determination to be long-term, though it had not yet been even a year.

"I am impressed with you as well, Haze," he said, using the pet name he'd given her when they were children. "How is this life suiting you? Are you finding yourself satisfied?"

"Very much so," she said, then wished she hadn't. In seven months, she would give up this life and take on the role of headmistress of her own school in King's Lynn. When she made that transition, she would need to play out that this life was not all she'd hoped it would be as justification for why she was leaving it behind. She opened her mouth to make an amendment but could not find the words. Instead, she turned the conversation back to Harry. "And how about you? Are you enjoying the role of husband and landowner?"

"Very much so," he said, echoing her words. "Though I've had more time to explore that of the latter role—we had little time together before she left for London." He set down his empty cup, waving her away when she moved to fill it, and settled on the settee, stretching his arms across the back. "Sabrina is more than I could have wished for, even with the amount of time we've spent apart. We are making a fine life together."

"It must be difficult having her so far away, then." Hazel was proud of herself for not saying the same thing with different words: "I hear marriage is always easier when partners live a hundred miles apart" or "I shall have to hear this from Lady Sabrina to believe it."

"It is horrible," Harry said, shaking his head and then leaning back so he was staring at the ceiling. "She stayed at Falconridge the first few weeks of our marriage, then had to go on to London. I am excited to have a few weeks with her, but I dare not stay for long."

Hazel laughed. "Afraid the estate will crumble without your supervision?"

He continued to stare at the ceiling. "Afraid London will swallow me again if I stay too long."

Hazel looked into her cup. What was she to say to that?

He looked back at her, arms still spread along the back of the settee. It was not difficult to see what Lady Sabrina saw in him physically; he'd always been a fine specimen of the sex. "I have been without a drink for ten months now—I do not even keep liquor at the estate. I ride the perimeter every day and have even begun attending church."

She wrinkled her nose at him. She had not been to church since the Christmas service. "You are funning me."

Harry laughed and shook his head. "I am not."

"Lady Sabrina requires church attendance, then?"

"No, I go of my own volition," Harry said. "I will admit she did have to convince me when Sunday morning came, and I would prefer we stayed in bed longer, but I have been."

Hazel looked into her teacup, refusing to let her thoughts follow his suggestive commentary about wanting to linger in bed with his new wife.

"I have found value in believing there is a God who believes in me. I have had a few particular experiences that have given me greater . . . propensity to believe. There is peace in finding purpose."

"Purpose?" Hazel repeated.

"To life," Harry said. "To the people in our lives. To the way we live each day."

"Gracious, you sound like a philosopher."

"Hardly," he said, shaking his head. "I take it you and Duncan are not churchgoers then?"

"Actually," Hazel said, shifting awkwardly in her chair. "He is very religious, which is frankly odd considering his analytical approach to everything else. Catherine enrolled Duncan in a school headed by the local vicar when he was young, and he began attending Sunday service at the vicar's suggestion, though it was not required. He has attended ever since."

"Catherine?" Harry said, lowering his chin. "His father's mistress enrolled him in a church school?"

The word "mistress" grated, but it is what their mother had called her and what the situation painted Catherine to be. "She played the part of a mother for Duncan." She paused and shook her head. "I cannot make sense of it, truth be told. She moved in with them when Duncan was five years old and was Duncan's sole support after his father's death six years later. She taught him to read, gave him his first lessons on factoring, and enrolled him in school. She owed him nothing, yet she was devoted to him for the rest of her life."

"Really?" Harry said, sitting up and clasping his hands between his knees. "How very un-Mayfield of her to be devoted to a child, let alone a child that was not her own."

Hazel laughed, in part to cover her discomfort at sharing Duncan's personal history with someone she did not entirely trust. "Mother was devoted to you and Hannah."

She'd spoken the words lightly, but they fell like stones, and Harry's smile fell with them. "She doted on us to make up for Father's meanness," he clarified. "Which is not exactly the same thing."

The silence arched and twisted for a moment, and Harry must have felt it too because he rescued her from having to respond.

"I really am sorry for the part I've played in your hardships,

Haze. I have not been good to you the way a brother should have been. Not when we were young, not when we were grown. I genuinely hope we can become more to one another than we've been before."

She could not keep the skepticism out of her expression, but she nodded her willingness to consider it, then felt cruel for hesitating. Had Harry ever hurt her? He'd been irresponsible in matters that influenced her life, but how much of the distance between them was due to their limited interactions and her own jealousy of what seemed like excess he did not appreciate? If that were true, then the trouble between them was not so much his doing as it was her perception.

Harry smiled and spread his hands as though making a peace offering, which was exactly what he was doing. "And are we not lucky to have the chance to build something new? Falconridge is not so very far away, and I would like very much for Sabrina and Duncan to meet."

Duncan!

Hazel looked at the clock. It was 5:41. She pushed up from her chair, which caused Harry to jump to his feet, his eyebrows drawn together in alarm. She took a lurching step, but then realized there was nothing she could do to stall this meeting.

"What is wrong?" Harry asked, his eyes wide.

"Before Duncan gets home—he'll be here in ten minutes or less—I need to . . . prepare you to meet him."

Harry's eyes shot up his forehead. "Well, that is a rather ominous introduction."

# Chapter Twenty-Five

That is why Scotland is so very vindictive of Britain's rule."

Cousin Harry—Hazel's twin brother, though they looked nothing alike—nodded as he took another bite of his pudding, an excellent date cake with lemon glaze. Cousin Harry had proven a good listener, which was a talent Hazel had not alerted Duncan to expect.

"Frankly," Duncan continued, "I am impressed with your interest in this topic, Cousin Harry. Hazel had made it sound like you did not have a great deal of interest in intellectual pursuits."

Cousin Harry looked at Hazel sitting at the other end of the table that sat six, though it had only actually sat six people the one time the vicar and his wife and Mr. and Mrs. Randall had come to dinner a few weeks earlier.

"Did she?" Cousin Harry seemed to be asking the question of Hazel though Duncan was the one who had been carrying the conversation. Hazel had eaten rather quietly tonight. Duncan hoped he had not left her out. He wished he'd thought to ask sooner.

"She also said she was the more attractive of the two of you, but I find that a difficult comparison to make as the two of you look so very different. It would take specific preference for one type of coloring over the—"

Cousin Harry covered his mouth with his napkin but then burst out laughing a few seconds later.

Duncan stiffened and focused on his pudding as anxiety halted his confidence. He had wanted to make a good impression. He began pulling his thoughts inside himself. *Cut a bite, put it in your mouth, chew three times, swallow. Cut a bite, put it in your mouth—*

"He is not laughing at you, Duncan," Hazel said. "He is laughing at me."

"It is unkind to laugh at people," Duncan said, still looking at his plate.

"He does not mean it poorly," she explained.

Duncan risked looking up between them, wishing he could better understand expressions. Hazel was smiling though, and he trusted she would not be laughing at him as she had never laughed at him before. Or told him false. Cousin Harry was still laughing, enough that he seemed to be having a difficult time catching his breath. In Duncan's life, laughter usually came at his expense.

"Forgive me, Duncan," Cousin Harry said, shaking his head and waving a hand through the air. "I mean no unkindness, I assure you."

Duncan returned to his pudding, unconvinced, and now wondering if Cousin Harry had been laughing at him silently the whole meal.

It had been Cousin Harry who said he'd hired a Scotsman as his new steward, but then he'd known so little about the Picts.

If he hoped to make a good impression on his new employee, having a solid grasp of the history of their two countries' disagreements was important. He'd seemed genuinely interested when Duncan had begun explaining the invasion of the Romans upon the order of Julius Caesar that lead to the initial conquering.

However, Duncan also knew he sometimes remedied his own discomfort by speaking too much on a topic of his own interest and not properly engaging other people in the conversation. Had he done that and not noted the signals that the company was growing bored with his conversation? He was embarrassed to think he'd done this with Hazel's brother. Good impressions were incredibly difficult to control since it was at the other person's discretion to judge one's actions.

"My brother has repulsive manners, Duncan."

Cousin Harry snickered again and raised the napkin to his mouth.

"Perhaps it will help if I explain why this is humorous," Cousin Harry said, leaning forward.

Duncan risked a glance, though he did not meet Cousin Harry's eye.

"Hazel told you she was more attractive than I, which put her in a superior position despite the assessment being a purely subjective one since beauty is in the eye of the beholder."

Duncan considered that and remembered marking the comment as clever back when Hazel had said it on their first meeting at Howard House.

"And she is completely right about my lack of interest in intellectual pursuits," Cousin Harry continued. "But for you to say as much out loud puts her in an awkward position because it was an unkind thing for her to have told you. Most people would not have repeated it in my company. That you did, turned an unflattering light on my dear sister's assessment of me."

He balled up his napkin and threw it toward Hazel. Hazel amazingly snatched the napkin out of the air, balled it up again, and threw it back, which made Cousin Harry laugh all over again.

Duncan looked between them. "You are laughing because the things Hazel told me about you were meant to be private." He looked directly at Hazel. "I broke your trust."

"No," Hazel said, smiling at him in that way that relieved him of worry. "You did not break my trust. It simply shows a negative side of my character quite brightly, and nothing pleases Cousin Harry more than putting me at a disadvantage."

This set Cousin Harry laughing again, but Duncan tried to factor it all out. "He likes you to feel badly?" Duncan asked. "That is unkind."

She cocked her head to the side and raised her eyebrows in Cousin Harry's direction. "It is unkind, isn't it?"

"This is glorious!" Cousin Harry said, still smiling. He did have a very nice smile, though Duncan preferred Hazel's.

"I am afraid I do not understand all this," Duncan said, placing his napkin over his now-empty pudding dish. This was the sort of thing Mr. Shopledge had meant when he said Duncan's brain was broken. Hazel and Cousin Harry both understood the humor and the context of this conversation, while Duncan was confused and annoyed by his confusion. "Could we go into the parlor and talk more about the Picts? I have an excellent history of Scotland with a detailed map that shows the primitive placements of the leading clans prior to the Jacobite uprising of 1745."

"I would love to stay," Cousin Harry said as he looked at Hazel, who narrowed her eyes at her brother. Was she angry or teasing? Duncan usually found her much easier to read than other people, but she interacted with Cousin Harry differently than she interacted with anyone else. "But I should have left before now if I hope to get a room. I do thank you for the education. I have a variety of things to converse about with Mr. Fergis upon my return to Falconridge."

"You are getting a room for the night?" Hazel asked.

"There is a decent inn outside of the village, Fox & Foundry on Belstead Road. I hope to stay there and finish my trip to London tomorrow."

"Fox & Foundry is five miles to the north," Duncan said. He had often walked the path that wound through the woods behind the stable at Fox & Foundry, referred to as Foundry Inn by the locals, though he did not do so much walking these days as he preferred to be home. "There is a high probability that their rooms are taken this time of night as they are located so near the road to London and is therefore popular among travelers." He checked the time on his watch. It was almost nine o'clock. "It shall take you several minutes to have your horse saddled at the public stable as I imagine you did not leave it saddled for all the time you've been here, and then it will be some time before you arrive at Fox & Foundry, which increases the likelihood that they will have no available rooms."

Cousin Harry shrugged. "If they are full, I shall keep going until I find another room."

"That is idiotic," Duncan said.

"Duncan," Hazel said in a reprimanding tone. She put out her hand but did not touch him and instead let it drop to her side. He would not have minded if she had touched him as his experiment regarding touch with Hazel was going very well, but he knew she avoided initiating touch because of his early reactions and the reactions she had observed when other people touched him.

"You should stay here," Duncan said, nodding. It was the sensible solution, though the house was small and did not have a guest room. His room, however, would be adequate, and Duncan did not mind sleeping on the sofa in the parlor. "That is the logical solution and both appropriate and expected in light of your familial relationship to Hazel. I shall be very comfortable in the—"

"Excellent suggestion!" Hazel all but shouted, causing both Duncan and Cousin Harry to startle. She smiled in a way that looked rather queer as she rose to her feet. Cousin Harry and Duncan rose, as was proper when a woman stood.

"I shall have Corinne ready the upstairs guest chamber."

Duncan looked at her. "We have no—"

"Do you need to see to your horse?" Hazel interrupted in the same loud voice. She stared at Cousin Harry, who looked back at her from the opposite side of the table, his expression also queer.

The similar expressions showed more of their similarities of feature, but Duncan still could not determine which of them was the most attractive. Hazel, he thought, but then he was attracted to women in general, and so it was reasonable that gender alone would keep her the winner of the debate.

"You left your horse at Hanifords, I presume?" Hazel continued, eyebrows raised in what seemed like an exaggerated expression. "If he is to board overnight, you will want to make arrangements and perhaps fetch your bag, assuming you brought one as you were anticipating an overnight stay at the inn."

"Uh, yes, I did pack a bag." He pointed over his shoulder, and Duncan followed the directional indication but could see no bag. Perhaps he meant to point in the direction of the public stables, but if so, he was flat wrong. Hanifords was due west, and Cousin Harry was pointing north to northeast.

"I should like to see to the horse if you are sure it is no trouble for me to stay," Cousin Harry said. "I did not mean to intrude."

"No trouble at all," Hazel said.

Duncan leaned toward her. "Are you angry?" he asked in a quiet voice, feeling nervous about her confusing and changing reactions over the last few minutes.

"Stop talking, Duncan," she said, still smiling.

Cousin Harry looked between them as Duncan stopped talking.

"Well," Hazel said, making a shooing motion to her brother with both hands, "you had best get to it, and I had best pass on the instructions to Corinne so the guest room is ready when you return."

Duncan nearly reminded her, again, that they had no guest room, but she had told him to stop talking and she was acting strangely, so he did not dare act against her orders.

Cousin Harry seemed hesitant as he left the house, but he did as she'd instructed. He likely did not dare act against her orders either.

Hazel remained standing, which dictated that Duncan remain standing as well since, unlike Cousin Harry, his manners were not repulsive. When the front door closed, Hazel limped to the bellpull and gave it a tug so as to draw Corinne's attention to the dining room.

The pulls situated in each room were quite a fascinating system. One Duncan had not encountered before moving into Lavender House, though he knew of their existence, of course. The pulls were connected to a series of wires loosely run through the walls and into the servants' quarters where they were attached to a bell, below which was a label that indicated which room the pull that rung the bell had originated from. When the bell rang, Corinne could look to see which bell was reverberating and know in which room she was needed. Such a simple yet ingenious invention.

Hazel turned to Duncan, drawing his attention away from the bellpull. "I do not want Harry to know we sleep in separate bedrooms."

Duncan inferred he was being given permission to talk again, even though she had not expressed the idea in a way that would more naturally invite a response. He took a risk by following his assumption. "But we do sleep in separate bedrooms."

"Yes, I know, because this is not a real marriage, but I do not want Harry to know that it is not real."

"But it is real. We are married, and it is not uncommon for husbands and wives to have separate bedchambers."

Hazel closed her eyes, and her mouth tightened a moment before she opened her eyes again. "For the first time in a very long time, I am . . . even with my brother, or at least it appears that I am. Can you understand that?"

Duncan had to think about what she'd said very closely—how was she defining "even"? Why was being "even" with Cousin Harry important enough for her to want to pretend they shared a bedchamber? It was a complex puzzle.

She interrupted his thoughts before he'd reached a conclusion, her voice filled with anxiety. "Harry and I are both married now, and I am no longer his responsibility because I am financially independent of his care, such as it was," Hazel explained, her face softening, which helped Duncan relax. "Uncle Elliott made us promise not to reveal our arrangement to anyone, and if Harry knows we sleep in separate rooms on separate floors, he will suspect something. Frankly, I will be surprised if he doesn't already suspect something." She took a breath before asking, "Do you understand why we must pretend we are like any other married couple while Harry is here?"

Duncan felt his muscles tighten. "I am not very good at pretending."

"I know," she said with a sigh, then looked at the door as Corinne came in. Hazel straightened and lifted her chin. He'd noticed she usually did so when addressing one of the servants. He believed it made her feel more authoritative, even though Corinne was now also her student and he believed they were also friends.

"Ma'am?" Corinne asked.

"My brother shall be staying the night with us. In Duncan's room." She limped toward the servant while explaining that she wanted Duncan's room cleared of his personal belongings and the bed set with fresh linens.

Hearing her explain the instructions that would interfere with his room made him anxious. He did not like people to touch his things, and suddenly he did not like the idea of another man sleeping in his bed, even on fresh sheets.

He wondered if perhaps it would be better for Hazel to sleep in his room; he could help her up the stairs and she could sleep in the bed while he slept on Elizabeth's couch. Her room would then be the one disturbed by her brother, which seemed fairer anyway. Hazel was not nearly as particular about her things as he was with his; at least, she had never expressed feeling so particular.

He was about to suggest his alternative plan when she said, "Duncan shall sleep with me."

Corinne's cheeks turned pink—apparently she did not like pretending either.

Duncan had already opened his mouth to speak when he realized something he had missed in his initial assessment. According to this arrangement, he would be sharing Hazel's bedchamber tonight, and there was no sofa in that room, which meant he would be sharing Hazel's *bed*. A thrill of anticipation shot through him as though he'd just stepped into a hot bath.

Sharing Hazel's bed would be an excellent opportunity to experiment upon his hypothesis that sharing touch and close physical proximity with Hazel was not uncomfortable for him.

"I shall help clear the articles of my possession from my bedchamber," Duncan said as he began taking long strides toward the door. "I shall have Elizabeth locked in the kitchen for the night, she will understand the reasons, and I will move the clothing I need for tomorrow into Hazel's bedchamber as well."

He hurried from the room before either women stopped him, then paused at the bottom of the stairs, worried Hazel would have also realized what she'd proposed. Aside from the murmuring of the women's voices, however, there was no indication he was being called back with an alternate plan.

He took the stairs two at a time to the top floor while calling for Elizabeth, who, contrary to his pronouncement of her understanding, would not take kindly to this at all.

# Chapter Twenty-Six

*H*azel muttered to herself throughout her bedtime routine while Duncan waited in the parlor, likely pacing back and forth. His eagerness made her uncomfortable.

Harry had returned from the stable only minutes after Corinne had pronounced the room ready for him, dripping from the rain that would have made his ride to the inn miserable. The three of them had visited in the parlor until Hazel ran out of patience with Duncan's inability to stop talking about the Picts and suggested they all turn in for the night. After Harry had gone upstairs, she told Duncan to wait in the parlor while she got ready for bed.

Sharing a bed was one thing, sharing her bedtime routine was quite another.

The last thing Hazel did each night before bed was minister to her poor foot, and though she wanted very much to skip the task tonight, she did not. She sat on the edge of the mattress and removed the ties of her boot, one tie on the top like any shoe, but with additional ties on either side that allowed her to adjust the fit. None of her other boots had included that sort of specification, and this new design kept the leather from rubbing against different parts of her foot.

She eased off the boot, grimacing at the resulting ache in her foot. From the drawer of the small stand beside her bed, she removed the bottle of olive oil, with a little lavender oil mixed in, and poured a generous amount into her cupped palm before rubbing her hands together to distribute it evenly.

Once her hands were properly oiled, she began the kneading process on the twisted appendage. Despite her nightly attention, her foot was always dry, and sometimes it developed extreme cracks that were the very devil to heal.

When she had been fourteen, she'd developed an infection in her foot that had required the school to call a physician. She had never seen a doctor for her foot before, only the school cook who doled out an array of salves and advice such as garlic compresses and chewing more slowly at mealtimes.

Hazel had been embarrassed to show her foot to the physician, but he had said the twisting of her bones and ligaments contributed to poor circulation that kept bad blood trapped in her foot. He'd bled the foot just above the ankle, which she was not sure had helped, but then he'd showed her how to improve circulation using the oil-and-massage technique. She'd performed the routine every night since and never developed another infection, though there were still blisters to address from time to time and cracks, especially in the winter.

At the beginning of her treatment each night, she had to grit her teeth through the pain of it, but after a few minutes, the pain faded, and the relief set in. In the years of her self-treatment, the shape of her foot had changed, but only a little. Her toes were not so stiffly curled, she could manually separate and straighten them whereas they had seemed like stone before, and the arch of her foot was not so tightly bound.

When she finished the treatment, she wrapped her foot in a linen dressing and spent a shorter but equally satisfying time massaging her good foot. She relied so fully upon the strength of her left foot that this ministration was as important as the attention given to her right.

After she'd finished with both feet, she cleaned her hands with some alcohol and a cloth she kept in the same drawer as the oil and put away all her supplies. She then adjusted herself in the bed and pulled the cord to alert Corinne to tell Duncan she was ready.

Hazel suspected Corinne felt awkward about her role in this arrangement, and she wished she could apologize for all the discomfort but knew that would make it even more uncomfortable for both of them.

She was smoothing the bedcovers over her lap when Duncan burst into the room as though someone had warned of a fire. His eyes were bright as he searched the room and then stopped to look at her. Really look.

She looked away first as she adjusted her position against the headboard, hating the awkwardness and fearing there would be more of it before it improved.

He remained in the doorway, hand on the knob of the door that was still open. "Your hair is down."

Hazel fingered the end of the braid thrown over her shoulder. "I sleep with it in a braid. Most women do."

"Catherine did not," he said, still standing there. "She twisted it on her head and wrapped it in a scarf that she knotted in the front."

Hazel was not sure if she was supposed to comment on Catherine's hair preferences but did not want to engage in conversation right now. Due to Duncan's excited mood, he could go on indefinitely. He always talked a great deal when he was anxious or excited. "Would you please close the door, Duncan, and come to bed . . . er . . ."

He closed the door and immediately began fumbling with his cravat while kicking off his shoes. She had to close her eyes against the eagerness of his movements, and then took a breath, hoping it would give her the strength to say what she'd wished he'd known without her having to point it out. That he could not understand some things without it being specifically stated was annoying.

"This arrangement does not change my feelings regarding physical intimacy," she said while looking at the bedclothes.

"I did not expect that it did."

Her eyes snapped up. "You didn't?"

"No." He unwound his cravat from his neck. His feet were already bare.

She looked into her lap, feeling foolish for having presumed. "All right, then, go about your . . . undressing or dressing or . . . well, get ready for bed . . . er, sleep."

She heard his movements slow and dared to look up. He stood in the center of the floor, his shirt in one hand, his feet bare on the rug and his arms at his side. She looked away from his naked torso, heat rushing up her face.

She hadn't seen a man without a shirt since the time Harry had undressed to his shorts and dove into the pond, splashing her in the process. Harry had been thirteen years old, skinny and smooth-skinned. Duncan was not quite so skinny, though he was not portly, and his chest was covered with curling dark hair that looked disarmingly soft and tapered down the center of his stomach.

She looked away and pointed to the chair next to the bureau. "Corinne put your nightshirt, there."

She kept her gaze averted until she heard him moving toward the chair. Then she looked again, watching his back as he unfolded the nightshirt and slipped it over his head. He fiddled with the front of his trousers, which then slipped down his legs and pooled at his feet. The warmth in her cheeks was not only from her embarrassment, but then it was natural to be curious, wasn't it? When would she ever have another chance to see a man in such a state? Seven months from now, such opportunities would never present themselves again.

He collected his clothing from the floor and folded the articles onto the chair. Then he came to the side of the bed opposite of Hazel. He did not get under the covers but stood there for several seconds.

Hazel snuggled down into the bedclothes, but still Duncan did not get into his side of the bed.

"Are you all right, Duncan?" Hazel finally asked.

"It does not hurt when you touch me," he said fast and loud.

Hazel paused, trying to determine the context of his words. "What?"

Duncan stared at his feet and took a breath, his head bowed so she could see only the unruly swirls of his hair caused by his having disrobed so quickly. "I do not like to be touched, especially when I am not expecting it. A shock goes through my body and makes me feel very anxious. Catherine taught me how to tolerate some interactions, like shaking hands, but touching is not something I enjoy. Sometimes, though, when you touch me, I understand what other people must feel when they . . . put their arms around each other. I have been experimenting and had hoped—"

"Experimenting?" Hazel said, shocked enough to speak.

"Every scientific discovery is made through hypothesis, trial, error, reconfiguration, and new attempts toward proving the theory. My hypothesis is that I can enjoy touch when it is shared with you, and so I have been using trial and error to see what types of touch are enjoyable and which ones are uncomfortable."

"I do not touch you, Duncan. The times I have, caused you to jump and reprimand me."

He lifted his head, his disheveled hair falling loose around his face. He looked just to the side of where she lay in the bed. "Those are the types of touch I do not like, the kind that send shocks. On our wedding day, we shared a kiss, and it was very pleasurable. At church on Christmas Day, we sat very close together in the pew. I could feel your leg touching mine through your skirts and my trousers. Your shoulder rested against mine as well. It did not hurt.

"Sometimes, when I hand you a book or you give me a cup of tea, our fingers brush against one another, and it does not shock me. I have placed my hand on your back when we go into a room, offered my arm when we are walking, and once you brushed my hair from my forehead and told me I needed to get a haircut."

Hazel did not remember any of those specific instances besides the kiss on their wedding day. She mostly remembered the few times she had touched him and he had jumped as though she'd burned him. Hearing his account of the interactions he had been cataloguing for months made her feel something she did not fully understand. Desired? Not quite.

"My ultimate goal has been to hold your hand, as that is an action I very much disliked when I was a child, but to do so would draw attention to the experiment and could therefore skew the results, so I have not initiated that action. Sharing a bed for the first time since making our vows seemed an excellent opportunity to try a new level of experimentation, however."

"A new level, meaning . . . holding my hand?"

"Without entwining the fingers."

Hazel was silent for a few seconds, trying to make sure she thought through this fully before she responded. "Is that what you meant when you spoke of physical intimacy all those months ago?" It couldn't be; she'd spoken of pregnancy, and he had not been confused about that. He did understand what sexual relations were, didn't he?

"Oh, no, back then I was specifically focused on full intimate connection, but you explained that it would take an emotional investment on your part, and in hindsight, I have wondered if perhaps such intimacies would be too overwhelming for me if I am unable to even hold your hand without discomfort."

"You no longer want physical intimacy, then?"

"I am still excited by the prospect, as is natural and understandable in a healthy male, but I understand it is not a simple choice for you to make with a man like me, and I am content with continuing my experiment with the scaled goals I mentioned. I believe it to be a more reasonable course."

*A man like him.* Was he so aware of his limitations? She wanted to reassure him that those limitations were not necessarily negatives, but she sensed the need to stay on topic. "And this scale includes holding my hand?"

"If you are agreeable."

Hazel pinched her lips together to keep from laughing. He would never understand that she was laughing at herself for jumping to conclusions and not at his remarkable innocence. She took enough time until she could speak evenly, then she leaned forward and pulled back the covers on his side of the bed.

"Duncan, please turn down the lamps and come to bed. I appreciate you confiding in me regarding your experiment, and I accept your terms. I would like to hold your hand."

"Not with fingers intertwined," Duncan insisted.

"Not unless you determine it an acceptable acceleration of the experiment. I shall let you make the decision."

Duncan nodded and then hurried to first turn down the lamp on the bureau and then the lamp on his side of the bed.

Hazel blew out her candle, then wriggled herself down beneath the covers, lying flat on her back. Feeling both ridiculous and invigorated, she moved her hand toward Duncan, who was similarly situated on the other side of the bed. When her arm was roughly at a forty-five-degree angle from her body, she stopped and let it rest on the empty section of mattress between them. She heard the brush of his arm against the bedclothes as he too moved his hand toward the center. When he first touched her arm, he pulled away sharply, and she thought the experiment had failed.

"I am sorry," he said quickly. "It is because of the dark."

A second later, his pinkie touched hers, and she felt a wave of warmth begin to expand from that tiny touch, up her arm and through her body. He kept the contact in place for several seconds, then moved his hand to cover hers, palms together.

The resulting warmth she felt was stronger and deeper than mere body heat could explain. She swallowed in the darkness and stared toward the ceiling, focusing on taking deep, even breaths while she waited for him to say something. Then, so slowly she did not notice it right way, she felt his hand move so that his fingers lined up with the spaces between hers. He curled his fingers into the spaces, and she curled hers as well until their hands were most certainly intertwined.

She could hear his slightly elevated breathing in a room she'd only ever slept in alone. She thought of Harry upstairs and what he would say if he knew that below him these newlyweds were feeling rather overcome with the sensation of holding hands for the first time. He would laugh, certainly. But he did not know. No one knew what her and Duncan's relationship was like—no one needed to. She did not need to justify or explain it, but she could enjoy these sensations.

"So?" she asked after a full minute had passed. "Has this next level of experimentation proven your hypothesis?"

"I believe so," Duncan said, the sound of his voice making her swallow again. He was so close. "Your touch is definitely different from that of other people. I do not feel the need to escape it."

Hazel took inordinate pride in such an accomplishment and turned her head in his direction though she could only just make out the shape of him in the darkness.

"Might I try something?" she asked.

He was quiet for five full seconds, and when he spoke, he sounded nervous. "What?"

"When I was very young, before I was sent away to school, my sister and I shared a bed, and sometimes she would wake up frightened in the night. I would tickle her arms, just run my fingers up and down as she fell back asleep. It was very soothing for her." It had only been recently that Hazel had begun to remember positive memories from her childhood.

"Is it a light touch or a scratch?"

"Light touch," she said, smiling into the darkness. "I can show you if you want to turn your arm over. And if you do not like it, you need only say so and I will stop."

He hesitated, but then disengaged his fingers from hers and turned his palm upward.

She rolled onto her side but did not scoot closer so as not to invade his space more than was necessary. This felt rather like trying to earn Elizabeth's trust, but she hoped he would be more receptive than his cat had been. She started at the wrist, and he startled but did not pull away. She paused, but he did not tell her to stop and so she continued. She lightly traced his arm up to his elbow, then back down to his wrist, braced for him to pull his arm away at any time. She continued the action for several minutes, until she heard a deeper breath from the other side of the bed. She paused and listened until she heard it again.

"Duncan?" she said in the softest whisper she could manage.

He did not respond.

Hazel smiled in the dark as she rolled to her other side and closed her eyes so that she might join him—her husband—in sleep. It had been a day of surprises, and none of them—surprisingly enough—had been bad ones.

# Chapter Twenty-Seven

Something changed between them after Harry's visit. Duncan returned to sleeping in his room, but sometimes Hazel sat beside him on the settee in the parlor, and once, he spontaneously took her hand when they were sitting beside each other. She did not stop him. They did not have a conversation about these events, but she became very aware of every brush of his hand, taking of his arm, and touch of their shoulders when they sat in the evenings.

He started going to the pub for a simple plowman's lunch three days a week at her suggestion. Hazel's motivation was, in part, to help preserve the relationship Duncan had with Delores, but it was also with the hope that if Delores knew Hazel had encouraged this, she would be more open to a connection with Hazel.

The second part of that goal, however, did not happen. Hazel extended invitations to tea that Delores refused. She sent baskets of sweets from Cook with Duncan, and Delores never sent a thank you. The only effort from Delores's side was that she would sometimes send fish for Elizabeth. Hazel asked to be the one to give Elizabeth the treat, however, which did invite a more friendly relationship with the cat.

With spring came the reason for Lavender House's name— the entire perimeter of the grounds was rimmed with lavender bushes that burst toward the sky first in green stems, then in tiny purple blooms that further filled them out. Hazel dried some of the stalks for sachets she tucked into the corner of her wardrobe and beneath her pillow.

She liked lavender oil for her foot and preferred the scent over more fruity or floral perfumes, but came to feel as though it belonged to her. There was something robust about the blooms, strong and healing. Though she tried not to think about it, she knew she would miss this house when she left Ipswich, miss being surrounded by the herbal shrub that so resonated with her increasing sense of self and identity.

The parlor school continued, and Mrs. Randall proved to be an excellent partner. She brought her four-year-old granddaughter with her two days a week, and the young girl was learning her letters at an incredible speed. The women and girls were thriving, growing in confidence, and working hard at their studies.

Rachel, Corinne's niece, took a position in an estate house a few miles to the south. That she was hired as a house maid instead of a kitchen maid had her mother beaming—front of house staff were expected to have more education and poise.

The simple success of these accomplishments made Hazel more and more excited about her own school, but also increased her awareness that there were things she would miss about this life in Ipswich. To miss them now by focusing too much on the future was foolish, and so she enjoyed her days with the parlor students and her evenings with Duncan and kept her thoughts about the future in a separate compartment from the present in which she was living.

Cordon Academy's spring term ended in May, and Hazel's ownership of the school, as well as the name change to the Stillman School for the Advancement of Young Women, was announced at the final teacher's tea of the year. Hazel wished she could have been there but had to settle for Sophie's letter, which was three pages long and full of details that made Hazel both green with envy and deeply grateful for Sophie's willingness to lead the transition.

On the Saturday evening following Sophie's letter—the next time the discussion topic was of her choosing—Hazel chose to discuss Sophie's letter and the school. It would not be Duncan's favorite topic, but then she was not all that interested in discussing the unification of Upper and Lower Egypt during the First Dynasty, and they had discussed it on three separate occasions due to Duncan's fascination with the political maneuverings of that time.

"Sophie is determining which teachers will stay on for the reduced terms and which we will need to replace come next winter, when we will be ready for full enrollment. I worry we will lose the more proficient and ambitious faculty." Hazel set the letter in her lap, still tingling from the excitement of reading it even though she'd read it four times already.

"Why would they not stay on?" Duncan asked from where he sat across from her.

His hair, which he combed back with some sort of pomade each morning, was coming loose from its holdings, resulting in a more devil-may-care arrangement around his face she found quite attractive. The wavy locks softened his features, and looking at him now, with the energy of the day still coursing through her,

Hazel felt the oddest desire to cross to him, sit on his lap, and brush the unruly hair from his eyes herself. That the thought did not make her blush must be due to the excitement of officially owning the school. *Her school!*

"It is your turn to answer," Duncan prompted her, drawing her back from the thoughts that had gone so far astray.

"I'm sorry," she said, shaking her head. "What was the question?"

"I asked why the proficient and ambitious teachers would not stay on."

"Because I am young and untried," Hazel said. "The teachers of the advanced subjects will have limited options regarding positions at other schools but will pursue whatever opportunities they can. I expect we will lose a few, which will put Stillman at a disadvantage."

She smiled as she said the name and then repeated it three times in her head: *Stillman School for the Advancement of Young Women, Stillman School for the Advancement of Young Women, Stillman School for the Advancement of Young Women.* It was a bit of a mouthful, but she already thought of it as just Stillman School, which had a nice ring. She suddenly remembered that her name was no longer Stillman, but Penhale. "Penhale School for the Advancement of Young Women" did not sound like her school, however.

"The teachers of the more traditional subjects have a better chance of finding a position with a school that is secure, so I imagine they will explore their options, which may leave us heavy in advanced topics and weak in the basics, which are necessary for building a solid foundation of scholarship."

"Advanced teachers should have no trouble teaching the more foundational subjects, such as you are doing in the parlor school."

"That is true," Hazel conceded. "I shall ask Sophie to discuss that option with the teachers we are inviting to stay. Sophie has also found a builder to renovate the east dormitories and perform a few repairs to the classrooms and teacher rooms. I think I shall do the teachers' parlor in shades of green and gold. Sophie hasn't been able to walk him through the rooms, of course, due to the term being in session, but we hope to begin the construction phase by the end of the month."

She bit her tongue to keep from saying she wished she could be a part of everything that was happening in King's Lynn.

"So," she said, straightening in her chair and leaning forward to collect the folder where she kept all her notes about the school. "I would like your feedback on my proposed curriculum."

"I hope there is a course on the history of mathematics," Duncan said. "That continues to be a portion of your education that is decidedly lacking."

"I know, I know," Hazel said with a smile. As though she would ever forget his thoughts on that particular topic. "Sophie and I have agreed on two tracks of focus. They will share some of the core topics like writing, etiquette, and French, but will also include their own specific courses that focus on either Science or Classical." She handed him a paper that outlined the separate tracks, and his hair fell forward as he leaned in to take it. His fingers brushed hers, and they shared a look across the paper before resuming their places in their chairs and in the topic.

They discussed the curriculum for an hour. Duncan remained in his chair, which meant he did not find this topic very interesting; when he was excited, he paced. Hazel did not need his excitement, however, and he participated fully, though he fixated on the need for a history of mathematics class and went on for nearly a quarter of an hour about how that particular class could be worked into both tracks. He did not stop campaigning until she agreed to discuss the possibility with Sophie. Some of his ideas were excellent, however, like adding an "innovations" class to the science curriculum that would focus on the newest discoveries and inventions as further industrialization was introduced.

When she had covered all the topics she'd hoped to address, she put the notes back in her folder and pushed herself up to standing. She shook out her bad foot, which was tingling from her having sat for so long, then limped to the writing desk where she stored the folder alongside the items she'd been given as payment from her parlor students.

She ran her fingers over a sampler. Margret Bushwell had stitched the first two lines of Psalm 23, something the girl could read now because Hazel had taught her how. What she gave to these students here in Ipswich was so little compared to what she would offer at Stillman School, yet in some ways it helped them even more than it helped those girls who could get the most advanced learning but who could do little with it in a world that did not allow them entry. Yet.

"What are you doing in here?" Duncan said, causing Hazel to look up and see Elizabeth slinking around the doorframe. The cat was not allowed in the main rooms of the house, only the kitchen and Duncan's room, but now and then she managed to slip through the baize door in order to explore the forbidden. Hazel was in such a good mood that she did not even mind and, instead of demanding Duncan return her to the kitchen, she limped toward the chair where, if she were lucky, Elizabeth would jump onto her lap and they could take another step forward in their relationship.

She reached the chair just as Elizabeth darted toward the

furniture, and a horrendous yowl cut through the air. Hazel's good foot rolled off Elizabeth's tail.

"Elizabeth!" Duncan yelled, reaching for the cat streaking from the room.

Hazel tried to keep herself from falling, but her bad foot buckled beneath the sudden weight she placed upon it. Her balance beyond saving, she tried to grab for something to support her, but her knee twisted. She crashed against the center table at the same time Duncan called her name and lunged toward her.

He was too far away to catch her, so she fell hard against the table, then rolled between the table and the settee. She ended in a heap on her side, moaning as pain throbbed through her. She had not fallen since the night before Duncan had come to Cordon Academy, but she had not forgotten the pain or the fear of it.

Duncan picked up the table between them and threw it to the side, literally, before falling to his knees beside her. He helped her roll onto her back. "You are hurt."

"Yes, I am hurt," she said through gritted teeth. *And embarrassed, and angry at the stupid cat!*

Corinne appeared behind Duncan. "Goodness, what's happened?"

"Elizabeth," Duncan said simply.

Corinne tsked. "Let's get you into a chair, Mrs. Penhale."

Duncan came around to her shoulders and put his hands beneath her arms, while Corinne adjusted Hazel's tangled skirts. Hazel cried out when Duncan lifted her up.

"Lower her back down," Corinne instructed Duncan, who promptly obeyed. To Hazel, she asked, "What hurt just then?"

"My ankle and my knee," Hazel said, gesturing toward her right leg—the same knee she'd injured the last time she'd fallen. Because of the misalignment of those joints, they were always more susceptible to injury. "It's happened before. Help me prop my back against the chair, and let me catch my breath."

Duncan moved the chair behind her so she could lean back, and she took several deep breaths to center her thoughts. Then she leaned forward and manually straightened her leg. It hurt like the devil, but making the adjustments herself was better than having someone else do it.

Corinne reached for one of the ties of Hazel's boot. Hazel's calf was already beginning to swell.

"No!" Hazel yelled, slapping the woman's hands away. "Leave it."

She leaned forward, noting a twinge in her hip but not letting the pain show on her face. She gathered her skirts above her knee, then reached underneath to unclip the garter and roll down the stocking. Her knee was badly swollen, softening the usual ridges of the joint.

This was worse than last time. "I need . . ." She shifted her weight, and a bolt of pain shot up her leg, causing her to fall back against the chair and take a sharp breath. When she opened her eyes, she saw two worried, round-eyed faces looking at her for instruction. "I need . . . linen strips to bind the knee," she said.

"I'll fetch them," Corinne said, rising to her feet and hurrying from the room.

"Duncan," she said to draw his attention away from her knee; he had never seen so much of her body before.

He slowly looked from her knee to her face. There was color in his cheeks, which, in another situation, might make her blush in response, but she was too overwhelmed by all the other things she was feeling.

"Do you think you can carry me to my bed?"

"Yes." He did not move, however, except to look back at her uncovered leg, the stocking rolled down to the top of her boot.

"Right now," she added. She could probably walk, but if she didn't have to . . . "This hard floor is doing nothing to help my discomfort."

"Oh, yes, of course."

She put her skirts back over her legs, tucking the excess fabric between her knees so it would not get tangled again.

He knelt down by her side but did not seem to know what to do.

"Put one arm under my knees, yes, like that. The other arm goes around my back, yes, there. Now, stand up and pull me toward your chest as you do so."

She clenched her teeth to keep from hissing at the refreshed pain that seized her leg when he lifted her. She clasped her arms around his neck, pulling herself tight against his chest in order to keep herself as motionless as possible.

He walked carefully from the room, easing her through the doorway so she did not hit against either side, and then easing her through the doorway to her own room a few moments later. He gently set her on the bed, but he did not let go. Neither did she. They remained in what was almost an embrace, until she lifted her head and looked into his face, which was only a few inches from hers. His eyes were closed as though he were focusing all his attention on something specific. She was so close to him that she could feel the rapid beat of his heart.

"Duncan," she said in a whisper.

He opened his eyes and looked at her, but said nothing.

She could feel his breath against her neck, and she shivered for a different reason than the pain in her leg, which seemed to have lessened while she was in Duncan's arms, so close to his face, so close to his heart.

A bolt of pain shot through her again, breaking the spell. This was not the time. There would never be a time.

"You can let me go now."

"Certainly."

They released one another, and he stood up but did not move away from the bed.

Corinne bustled into the room with an armful of linen strips and a jar of ointment. "Cook said this would help with the swelling," she said as she dumped the items onto the bed before coming around and stepping in front of Duncan, forcing him to fall back a few steps. "That is all, Mr. Penhale," Corinne said. She set about propping pillows behind Hazel's back for support.

"I want to help," Duncan said.

"Go on to bed," Hazel said. "Corinne will fetch you if there is anything else we need."

"Are you sure I cannot help?"

"I am sure, but thank you for all you've done. Good night."

Duncan sighed and turned from the room.

# Chapter Twenty-Eight

$\mathcal{J}$t was a long night, and in the morning, Hazel's knee had nearly doubled in size, and her ankle was black. Duncan did not go to his office, and when Mrs. Randall arrived for the day's lessons, he brought her into the bedroom. She took one look at the knee and immediately sent Duncan for her husband. Hazel's protests did no good, and within the hour, Mrs. Randall had sent the parlor students home and Dr. Randall was sitting beside her bed.

"Mr. Leavitt's boot likely saved you from a worse fate than this," Dr. Randall said after inspecting her boot. "The supports built into the ankle will need to be repaired before you can wear it again, however."

"I shall have Corinne take it to him this afternoon," Hazel said.

Dr. Randall lifted her foot, turning his head to assess it. "When the swelling goes down, I would like to make a better assessment of your foot." He pressed on the inside of her foot, then glanced at her tight expression and withdrew the pressure. "There may be some therapies that can improve the alignment and allow you to build strength into the muscles that play into balance."

"I massage it every night."

"That is obvious. If you did not do so, your foot would be little more than a knot of wood at the end of your leg. You have done very well with your own ministrations, but additional treatments may bring even greater improvement."

"I imagine these additional treatments will include bloodletting and cognac."

Dr. Randall laughed and began rubbing some of Cook's ointment on Hazel's bruises. "I am rather skeptical of bloodletting for matters of structure, like this, and though cognac can be a good treatment for ailments of the lungs and stomach, it does little for muscle and bone. What I have in mind is a more rigorous massage that can further stretch the tendons and, perhaps, the resetting of a few of the bones. I think there is a fusion of sorts in the lower metatarsals."

"That sounds painful," Hazel said without hiding her trepidation.

"Oh, it will be painful." He smiled at her. "But are you not in pain anyway?"

"I see your point, but for now, I would like to focus on being able to walk again. How long until I can try?"

He began wrapping the ankle tighter than she normally would while explaining that the pressure would keep blood from pooling but that she should check every hour to make sure her toes were not turning purple. If they did, she should loosen the binding immediately. Then he stood and allowed her to slide her foot back under the covers.

"Five days in bed, no weight-bearing on that foot," he said. "And then crutches for at least a week. I do not want undue pressure on this leg until you know you can properly bear weight. You have a cane for when you no longer need the crutches?"

Hazel nodded, then gave a heavy sigh. "Crutches. I swore I would never use crutches again once I could walk on my own." She mourned the idea of staying in bed. What about the parlor school? What about . . . well, that was the only responsibility that would be affected, but it was a big responsibility! She did not want her clumsiness to interfere with her students' education.

"Should you impede the healing of your right leg or injure your left leg, the repercussions will be far more inconvenient than a week on crutches. You might want to think of keeping the crutches on hand even after you've healed. Using them on occasion will ease the pressure on your joints and perhaps give you greater mobility."

"There is no greater mobility than walking on my own."

"There is no greater *independence* than walking on your own," Dr. Randall amended. He picked up his bag from the side table. "Just consider the possibility, Mrs. Penhale. You suffer from a condition that resigns many people to a bath chair by their third decade of life because even ordinary actions, like walking, take a toll upon misshapen bones and joints.

"Anything you can do to lessen that impact—such as not stepping on cat's tails"—he smiled, and she could not help but smile back—"should be considered an effort toward your future independence. I shall instruct Duncan on where to procure a set of hardwood crutches that will be suitable for indoor and outdoor use. Promise me you will obey my instructions."

"I will. Thank you, Doctor."

Duncan brought the crutches into her room that afternoon, beaming with pride at his accomplishment. The crutches were padded with leather straps that fit around her forearms and a handle she could grip in such a way that allowed better dexterity than if the crutch had fit under her arm.

*Only for a week,* she told herself, but she did not forget what Dr. Randall had said about a bath chair and the unnatural impact she inflicted on her body with every step.

Mrs. Randall arrived promptly at nine o'clock the next morning, and they made a plan for the next week of parlor school. Mrs. Randall would manage the students but send them to Hazel's room for their readings and recitations. Corinne helped Hazel dress each morning and do her hair so that she looked as presentable and professional as possible, despite being in bed. Such a thing would never be tolerated at Cordon Academy, but the parlor students did not stand on such formality and would pull the chair up to the bed without discomfort.

Duncan ate his dinner in the dining room each night while Hazel ate from a bed tray, but then he came to her room for their evening discussions. He could pace fourteen steps in her bedroom, which was an acceptable count. That first week included a discussion about the railway—again—the significant impact of industry on the city of Manchester—Hazel's choice—and the religious practices of followers of Confucius—Duncan's choice after he'd found a periodical regarding Confucianism.

By the time Hazel was freed from her confinement, she could not wait to master the crutches and reclaim the independence she'd missed so much.

True to Dr. Randall's word, she found she could soon move

faster on her crutches than she could on her feet, and though her shoulders and back often ached at the end of the day, it was a strengthening sort of ache she began to welcome. Her ankle improved sooner than her knee, which allowed her to wear her boot again instead of wrapping her foot in linen and covering it with a sock.

She took to massaging her knee at night along with her feet, but it was almost three weeks before she dared walk without crutches, and even then, she found herself using her crutches around the house more often than not. She had only to imagine a bath chair in her future to see the crutches as something other than a limitation.

In an ironic twist, she learned through letters with Harry that he'd had a severely broken leg just one year earlier, which had sentenced him to bed for weeks, after which he'd had to walk . . . on crutches. It was a strange connection to share, yet when he explained his feelings of dependence and humility, Hazel found herself feeling understood by the brother she had been sure could never understand her.

Summer passed, another parlor student took work as a laundress, and two more girls from the parish joined the school, though Diane, Corinne's sister, stopped coming for the daily lessons because her neighbor was no longer able to watch her younger children in the mornings. She still came once a week to borrow from the collection of children's books Corinne and Duncan had helped Hazel build up. Diane's children would grow up with stories and words they would never have had otherwise.

Duncan began cutting lavender stalks every few days and putting them in the parlor. He said that lavender had become his favorite scent. Hazel kept to herself her own affection of the flowers, though she did not dissect her reasons for keeping their shared love of the herbal flower to herself.

Only six teachers agreed to stay on for Stillman School, and only eighteen students remained enrolled for the summer term. The financial impact was less of a concern than the loss of support, but at least the six teachers who remained were willing to teach a wide variety of subjects. And sixteen of those eighteen summer students signed on for the fall semester. Sophie felt positive about the renovations and the school itself but was concerned about the lack of support from the community.

Hazel began a campaign of letters she sent to numerous business owners, clergy, and prominent households in King's Lynn, explaining the mission of the Stillman School. She also offered day classes to local girls where they would live at home but attend school four days a week.

By the time fall term began, there were thirty-seven students enrolled, twenty-two of whom were boarding. Hazel interviewed teachers via written correspondence, and four more teachers were hired, with another three—all of them specializing in advanced topics—agreeing to come for winter term. It was exciting and encouraging, and yet the need to keep the Stillman School contained in a specific compartment of Hazel's brain became even more important if she wanted to enjoy her time in Ipswich.

And she *was* enjoying her time in Ipswich very much.

Too much?

Duncan worked on his accounts every morning. He still visited with his associates in town, but he had developed the habit of checking in with his tenants multiple times in the week. When he relayed the exchanges to Hazel, she told him she feared he was becoming a nuisance.

"No, I am sure they like knowing I am such a conscientious landlord."

"Not if you are interrupting their work," Hazel said.

"I want them to know I am available to address any concerns."

"You can do that without bothering them. They all know you are keeping an office in the building, so they know where to find you if they need help, and that is sufficient."

"I will consider it, but I do not think you are correct about this."

"Ask Delores and Mr. Ludwig."

"Mr. Ludwig?" Duncan said, sounding incensed.

"He does not like you, so you are more likely to get an honest answer."

"Delores likes me."

"Yes, she likes you enough to also give you an honest answer. Friends and enemies are those more likely to tell you the truth. The neutral parties, such as the other tenants, will not want to offend you, and therefore they will keep their annoyance to themselves. But from what you have relayed to me of their reactions, I think they are annoyed."

"Hmm," Duncan said, returning to his dinner. "I shall ask Delores, but I will not ask Mr. Ludwig."

Hazel smiled to herself and took another bite of her potato, looking across the table at Duncan and feeling a rush of tenderness for his good heart.

She peeked at the corner in her mind that contained Stillman School and felt regret at the reminder that her future there would take her away from Duncan. They would still see one another, at Christmas at Howard House perhaps, and maybe they would visit one another from time to time, but it would never be like this, and that made her feel heavy. She turned away from that corner and focused on the fact that she was Mrs. Duncan Penhale, a respectable woman running a school in her parlor and keeping a home.

They finished dinner and retired to the dining room. Hazel leaned her crutches against the side of her chair as they sat, settling in for an interesting conversation regarding a subject she had been considering for a few weeks now.

"What is the topic of our discussion tonight?" Duncan asked, sitting on the front portion of his seat. From that position, it would be easy for him to jump to his feet and begin pacing when—or rather, if—the topic warranted the excitement.

"Dogs."

Duncan sat back in his chair. "I do not like dogs."

"I want to hear about the day you were bit by the dog."

"Why?"

"Because, though you have told me some details here and there, I feel there are things missing from the story. And as it is connected to such a significant event of your life, your mother's death, I want to make sure I understand it."

"The dog bite is not connected to my mother's death. It simply took place the day before Mother went for bread and was killed by the carriage. It only feels significant because I remember the two events together, but they have no bearing on one another and are therefore not correlated other than chronologically."

His tense posture made it clear he did not want to discuss this topic, but Hazel persevered. "You mentioned once that you heard your parents talking about sending the dog away. When did you overhear that discussion?"

"The night of the dog bite. I was hiding in the cupboard." He stood and began to pace. Usually his pacing was due to excitement of the topic they were discussing, but tonight it seemed to be prompted by anxiety.

Seventeen steps, turn, seventeen steps, turn.

"So, they did not know you could hear them?"

"No. They did not like me to hide in the cupboard, so I would wait until they thought I was asleep, and then I would pretend they were statues who could not tell me *not* to go in the cupboard and I would sneak in when they were not watching."

"You preferred the cupboard over your own bed?"

"Yes."

"Why?"

"Small spaces made me feel hidden. No one could see me. No one could touch me. It was dark and safe in the cupboard. It smelled like soap."

"A kitchen cupboard, then?"

"Yes."

"All right," Hazel said, settling in and being very attentive. "I want to hear everything you remember from those two days, the day you were bit by the dog and the day your mother left the apartment and was killed by a carriage."

# Chapter Twenty-Nine

*H*azel stood on the small front porch of Lavender House on Monday afternoon and swallowed, gripping the handles of her crutches in her sweaty hands.

"Are you certain about this, ma'am?" Corinne asked.

Hazel shook her head. "Not in the least."

She moved the crutches ahead six inches to the edge of the front step, planted them securely, and then swung herself forward, lifting her right foot enough that it would not drag while bringing her left foot even with the crutches.

Using the crutches around the house had become a daily convenience since her fall, even if only for an hour or two, and she'd become quite good at managing them indoors. She had been practicing stairs in anticipation of this expedition, but she'd never used her crutches outside of the house. Never let anyone but Duncan and the servants see her. Duncan had nothing but praise for her progress with the crutches and regularly encouraged her to use them to explore the city, but she had declined. She didn't wish to be a spectacle.

The Burrow Building, however, was seven blocks away, even

further than the church, and she had to get there and back, which was a daunting journey. Delores's unwillingness to come to her all these months, combined with what Hazel had learned from Duncan's recounting of the day his mother died, had formulated an important enough question to necessitate this expedition. And although there were a dozen reasons why the answer was none of Hazel's business, she wanted to know. Then she could decide if Duncan should know.

Hazel looked at the stairs and swallowed her growing anxiety. "If you will put your hand on my back while I take the stairs, Corinne, just so I know that you're there if I lose my balance."

"Of course, ma'am."

The warmth of Corinne's broad hand in the center of Hazel's shoulders lent enough confidence for Hazel to carefully navigate her way down all four steps. Once on the cobbled walkway, she focused on the ground ahead of her instead of whether or not anyone was watching.

"Please walk ahead of me, Corinne. It will clear a path, and I can watch you instead of having to navigate."

"Yes, ma'am."

Hazel focused on the back of Corinne's skirt and did not look at anyone they passed on the street. She was careful to keep her back as straight as possible and tightened her stomach muscles to help ensure her balance. When they passed the church, she celebrated the accomplishment in her mind. *Only two blocks to go.*

"There it is," Corinne said after what felt like miles. "We just need to cross the road."

Hazel's shoulders and hands were aching, and she tried to hide her heavy breathing as she looked up from the street. There were people on both sides of the road and two carriages moving down the middle, the wheels carving divots in piles of horse manure. A man on horseback caught her eye, then looked away as though he hadn't seen her. She took a breath and used her left foot to stand up straighter as she assessed the best place to cross.

"How about there?" she said to Corinne, leaning on her left crutch so she could point with the right.

Corinne nodded and moved that direction.

Hazel took careful steps so as to avoid the worst of the mess in the street.

A carriage stopped, allowing them to pass, the horses huffing and snorting only a few feet away. She imagined the driver was impatient with her slow progress but did not risk a glance to confirm it. Once on the other side of the road, she grinned at Corinne triumphantly. For the next section of the journey, she divided her attention between the cobbles in front of her and the building Duncan owned.

The Burrow Building was long and made of butter-colored stone, which made it stand out against the gray color of the other edifices. There were timber-framed shop fronts along the street level. The shuttered windows on the level above must belong to the apartments such as the one Duncan had lived in. The building was in good condition, the woodwork sound, the paint in good repair, and the sidewalk in front freshly swept.

She felt a sense of pride that the property was so respectable and wished she could pass on the compliment to Duncan. Doing so would require her explaining how she'd come to see the building in the first place, however.

*I am an independent woman and can do as I like,* she told herself, but she still felt guilty for seeking information about his past without his knowledge.

"Here is the pub, ma'am."

Hazel looked at the sign hung perpendicular to the building

from an ornate metal hanger. "Ye Old Pub" was carved into the wood above the timber-framed entrance, the carved letters painted dark-green. A blue fish was also carved below the title, which Hazel found humorous since Duncan sometimes brought fish home from the pub for Elizabeth. The sign above the door just west of the pub said "Penhale Accounting."

"Would you hold the door open for me, Corinne?" Hazel asked, casting a wary glance toward Duncan's office. He was such a determined creature of habit that she did not fear he would leave the office before 1:30 and catch her here, but she felt bad for not stopping in and seeing him too. Though, if she did, he would have questions for her that she was not prepared to answer.

"Ma'am?" Corinne prompted, and Hazel nodded her thanks as she swung through the open doorway, pausing to allow her eyes to adjust to the dim light of the interior.

The pub smelled like stale grease and sharp whiskey. It took a great deal of effort not to wrinkle her nose as she took in the rest of the room and the occupants—four men seated at a table, all of whom were looking at her. She nodded at the men in greeting and then swung her crutches toward a table against the wall nearest the window. The pub was small and felt very cramped.

She moved smoothly into the bench while Corinne sat at a different table. Hazel tried to make herself comfortable but worried she could never be comfortable in a place like this. At the same time, she felt a whirring sense of triumph. She was twenty-nine years old and had never been inside a *pub* before. She'd also had to walk several blocks to get here, on crutches no less. It felt like quite an accomplishment for Hazel Stillman Penhale.

"What are you doin' here?"

Hazel looked up to see Delores staring down at her, hands on her hips. "I wanted to talk with you, and you have either refused or ignored my invitations. I had no choice but to come."

"I am very busy."

Hazel made a pointed look around the room. The four men had gone back to their pints. Corinne sat quietly at the table with her hands in her lap. Hazel met Delores's eyes again and waited.

"I've supper to prepare for in the back," Delores said.

"I am not leaving until we've had a chance to talk."

Delores scowled and turned around. "Stay as long as you like." She took a step away.

"Are you Duncan's mother?" Hazel blurted out when she realized that Delores may very well leave her sitting there alone.

Delores kept her back to Hazel for several seconds, but the four men were looking in their direction. Hazel felt sure that was what convinced Delores to turn around.

Delores stared at Hazel for a long moment, her eyes unreadable, but Hazel didn't sense anger behind them. She relaxed, but only a little. Delores walked slowly to the table but did not sit. Hazel hated having to look up at her, but held her eyes all the same.

"Why would you think that?" Her voice was soft. Scared? "That I'm his mother?"

"You care for him a great deal, and you and he share certain mannerisms and physical traits." Hazel pointed at her own nose in order to indicate she'd noticed that particular feature between them. "I think that is one reason why you do not come to the house. You do not want me to make the connection."

Delores swallowed and stared as she sorted out whatever thoughts were going through her mind.

Hazel did not look away, but the longer the silence lasted, the better she understood why Duncan found it difficult to maintain eye contact sometimes. She felt as though she could see all

Delores's feelings: fear, surprise, compassion, anger, annoyance. Adding Delores's feelings to Hazel's own was rather overwhelming.

When the moment had stretched to the point of awkwardness, Hazel pushed a bit harder.

"He heard his parents fighting the night before she left. He liked to hide in the kitchen cupboard sometimes when he felt scared or anxious, and he heard his mother say that she could not stand it, that *he* had to go somewhere else so they would be safe. He thinks she was talking about the dog that had bit him the day before. He thinks she was asking his da to make sure the dog was killed for having attacked him."

Delores began to twist her apron with her fingers and finally looked away, staring at the tabletop.

Hazel continued. "You did not come into his life until after Leon had died, but you said you knew his father. Duncan hasn't made that connection either. He thinks you and Catherine were old friends, but Catherine was the daughter of a viscount."

Delores said nothing.

"After Catherine died, you made sure Duncan was taken care of. You made sure he had dinner every night, you encouraged him to observe different craftsmen around town when he was looking to find an occupation, and you have helped him sort through interactions with people that he did not understand. You were the one who told him to write to me after he met me at my uncle's house."

Hazel waited, again, for Delores to answer.

When she did not, Hazel continued. "Are you Duncan's mother, Delores? Did you come back because you heard of Leon's passing and felt a pang of conscience to have abandoned your child to the woman he could not marry because Leon had still been married to you?" The one part Hazel couldn't understand is why Duncan would not recognize his mother; but if her appearance had changed enough then perhaps that might explain it.

"I am not Duncan's mother," Delores finally said, so soft that Hazel almost did not hear it. Then she did not believe it. She had been so sure.

"Abigail was my sister," Delores said. "Younger by near ten years, beautiful and good-hearted . . . in most ways."

Hazel hurried to recover from her surprise. "Would you please sit down?" she asked in a quiet voice.

Delores considered the request for a long moment, then she sat on the bench across from Hazel. She continued to stare at the tabletop. "You mustn't judge her too harshly for leaving."

So, she hadn't been killed in a carriage accident. Hazel had been right!

"Mustn't I?" Hazel said before thinking better of it. If she wanted this woman's cooperation, it would be best not to malign her sister. But who better deserved to be judged harshly if not a woman who had walked away from her husband and child?

"I have said for near twenty years that I love Duncan like my own son, but it ain't entirely true. I don't love him the way Abigail did. I think it's easier for me to care for him than it was for Abigail."

*Abigail,* Hazel repeated to herself. *Abigail Penhale.* "What do you mean by that?"

Delores glanced at her, then back at the table. "Those things about Duncan's mannerisms that make people uncomfortable now were even harder to tolerate when he was a child. He would throw tempers over the smallest thing, like having to wear shoes or getting his hair combed. Abigail would try to hug him, and he'd kick her away and scream as though she'd burned him. It ate her up month by month and year by year. She jus' wanted to love 'im."

"Touch is often difficult for him," Hazel said.

"It is difficult to mother a child you cannot touch."

"Difficult, yes, but to leave him? How can you defend that?"

"You canna understand what it was like," she said sharply, cutting a glaring look at Hazel. "You wasn't there."

Hazel startled at the bite of her words, but then nodded. She hadn't been there, and she wasn't a mother. She couldn't understand, but she could try.

Delores took a breath, then paused while the men at the other table burst out laughing at something. When they quieted enough for her to talk without having to shout, she began to explain.

"It weren't Duncan's fault, the way he was, but it was hard. We all lived in Manningtree back then—Leon, Abigail, and I grew up there together. Leon worked the shipyard after leaving the King's navy, and sometimes he hired on to crew a merchant ship, which took him away for weeks at a time.

"Abigail was left alone with Duncan, and it fell on her to manage his strangeness and try to calm him. The older he got, the more difficult he was to manage. That day with the dog . . . She'd convinced him to come outside by promising him a treat if he came to my shop—my husband and me ran a bakery then and my sister hadn't been out of the apartment for days because Duncan was difficult to control.

"The dog appeared out of nowhere, and Duncan started flappin' his arms and screamin' like he did sometimes, which upset the dog, who came after Duncan's bare feet. I heard the screamin' but dinna know it was Duncan, course, 'til I came onto the street. Abigail had kicked the dog away, and he'd run off, but Duncan was hitting his head against the cobbles in between pushing Abigail away. She was crying and begging him to stop, but he was too big for her to pick up.

"I hurried across the street to help, and I was able to grab him, surprised like, and hold him tight. He fought me, but he finally stopped and curled into a ball right there in my lap. His head and his ankle was bleeding, and his knees was all skinned up from his fit.

"There were people stopped to watch the spectacle, and a constable finally come and helped us get him home. The constable said Duncan were mad and needed to be in a hospital or foundling home. It weren't the first time someone had told Abigail that, but she sort of got stuck on the idea that they would all be safer if'n he were in a place like that."

Hazel knew the sort of home Delores was referring to—a home for orphaned or abandoned children. Disabled children, like she had been, were often abandoned at such places. They lived in poverty and often died young due to poor living conditions. The thought of Duncan being taken to a place like that made Hazel's throat tight. The image of a child hitting his own head against the cobbles because he could not sort his feelings or express them was no less disturbing.

"The conversation he overheard in the cupboard was about him being sent to a foundling home, then? Not getting rid of the dog," Hazel summarized. Her stomach felt heavy. "And when Leon would not agree, Abigail left."

Delores nodded, looking at Hazel now. "She only meant to stay with me a few days. She ha' not slept well in weeks and was still awful sick."

"Sick?"

A guilty look crossed Delores's face.

Still awful *sick*. Unable to pick up Duncan.

"She was pregnant," Hazel said.

"It dinna help her to think too straight," Delores said, still defensive. "She'd planned to stay with me a few days, get rested, and then go back and talk to Leon."

"Leon knew where she was?"

"'Course," Delores said. "Where else would she have gone but to her sister's place on the other side of town?" She paused and looked at the table again. "But a few days turned into a week, then two. Leon started comin' 'round and askin' when she was comin' back. The baby inside her got growin' bigger, and her worries grew with it."

Hazel groaned in her throat, picturing the five-year-old wild boy banging his head on the cobbles and kicking his mother away. She closed her eyes and swallowed tears for the impossibility of the situation. "What did Leon say about her staying away?"

"He was none too happy about it, he cunna work, what with no one to look after Duncan, but it were his baby too in Abigail's belly. He left each time he visited without knowin' how to fix things." She paused for a breath.

"After a few weeks, I made her start helping me in the bakery. She needed to be doin' something, and we'd lost one of our girls. Even with that big belly, she was a pretty thing. She caught the eye of one of the customers, and they got to talkin' and such. I dinna think too much 'bout it other than it was nice to see her smilin' again—she had a beautiful smile."

Delores began drawing circles with her finger on the table. "One morning, she dinna come down to the bakery, and when I went to look in on her, she was gone."

The compassion that had been building in Hazel's heart began to sour. "She left with this man?"

"I dinna know," Delores said, the defensive edge returning to her voice.

"She didn't leave a note?" Why would she not leave a note so her family would at least know what she'd done?

"Abigail dinna write," Delores said, wrinkling her nose. "Not all of us got fancy schoolin' like you did."

Hazel blushed, embarrassed to have assumed. Duncan's mother, raised forty years ago in a small port town, would not have had the opportunities Hazel had been given. Like the parish girls she'd been teaching these last months, Abigail had been raised to work—*In the sweat of thy face shalt thou eat bread.*

"But you eventually learned where she went."

"More than a year later she came to the bakery, her husband and baby in arms."

"Husband?"

Delores pinched her lips together. "Her man took her to a new place where no one knew 'em, and they claimed they was married. Everyone thought him the father of the child, and Abigail, well, she was happy and, so while I dinna take to her lyin' like she did, I could see why she done it.

"By then, Leon had taken up with Catherine, and Duncan was doing better. I think Abigail's sadness had made things worse for him too. Leon was angry with me, o'course, and then one day he came to the bakery and said he and Catherine were takin' Duncan to Ipswich. He'd a friend from the navy who was gunna help him find work there, and Catherine's uncle had a place where they could live that would make things better for all of 'em.

"Catherine were teachin' Duncan to read then, and Leon was so proud o'that." She smiled sadly. "He said maybe the trouble all along was that Duncan needed learnin' to fill his mind. Catherine wrote to me now and again, telling me how they was, which is how I knew where they lived back then—my daughter would read me the letters. Catherine told me of Leon's dyin' and, as my husband had died too and I'd lost the bakery for it, I came to Ipswich. My daughter were married then and dinna need me no more. I thought I might could help Catherine some with my nephew and get a new start for my own self."

"Leon and Catherine didn't marry because he was still married to Abigail."

Delores nodded, obviously uncomfortable with that part of the situation. "I'd thought they'd tell a lie like Abigail and her new man had done, but they dinna do that. Duncan was twelve years old when I come to Ipswich and smart as anyone I'd met. I worked at a bakery the first couple of years but then hired on here when they was lookin' for a woman 'cause Catherine was sick, and I thought it best to be close by."

Hazel did not know what to say for several seconds. She wanted to hold tight to morality and fairness and doing what was right. But what was right? Certainly, Abigail should have stayed and learned to deal with her son, but she'd been pregnant, and Duncan was physically aggressive. Could Hazel hold it against her to want to protect the unborn child?

Running off with another man was also wrong, and yet Abigail leaving had opened a place for Catherine to step in and make important changes in Duncan's future. Neither of his parents were educated; what would have happened to him if he'd never gone to school and learned how to use the beautiful brain he'd been given?

*Catherine.* Hazel felt tears well up in her eyes. She still didn't understand what had brought the youngest daughter of the fourth viscount of Howardsford from London to Manningtree to take up with a married shipyard worker and his strange son, but she'd changed Duncan's life. She'd stayed even after Leon died.

"Catherine accepted your help," Hazel said, another

remarkable detail she could see now that she understood the history.

Delores nodded. "She was nervous of me at first, but lonely too, without Leon. Duncan warmed to me quick, but he dinna remember me from all those years before, and Catherine and I decided not to tell 'im anything 'bout who I really was."

"When did Catherine get sick?" Hazel asked. Duncan had never spoken about her illness, only that he'd been fetched at school when she'd died.

"She started gettin' headaches 'bout a year after I came, got worse and worse. That last year, she lost sight in her one eye, and when she finally went to see Dr. Randall, he said it were a tumor in her head and there weren't nothing she could do. That's when she found the away school for Duncan. She dinna want him to see the end of things for her." Delores took a deep breath and let it out. "Duncan dinna want to go, fought so hard against it until Catherine almost gave up, but the vicar stepped in and made it happen, said Duncan needed the learnin'."

"Catherine got bad fast after Duncan weren't there. I think she was done with livin'. She missed Leon something fierce, missed her family, missed Duncan. She drank more and more, and one morning, she dinna answer the door when I checked in on her like I did before opening the pub. I ran for the vicar, and he fetched a constable, who broke the lock on the door so we could get to her. She'd died in her sleep, poor thing, looked like an old women though she weren't more than thirty."

Hazel was silent, spent of ideas about how to acknowledge the woven tragedies of this tale.

Delores stared at the table and continued, "I've thought a hundred times to tell him all the truth about the people who's loved him, but I can't think of how that would help him now."

She paused for a breath. "And I ain't never been able to forget that little boy hitting his head against the cobbles." She shivered.

Hazel nodded, though reluctantly. How *would* knowing any of this help him?

"Where is Abigail now?" she asked gently.

Delores shrugged. "Three times over these last years I've had someone come into the pub and ask me if I got a sister up in Haven or Portsmouth or Leeds—guess she and her family moves around a fair bit. I'll say yes, and they'll say, 'She said to tell ya hello if I ever came through.' Best I can guess is someone from Manningtree told her I'd come up here. Though I know you might not understand it, and God might strike me for saying so, I'm glad to know she's found some happiness in her life."

She looked up at Hazel, her gaze piercing enough that Hazel felt herself growing tense. "Yer gunna leave him too," she said, that sharpness Hazel remembered from the parlor seeping into her tone. "I know yer playin' at somethin', trying to get yer share and then yer gone, ain't ya?"

Hazel swallowed the impulse to defend herself, but Delores was right. Hazel *was* going to leave Duncan, but not for the reasons Delores thought. She was going to leave because it had never been her intention to stay, because being here at all was only a means to an end, because their marriage was not a real marriage the way everyone thought, even Delores.

When Hazel said nothing, Delores's eyes narrowed, and Hazel took that as her cue to end the interview. She slid herself to the edge of the bench.

"I won't tell him any of this," Hazel said as though it was so very magnanimous of her to protect him from his own sad history. Would she be adding to that sadness in a few months' time? "But I appreciate you telling me the truth. It answers a lot of questions, and I admire very much all you have done for him. Thank you for that."

"Dunna thank me, I dinna do it for you."

Hazel felt the heat rising in her neck as she pushed up from the table.

Delores did the same, still glaring, and took a step closer. Hazel lifted her chin defiantly toward the woman who towered over her by several inches. "Yer no Catherine, and I wish I'd never told him to write to you. If I'd thought it would come to this, I never wouldah done it."

Delores turned on her heel and headed for the back of the pub. The kitchen door banged closed, and Hazel couldn't help but flinch.

Corinne joined Hazel and helped her slide her arms into the leather arm braces of the crutches.

As Hazel followed Corinne onto the street, she thought on Delores's parting statement over and over until she felt sure she'd parsed what the woman had meant by it: Hazel was not Catherine, who had stuck by Duncan and done right by him no matter what. Hazel would leave Duncan when the opportunity to have a better life without him came around.

Hazel was *Abigail*.

# Chapter Thirty

*H*azel made it through dinner and Duncan's discussion topic of the rebellion against the Greek Ottoman Empire without revealing the discomfort she was feeling, but only just. As soon as Duncan began winding down from his excitement of the topic he had discussed that day with Mr. Marcum, who had a brother in Greece, she excused herself for the night. But she did not sleep easy.

The things Delores had told her swirled in her head, and though she felt sure that it would not benefit Duncan to know that his mother had abandoned their family because of her inability to care for him, or that he had a full-blooded sibling somewhere in the country, or that Delores had come back for him, it was difficult to keep these things to herself.

Would she want to know if the situation was reversed? She believed that she would, but she possessed the ability to process the complex motivations—good and bad—that had driven the choices others had made.

But this wasn't *her* life. It was Duncan's.

She had struggled all her life to make sense of the particular circumstances that had determined *her* life's journey and still felt burdened by them. Could Duncan, with his literal mind and limited understanding of emotion, make *any* sense of it?

The thoughts tumbled and swirled in her mind. She rolled on her side, then her other side, then her stomach, and then her back again, wanting the discomfort to ebb, but when her thoughts about Duncan settled, Delores's parting words came back, cutting like a blade: *"Yer no Catherine."*

Hazel had agreed to spend this year as Duncan's wife in order to secure her future. It was the only chance she would ever have to manage her own life. She had known going into this that the risk—and the hope of Uncle Elliott and Aunt Amelia—was that she and Duncan would decide to keep this arrangement for the rest of their lives. She could see the shimmer of that life. She lived that life, at least in part, every day, but it wasn't *real*.

She had been Duncan's wife for ten months, but she did not love him. While she knew he enjoyed her company and would likely prefer that she stay a part of his highly regimented life, he would not be the one giving up his independence if she stayed. He would not be giving up anything at all.

And he did not love her either. She was not sure that he could.

He liked to think and debate, to structure his life and explore ideas. But he did not ask how she felt about anything. He had given no indication in all the time they had shared that he saw her any differently than he saw other positive aspects of his life: his favorite hat, his furniture brought from his rooms, his cat.

"I cannot stay," she said to the voice inside her that suggested she should. "The school. My future." Those were the things waiting for her. Those were the things she was working toward. Those were the things she wanted, despite the comfort she'd found in this pretend life. Despite the security she felt sitting across the table from Duncan. Despite the rushes of warmth and tenderness she felt when he touched her hand, or fetched her crutches, or excitedly introduced a topic he was sure she could debate better than any man.

*Those things are not love,* she reminded herself, then she paused, a new question filling her mind. If she *were* in love, would she stay?

It was with these realizations in place that she admitted, fully and completely, that she'd made a mistake. Not in agreeing to Uncle Elliott's terms, but in the way she had lived these last ten months. She had not properly protected herself against the comfort and security she'd found here. She had not kept Duncan at a far enough distance. She had invested in this place and these people. In him.

Had she been wiser, she'd have kept herself apart from it all, managed her boredom and loneliness on her own rather than pulling people into her sphere. No connections. No parlor school. If she'd been wiser, she would not have to let go of anything when she left because there would have been nothing to let go of.

There was no way to go back and change what she'd done, but she could begin now to strategize her exit and hope that doing so for the next two months would make it easier on all of them when she left.

When the night sky lightened to dawn, Hazel got out of bed—grateful to be out of excuses to try to sleep—dressed for the day, and went into the parlor. She pulled a piece of paper from the supply she kept in her writing desk and ignored the tokens of payment from her students stored there.

She was halfway through her first letter—this one to Mrs. Randall, explaining that she needed to step away from the school—when Duncan came into the room, stopping just inside the doorway.

"You are awake early. Wonderful. Shall we have breakfast together?"

"No, thank you," she said, determinedly continuing her letter.

"But you are awake early enough that we can share the meal."

"Yes, but I am not hungry, and I have a great deal of work to do today."

He remained where he was.

"A good breakfast is an essential element of a healthy lifestyle. Dr. Randall says that if—"

"Duncan," she said sharply, cutting him off and looking up. "I have a great deal of work to do today, and I do not want to have breakfast with you. Please leave me to my correspondence."

"I've upset you."

"Yes, because I told you I don't want breakfast and you are still asking me to have some. It is rude."

"I did not mean to upset you."

"Well, you did." She turned back to her letter.

"You are being very rude, Hazel. I was only suggesting—"

"Leave me be!" she shouted, slamming her pen on the writing table. "I do not want to talk to you."

"I do not want to talk to you either!" He turned on his heel and left the room. She put her hands over her face, knowing that she would have to repeat a version of this exchange numerous times over the next several weeks as she pulled away. She would not participate in the evening discussions as often as she had been. She would not always share meals with him. She would not teach her school or read the books Duncan gave her. She would not stop all these things at once, of course, but she would, over the course of the next two months, begin extracting herself from his life.

And it was going to be awful.

# Chapter Thirty-One

"When did it change?" Dr. Randall asked from his chair in the exam room.

Duncan adjusted the periodicals Dr. Randall had given him until they were perfectly squared against the line of his knees, but the usual excitement he felt about reading them was not spinning in his chest the way it usually did.

Today was Wednesday, which meant he and Hazel would play cards or engage in puzzles, but he did not expect her to participate. For forty-four weeks, they had kept to the routine, and then things had begun to change. Now, at forty-nine-and-a-half weeks, everything was different. They had not shared a discussion for nine days. Hazel complained that she was tired or she was working on something for Stillman School or she had a headache. She did not look at him like she used to. She did not let him close enough to touch her.

"On the morning of September eighth, she got angry when I invited her to breakfast, and things have been different since that time."

"September eighth?" Dr. Randall repeated.

"That is what I just said." The less time he spent with Hazel, the less pleasure he felt in life. He did not want to talk to anyone if he could not talk to her, and he no longer enjoyed his work.

"That is around the time she wrote to Mrs. Randall, saying she no longer wished to continue the parlor school," Dr. Randall said.

"Hazel is no longer teaching the parish girls?"

Dr. Randall shook his head. "No, not for two weeks now. Mrs. Randall was quite upset about the letter and tried to talk to Hazel about it, but she simply said she had another project that was demanding her time."

"Stillman School for the Advancement of Young Women."

Dr. Randall pulled his eyebrows together. "What?"

"Hazel has purchased the school in King's Lynn where she used to teach and has changed the name to Stillman School for the Advancement of Young Women. She spends a great deal of time working on the details of the school. It has her very distracted."

Dr. Randall leaned forward, his elbows on his knees. "She owns a school in King's Lynn?"

"Yes."

"She has never said as much to Mrs. Randall. I'm sure Margret would have told me if she had. You say she purchased it? How? I thought she was simply a teacher before you married."

"She *was* only a teacher, but then—" He stopped, realizing he had nearly broken the promise about talking about the details of their marriage with another person.

"Then what?"

"I cannot discuss the particulars of our arrangement."

Duncan thought Dr. Randall's expression was one of perplexity, but he could not be certain. Hazel was the only person who he had ever felt confident of properly reading their expressions, but even that was difficult now. She seemed to always have the same look on her face when he saw her. A look of neutrality that made him feel sad.

"Duncan, I cannot help you diagnose what might be happening with Mrs. Penhale if you do not give me all the symptoms of the situation."

"I promised not to tell the details." Duncan did not break promises, but in this case he wished that sometimes he did. Or just this once. He had come to Dr. Randall because Dr. Randall gave him good advice, such as the touch experiment that had gone so well.

"Did you do something to upset your wife, Duncan?"

"I invited her to breakfast."

"Something else," Dr. Randall said. "Something that hurt or offended her?"

"I don't know."

"Have you asked her?"

"No."

"Perhaps you should."

# Chapter Thirty-Two

"I wondered, Hazel, if I might ask you a question."

Hazel looked up from her fish. Duncan was looking at his plate, and she could tell by his posture that he was anxious. She returned her attention to her plate as well and took a breath. She'd been anxious every day since her realization of what had to be done, and it was only getting worse as the one-year mark got closer.

"Certainly, Duncan."

"Have I done something to offend you?"

She sighed. "No, Duncan, you have not done anything to offend me."

"You seem to be angry with me."

"I am not angry. I am just very busy getting ready to go to King's Lynn. Our agreement is almost over, and so I am thinking about the future."

"The future when you leave Lavender House and go to King's Lynn."

"Yes, as was our agreement." She dared not look at him because she dared not risk opening up herself to any of the good feelings she sometimes felt toward him. Endearment. Tenderness. Pleasure.

"Our agreement also included evening discussions and participation in the aspects of life as man and wife, but we have not had a discussion for nine days."

"The evening discussions were not part of the terms, simply something we agreed to engage in, and we did engage in them for several months."

"Forty-four weeks."

Of course, he had counted them. "Yes, but I am too busy now, and the discussions no longer interest me."

He was silent for a few seconds, then said, "I would like to consider an extension of our agreement. I would like for you to stay in Ipswich."

She did not meet his eye. "I do not think that will work for me, Duncan. I'm sorry."

"But you are not certain."

"Actually, I am quite certain—forgive me for using unprecise words. I am eager to devote myself to the school, and Sophie is expecting me to be there on November ninth. She has been doing everything herself for several months, and I am needed there."

"It seems as though you have done very well at devoting yourself to the work these last eleven months and one week. Sophie has done a good job managing things thus far."

"It has worked adequately well for the development portion of this endeavor, but the renovations are nearly finished, and I need to do my part. Our agreement was only ever for one year's time, and that is nearly complete." She no longer had the appetite to finish the fish and put her fork across her plate.

"That is a reasonable explanation," Duncan said, still eating.

His head was bent over his plate, shoulders hunched as he cut a bite of the fish.

She allowed herself to think about how she would miss his excitement over mealtimes and the comfort of sitting across from him. She would miss the eagerness in his face when he discovered a new topic of discussion or when a particular book he'd been waiting to arrive at the bookshop finally did. Sharing this house with him had been the most enjoyable time of her life. Far more than she had expected when she'd agreed to Uncle Elliott's terms.

"You're a good man, Duncan," Hazel said, her heart heavy. As enjoyable as most of this year had been, part of her wished she'd never agreed to it. She could be teaching at some other school, never having experienced anything different than what she'd already known. Never wanting more. "I wish my decision did not cause you disappointment, but I believe you shall overcome that feeling soon enough."

"I am not so certain," Duncan said. He pressed his closed fist against his sternum. "I cannot imagine a more comfortable arrangement than that of this last year and am very regretful of seeing it come to an end." He pushed back from the table. "If you'll excuse me, I don't really feel like eating pudding tonight. I think I will take a walk. Good night."

Once he'd left the room, Hazel put her hands over her face, but she didn't cry. What would she be crying over? His disappointment at her leaving was based on his enjoyment of their discussions and the ease of his life since their marriage, not love. Not . . . devotion.

She stood from the table when Corinne came in with the night's pudding.

"Please give Cook my apologies. It seems neither Mr. Penhale nor myself are very hungry tonight."

Corinne stood there, a plate of cake in each hand. "Are you truly leaving?"

To pretend surprise at Corinne's knowledge was a waste of energy; she knew everything that happened—and did not happen—in this house. Hazel nodded.

"That is why you ended the school. Why you send so many letters to that school in King's Lynn."

Hazel nodded again. Mrs. Randall had been downright angry when she received Hazel's letter. She had stormed into the house and demanded a better explanation. Hazel had just repeated herself over and over again, holding her ground.

They had taught at Lavender House for another week, but then Mrs. Randall received permission to teach at the church, so the students no longer came to the house. She'd sent Hazel a letter with an update a few days earlier, along with an apology for the tension and a plea for Hazel to explain. She said she knew something must have happened, and she would like to help resolve it.

Hazel had not responded to the letter and attempted to comfort herself with the fact that she had done good while she had been here, and that Mrs. Randall would continue that good.

"And Mr. Penhale is not going with you," Corinne stated.

Hazel swallowed the pain that accompanied the necessary answer. "We are very different people, and we want very different things."

Corinne did not say out loud that she did not understand, but she did not have to. No one could understand. No one *would*. Hazel would be the wife who left Duncan behind. Everyone would assume it was because she could no longer tolerate his odd mannerisms. She would be Abigail, just as Delores had said.

Hazel looked away while blinking back the tears. "Thank you

for all you have done, Corinne. You have taken excellent care of this house."

"It has been a pleasure, ma'am."

Corinne left, and only then did Hazel limp back to her room, close the door, cover her face with her hands, and finally cry. How could she live this life for three more weeks? The last five weeks, ever since she'd made her decision to pull away, had been horrible. How could she see Duncan every day, endure the loss of her students, and act like she was unaffected? The façade was miserable to keep in place.

She went about her nightly routine, but then laid in bed for hours—again—staring at the ceiling, listening to Duncan move about the house once he returned from his walk, then settle into silence. She couldn't do this anymore. Everyone she'd come to care for here in Ipswich would hate her when she left, but she had lost them already. Why draw that out any longer than was necessary?

# Chapter Thirty-Three

*E*lliott and Amelia had just come in from a walk when Brookie approached with a silver tray in hand.

"A letter for you, Your Lordship."

"Thank you," Elliott said, taking the envelope and looking it over. "It is from Hazel."

"It is addressed to *you*?" Amelia said as she undid the ribbons of her bonnet.

"Indeed, it is," Elliott said in a haughty tone. "And it is about time."

Hazel had written primarily to Amelia all these months, and though Elliott was glad for their growing connection, he did feel left out at times. He began to take the stairs to the study.

"Wait for me, Elliott," Amelia said, still unwinding herself from the bonnet and coat she'd worn into the cold autumn day. "This could be what we've been waiting for."

Elliott took the stairs a bit faster for the joke of it, but not too fast to upset his knee, which still gave him trouble from time to time.

"Elliott!" she yelled, talking to the stairs behind him.

He looked over his shoulder to see her glaring at him, her skirts lifted so as to move more swiftly. He laughed, which elicited a smile from her.

He reached the study and stepped behind the door. When she entered, he grabbed her around the waist and pulled her in for a loud kiss on the mouth. She put her hands on his shoulders and pushed him away as he'd known she would, but then she softened as he kissed her again, light and soft and lovely. She put her arms around his neck and let the kiss draw out, as he'd also known she would.

"What a woman you are, Amelia," he said, when he drew back.

She smiled up at him, then turned in his loosened hold and snatched the letter from his hand. She stepped out of his arms before he could stop her and hurried to the desk, breaking the seal as quickly as she could.

"I have been expecting this letter," she said excitedly. She unfolded the letter, and a slip of paper fluttered to the floor. She bent down to pick it up, her excited expression turning into a frown as she read.

"What is it?" Elliott asked.

She handed it across the desk toward him and turned her attention to the letter. "It is a banknote."

"Why on earth would Hazel be sending me a banknote?" Elliott examined the slip of paper, which was, in fact, a note from Gurney's bank in Norwich where he had helped Hazel set up an account for her fifty thousand pounds. The note was in the amount of £2,900.

Amelia, who was reading the letter, gasped and brought a hand to her mouth.

"She did not stay through the year," Elliott said, calculating that the £2,900 was equal to approximately three weeks of the one-year contract which Hazel had agreed to live as Duncan's wife.

Amelia lowered her hand from her mouth and handed the letter across the desk. "I was so sure this would work," she said in a soft, sad tone. "They are so good for one another."

Elliott scanned the letter in which Hazel thanked him for the opportunity, apologized for not seeing it through the full year, and explained the refund of the dowry. If he felt she owed him more than a flat rate determined by weeks, she asked that he let her know. She expressed her respect for Duncan and her hope for his future happiness, but she was needed at the school and felt she could not stay away any longer without risking her investment. She would not be coming to Howard House this Christmas, as they would be preparing for winter term, but hoped to be able to visit in the summer.

Amelia dropped into Elliott's chair behind the desk, her shoulders slumped forward, her hands clasped together on her knees. She looked up at him, blinking back tears. "I was so sure."

Elliott took a breath, then crumpled the letter and dropped it on the desk between them. He sat in the chair across from her. "So was I, my dear. So was I."

# Chapter Thirty-Four

*H*azel stared out the window of the headmistress's office as Sophie hurried in, startling Hazel from her woolgathering. "The Brackhams are going to enroll both of their daughters for the winter term!" She flopped into a chair and let out a deep breath.

Hazel smiled. "Excellent news. Will the girls share a room?"

"No," Sophie said, raising her eyebrows to show her surprise. "Their parents want them in separate rooms so they will make friends with the other girls. How is that for a modern attitude?"

"Science or Classical curriculum?"

"Science for both. Apparently Mrs. Brackham always fancied things like chemistry and physics, but she was not educated past a governess and feels rather put out that she did not have a place such as the Stillman School where she could pursue her interests." Sophie's words brimmed with pride that Hazel tried to hold to for herself.

"I only hope the girls are as eager as their mother," Hazel said.

"Each girl wrote a letter expressing her interest, and they sound sincere. The younger one, Constance, is also musical and wishes to pursue courses in music and Latin." She fluttered her eyelashes at having interest in her field of expertise.

"That's wonderful news. That gives us, what, thirty-eight boarded students for winter term?"

Their current capacity was sixty-four—fifteen more than Cordon Academy had housed before—with the option of expanding up to eighty if there was enough interest to warrant repairs on the third level of the east dormitories. It would take a year or two to sort out the many details that went into operating a school. The fact that Hazel could afford to ramp up slowly toward the desired enrollment was a blessing.

"I've another tour on Saturday and received a letter of interest this afternoon." She dropped an envelope on Hazel's desk. "I thought you could respond to this one now that you're settled."

Hazel stared at the letter and tried to swallow the bubble of anxiety that rose up in her throat. "I shall do so tomorrow morning." She pushed herself up from the desk, taking a few seconds to steady herself. Her crutches were in her apartment, but the comfort she'd found using them around Lavender House had not traveled to King's Lynn with them.

In fact, very little comfort of her life in Ipswich had come with her. During the week she'd been back in King's Lynn, she had tried to capture the enthusiasm that Sophie spun like ribbons every time she came into a room, but it continued to swirl out of reach. Which was why Sophie had given the tour that afternoon and Hazel had sat in her newly renovated office and stared out the window.

She should be ecstatic: everything was on schedule, changing the school's name had gone smoothly, students and parents were excited about the advanced education available to their daughters, and Hazel had the independence she'd never dared to dreamed of.

"Hazel?"

She hadn't realized she'd begun staring out the window again and looked back at Sophie, who was now standing on the other side of the desk. "Sorry, what were you saying?"

"Miss Labrum, the physics teacher I've been corresponding with, wants to come next week. It's earlier than we had planned on, but I believe she can help us with the final vetting of students, and we can collaborate on our classes. What do you think?"

"I think that's a very good idea."

Sophie cocked her head, concerned. "Are you alright, Hazel?"

"Of course, just . . . tired I suppose." Though she had no reason to be tired. All she'd done for a week was sit at her desk and do what little bits of work specifically demanded the head-mistress's attention, which was not that much as it turned out because Sophie was still running things. Hazel had intended to take over as much of the work as she could, but found herself doing as little as possible every day and hoping that the next day would be the one in which she woke up ready to live her dream.

She'd received a letter from Uncle Elliott that she had not yet opened. Sunday—three days from now—was the one-year anniversary of her marriage to Duncan. The anniversary date should not matter, but the closer it came, the more she dreaded it and the less she could run from the memories. She had not even said goodbye to Duncan on the day she left.

Just like Abigail.

She pushed herself up from the chair, suddenly needing the sanctuary of her rooms.

"Shall we go over the ladies' luncheon details tomorrow morning, then? When you're better rested?"

Hazel had forgotten that she'd promised to review the details this afternoon. The luncheon was on Friday so there was no time to waste. It would be her first group presentation of the changes she and Sophie were making, and she should be spending every spare minute reviewing the goals they had set. "Yes, tomorrow morning would be ideal."

"Alright." Sophie moved toward the door and then turned back. "Are you sure you are well?"

A lump formed in Hazel's throat. She lowered herself back into the chair, overcome by emotions she had been refusing to feel.

"Or might I challenge that what is truly bothering you is that you are missing your husband?"

Hazel shook her head. "Certainly not. I am simply tired. I shall rest for the evening, and we'll discuss the ladies' luncheon in the morning.

"Hazel."

Hazel stared at the desk for two seconds before lifting her head and meeting Sophie's eyes.

"Choose happiness."

The lump in Hazel's throat doubled, and she closed her eyes in order to pull her remaining composure together.

Sophie continued, "Choose whatever future is going to make you happy. If you aren't happy here, then—"

Hazel stood, cutting Sophie off. "Do not speak nonsense." She turned to the door of her apartment that was accessible through her office. Having her rooms connected to the office had seemed like such a good idea in the planning phases—no need for her to navigate stairs—but not having separation from her office now felt rather confining.

"I shall see you tomorrow, Sophie."

"Hazel, I—"

Hazel walked into her room and closed the door behind her.

# Chapter Thirty-Five

The night was long and her thoughts were heavy and Sophie's words rang like the reverberations of a bell that would not still.

*Choose happiness.*

*Choose happiness.*

*Choose happiness.*

What was happiness?

How could she possibly know which path would take her to it?

How could she consider any future other than this school?

It was a dream, an incredible opportunity for any woman, let alone a woman who had spent her life learning and who could now spend the rest of her life sharing that knowledge with other girls who would one day take positions of power in this world. But the sparkle of that dream did not blind her the way it once had, and when she closed her eyes and truly considered what she wanted from a life that was, as Sophie had pointed out, up to her, it was not the school that came to mind.

It was almost midnight when she tied on her boots and put a dressing gown on over her nightdress. She took the lamp with her as she left her apartment, went through her office, and turned toward the teacher's wing.

Sophie's room was on the second level, and Hazel hesitated at the bottom of the stairs, before taking them carefully, one step at a time. She had navigated stairs every day when this had been Cordon Academy and she had been a teacher living in the teacher's quarters. Her new life had brought many luxuries.

Once she reached the dark threshold of Sophie's room, she gathered her confidence and knocked lightly, not wanting to wake any of the other teachers in the adjoining rooms.

Only a handful of seconds passed before Sophie opened the door, her lamp low and her eyes blinking.

"Hazel?"

She swallowed, feeling tears in her eyes. "What if I *am* missing my husband? What if, despite him and me and all the reasons against it, I have fallen in love with him?" She paused and took a choppy breath. "What if he cannot love me back?"

Sophie's concerned expression softened as she stepped into the hall and put her arms around Hazel, who sank into her and gave into all the emotion she'd been trying to ignore for these last weeks. For a few minutes, Sophie simply held and soothed her, then she led Hazel into her room, lit the small stove, and fetched a handkerchief.

"You have fallen in love with your husband, then?" Sophie asked. She pulled the bench from the end of her bed so she could face Hazel, who sat in the wooden chair.

"I don't know," Hazel said, shaking her head as she folded the wet handkerchief. "But that is why I am here, feeling . . . ridiculous. I need to make sense of what I *do* feel, and I don't know how. I never believed I would need to understand what love between a man and woman can truly be, and without knowing that, how can I know what it is I'm feeling?"

"Well, then," Sophie said, sitting up straight and smiling warmly. "You have come to the right place. We shall figure this out, you and me, and both be better for it. Let us begin with the resistance you feel toward admitting that you are in love with Duncan."

Hearing his name made Hazel swallow. This was not a conversation on the ethereal nature of love; this was about Duncan. A real person. A person she cared for deeply. "To love him will change everything."

"That is true," Sophie said with a nod. "But everything changing is not necessarily a bad thing."

Hazel looked up from the twisted handkerchief in her hands and met Sophie's eye. "Not a bad thing? After all we—well, mostly you—have done for this school? How could I choose anything other than this dream?"

"If a new dream, a better dream, comes about, why would you choose a lesser one?"

"How can I say this is lesser?"

"How can you say it is not?"

Hazel sighed, remembering the day she'd let Sophie read Duncan's letter and they'd had a similar discussion.

Sophie spoke before Hazel could. "A few years ago, you would never have believed you could buy a school to teach advanced studies for girls and staff it with female experts in every field. But you've done that. Why is it so impossible to believe that after a year of living with a man, you could find yourself in love with him?"

"Because I am not a . . . normal woman. I cannot live that life."

"Dear Hazel, you are the smartest woman I know. Do not insult your own intelligence by saying something so incredibly stupid."

"It would never work," Hazel said.

"What would never work?"

"A life with Duncan," Hazel said. "He is so . . . strange, and together we are ridiculous—my broken body and his broken brain. I am certain people laugh at us behind our backs."

"When have you ever cared what people thought enough to choose a different course? You fought to learn more than the teachers could teach you. You've taught mathematics for a decade despite plenty of people believing you could not possibly do so."

Hazel shook her head. "It is not the same thing. I am not explaining it right."

"Then take your time and explain it right," Sophie said. "What are you afraid of?"

Hazel stared into her lap and thought hard for two full minutes, then she raised her head and faced her friend. "I want to be happy *here*, at our school, doing what I had planned to do from the start of this crazy arrangement, but I fear this last year has ruined me for finding joy here."

"Because you found so much joy in your life with Duncan?"

Hazel felt her chin tremble. "I came to love it, Sophie, and I think I came to love him too." She clenched her eyes closed against having said the words out loud. Making them real. "I managed a home, and I was part of a community. Duncan and I had the most fascinating discussions, and I knew that everything he told me was the truth."

She thought back to that dinner where Duncan had asked her to stay and had said that their year of living as husband and wife had been the most enjoyable of his life. He'd meant it, and she'd known it. And then she'd left the next day before he'd returned home from the office.

"He didn't care about my foot, he didn't care that I wasn't sure if I believed in God or not, he just wanted me to be with him. He just wanted to enjoy my company."

"And you left," Sophie summed up.

Hazel nodded and swallowed. "And I left."

"Why?"

"Because it wasn't real," Hazel said, looking at the desk to avoid seeing Sophie's realization of the trick she and Duncan had played on everyone. "We agreed to live together for one year to satisfy the demands of my uncle. He set the terms in hopes that we would fall in love and want to continue that life, but I want *this* life." She waved her hand to indicate the school. "I do. But . . . I want that one too, and I can't have it, which casts this life, which was once so bright and shiny, into a pale light."

"And the life with Duncan is bright and shiny now?"

"No," Hazel said. "It is pale, too. I must choose one over the other, but whichever path I take means I shall miss the other, which will ruin them both." She paused and took a breath. "It is impossible. I knew from the beginning that I would leave. I never gave myself to him or to that life, not fully. To go back means it would have to be real, and I don't know if that is possible. I don't know . . . " She swallowed as the truth of her next words cut through her. "I don't know that he can love me, not really, not the way I want him too."

"And how do you want him to love you?"

"The way a normal man would love a normal woman." She growled and shook her head in frustration of how words were failing her. "He is not a normal man, Sophie. He can't look me in the eye for more than few seconds, and he fixates on odd things to the point where he can see nothing else. We talk for hours about how wind speeds are measured and why he believes the Egyptians deserve more credit for mathematical understanding than they are given. It isn't . . . normal. We have kissed once, on our wedding day, we have held hands only twice, and he still flinches if I touch him unexpectedly. It is not how it should be."

Sophie nodded, which gave Hazel hope that some part of this crazed explanation was actually making sense.

"My husband, Richard," Sophie said, an unfamiliar softness in her voice, "believed that animals naturally understood Latin over any other language, and so we would be walking down the street and he would go over to a horse or a mule or even a cow and begin whispering Latin in their ears. I would try to block anyone's view of him because it was completely addled. At night, he would wrap himself in three heavy quilts and sweat through them by morning. I would have to hang the quilts every day to dry them in time for him to sleep the next night wrapped up like a meat pie. And the smell . . ." She wrinkled her nose at the memory.

"Most of the women I knew tried to spend as little time with their husbands as possible, while I craved Richard's company more than any other person. When Jason was born, I was almost sad at the time he would take away from Richard, isn't that terrible?"

She blinked back tears and looked up at the ceiling for a moment to regain her composure before she looked at Hazel again. "Duncan is not a normal man. You are not a normal woman. Perhaps that makes you perfect for one another."

Hazel opened her mouth to protest, but Sophie put up a hand to stop her. "I loved the life I had with Richard, sweaty quilts and Latin horse-talking included, and I would give anything to go back to it if I could. I can't, and I have made peace with that, but I do not believe there is anything this school can give to you that will make up for what you will give up if you choose this life over the life you had with Duncan."

Hazel opened her mouth again, ready to say that it wasn't so simple as that, but Sophie continued to speak.

"It will not be perfect, people may laugh behind your back, but if the relationship makes you happy and if it challenges you to grow and become the best version of yourself, you should go back to that life. I will run your school for as long as you want to keep it and find another path if you decide not to divide your attention."

"I don't want to give this up," Hazel said, stubbornly holding on to the dream of her own school. Her own. And yet . . . she'd had a different school in Ipswich. In the parlor. Teaching simple skills had lacked the challenge she enjoyed, but it had been fulfilling in a different way. She had still been giving to her students what they did not have.

"I hurt him when I left."

"Let him forgive you for that."

"What if he cannot? What if he cannot love me? What if his brain cannot do it?"

"What if it can? What if it simply will not look the way you expect it to look?"

Hazel closed her eyes and dropped her chin. Sophie was right; she was letting fear rule her. She was letting ideals of a marriage relationship that she had never actually seen act as the measure for the only way two people could build a life. The fear was overwhelming, but realizing she feared both choices—staying in King's Lynn or returning to Ipswich—helped to calm her somehow. Both choices involved unknown factors she could not solve on her own.

"Sophie?"

Sophie raised her eyebrows.

"Will you pray for me? That I can know the right path?"

Sophie smiled but shook her head. "I will, however, pray *with* you."

# Chapter Thirty-Six

Duncan had found the days since Hazel left difficult; in fact he would say they were some of his very worst days. Even worse than the time he had spent at Resins School or had been bitten by the dog. With Hazel gone, he moved back to his rooms in the Burrow Building with his furniture, and Delores kept dinner for him every night, even on Saturday and Sunday since Duncan did not much feel like cooking the way he had before he'd married Hazel.

Elizabeth kept going back to Lavender House—Duncan suspected Cook was giving her scraps—and sometimes she did not come to his rooms at night. He worried about her. She had to be lonely out there on her own after being used to so many people around.

His rooms felt very small and crowded even though they had never felt that way before. He checked with his tenants every morning despite Hazel telling him that would annoy them, did his work, and then walked and walked and walked. He had not visited any of his associates since she'd left; the discussions did not seem exciting anymore. Nothing seemed exciting if he could not discuss it with Hazel later. His trousers were loose, his coat was too thin, and though he knew it wasn't Hazel's fault that everything felt so uncomfortable, he couldn't help but think that if she were here, it would all be better.

He often dreamed of her at night. One time, she was running toward him with the paddle of a rowboat in each hand—running! In another, she was lying on the other side of the bed they had shared at Lavender House, waiting for him to wake and tickling his nose with a feather. He'd been particularly frustrated when he'd woken from that one and found himself unable to return to it no matter how long he'd squinched his eyes shut.

He'd gone to the pub one evening, hoping to find someone there willing to debate with him the latest advancement of the railroad and what it would mean for travel in their country. The man he'd been told was an academic had not known a lick about steam engines, and another man had laughed when Duncan began pacing during his attempt to teach the first man the proper history. Duncan had wanted to punch the laughing man in the nose the way he'd punched Mr. Ludwig, but he'd left instead and walked for hours.

Today, after finishing his work, though he had only worked for half a day, he walked again. Past the blacksmith shop. Past the butcher. Past Dr. Randall's office. He stopped in front of the cobbler's shop where Hazel's improved boot had been made and remembered how he had put his hand on her back to help her into the carriage. The touch had been pleasurable, and he wished he could go back to that day and feel that pleasure again. His chest felt heavy, as though he could not fully fill his lungs with air. He walked some more.

The gray sky became dark, and it began to rain, but the deflated feeling in his chest continued. Though his stomach rumbled, he did not go to the pub to get his dinner. He did not want to see Delores. He did not want to suffer from the noise of the pub. He wanted to pretend that people were statues and could not talk to him. That he was the only person in the whole world.

Except he wanted Hazel to be there too. But she was in King's Lynn, even though he had asked her to stay with him. She had not even told him goodbye, which made him feel empty and cold when he thought of it. He had come home from work, and Corinne had said Hazel had hired a carriage and left. Though she had called her Mrs. Penhale. He had liked thinking of Hazel as Mrs. Penhale. He had liked everything about her. But she had not liked him. She had not even kept her promise to stay for a whole year.

When full dark came, he began to make his way back to the Burrow Building, hoping all the walking would make it easier for him to sleep. His path took him past Lavender House on Mill Street, and he stopped out front. He thought he might find Elizabeth and bring her home. She did not like to be carried and would probably scratch him if he tried to hold her, but maybe if the scratching hurt, he would not be so aware of the pain in his chest.

He stood outside the front gate and stared at the front windows, now dark and empty. He felt like the house, an idea he had learned from Hazel was a metaphor. The drizzle of rain increased to a downpour, but he stood there for several minutes longer, not wanting to go back to his rooms. The rain dripped off the brim of his hat and the end of his nose, seeped into his coat and chilled his skin beneath. He did not want to go back to his rooms. He did not want to be alone. He did not want to do anything at all.

A barking dog spurred him to walk again. He did not want the dog to bite him.

The windows of the pub were still bright when he turned the corner onto Lower Brook Street, but he did not go inside to get his dinner. He forgot to wipe his feet on the mat placed inside the first door that led to his rooms, which meant he tracked mud up the stairs. His boots made a squishy sound with each step. Rain dripped from his coat and hat. When he reached the top landing, he fumbled in his pocket for his keys—his fingers were very cold—but when he went to put the key in the lock, he realized the door was already unlocked and standing partially open.

His first thought was that Elizabeth had come home, but she would not use the front door. And she could not operate locks.

He pushed the door open two inches and stopped. There was light inside his rooms, but he had left no lamps burning when he'd left at nine o'clock that morning. He was considering going to the pub and asking Delores if she had lit his lamps when he heard a sound from inside his rooms.

Elizabeth?

But that did not explain the door or the lamps.

Then the door opened fully, and he took a step backward in surprise. He stumbled to a stop, catching his balance on the wall, and stared at Hazel.

In his rooms.

"You lit my lamps."

She smiled at him. "That is all you have to say to me?"

"Yes." Duncan's brain was not working as quickly as it usually did, but then it often did not work properly when something happened that he did not anticipate. Hazel being in his rooms was most certainly something he had not anticipated.

She limped to the side and spread her arm toward the interior of his rooms. "Why don't you come in so we can talk?"

Duncan stepped forward into his rooms, but stopped just

inside the door. He did not want to track mud and drip water on the rug.

Hazel moved to stand in front of him. She lifted the sodden hat from his head and leaned past him to hang it on one of the hooks affixed to the wall behind his back.

Duncan stood completely still, but when she was close, he inhaled deeply the scent that was so particularly hers—lavender. It reminded him of springtime and sunshine and the lavender stalks he had liked to put in the parlor when the flowers were in bloom.

She returned to her place in front of him and reached toward the top button of his coat. When her hand brushed his neck, he startled without meaning to, shivers sliding down his back.

She paused, her hands hovering in the air a few inches in front of him. "I want to help you undo the buttons of your coat."

Duncan considered this and remembered his experiment. Also, his fingers were very cold and that would make it difficult for him to undo the buttons. He nodded and then stared at the hollow at the base of her throat while she undid the buttons from the top to the bottom. When she finished, she reached her hands inside his coat and rested them on his shoulders. She looked at him, and he met her eyes, holding the look for several seconds and enjoying the sensation of her warm hands on his cold shoulders.

"You are completely soaked," Hazel said, not moving her hands and not looking away. "You'll catch a cold if you don't get out of these wet clothes and warm yourself." Her cheeks turned pink, which made him think that maybe she felt extra warm, as he was beginning to feel.

"You left Ipswich nineteen days ago without saying goodbye to me," Duncan said. "Your school is in King's Lynn. You said your future was there. Sophie was there."

"I was wrong."

Duncan furrowed his eyebrows. "You were wrong?"

Hazel pushed her hands back, sliding his coat off his shoulders. She helped him draw his arms from the wet sleeves, and then he hung the coat on one of the hooks. When he turned back, she was facing him again. He missed the feel of her hands on his shoulders.

"I thought the school would make me happy, Duncan. I thought it would give me purpose and security and that I would love the work, but I was sad and lonely, and . . . I missed you. I missed the life we made here."

"You said our life was not real."

"I was wrong."

"You are a very intelligent woman, and though I know I have accused you of ignorance and insufficient education on some topics, I do not think you have ever been wrong."

"I want a life here in Ipswich, with you, if you will have me."

"Have you? What does that mean?"

"I want to continue to be Mrs. Penhale." She stepped toward him.

She was very close now, and he felt himself tensing, but then she lifted her hands and he made sure he did not flinch as she pulled the knot out of his cravat, which opened his shirt at the neck and made him very warm.

"I will go to the Stillman School every month or so, or when Sophie needs me, and I will continue the parlor school here so that I do not have to give up teaching entirely. But I want to be here . . . with you. Make a *real* life. With you."

She pulled the cravat from around his neck by tugging on one side until the other end was free of his collar. She dropped it on the floor, and though he hesitated moving because he liked the way Hazel was making him feel, after a moment Duncan had to lean down and pick it up. He turned at the waist to hang the wet cravat on one of the hooks as quickly as possible.

She was smiling when he turned back to her, which he interpreted as her not being angry about him cleaning up after her.

His body was getting warmer, which made his still-wet clothing feel even colder. He shivered, and Hazel reached for his hand. She pulled him toward the stove, which made him warmer with every step. It was very smart of her to have started a fire before he returned, and though he had many questions about how she had gained entrance into his rooms and when she had arrived, he did not ask them.

He realized he was still wearing his muddy boots, and so he took them off and set them to the side of the fire where they would dry but not so quickly that the leather warped. He was standing in front of the stove in his socks, pants, and shirt that was open at the neck.

"I feel very confused," Duncan finally said.

"I feel very awkward," Hazel said, shifting her weight from one foot to the other

"Why?"

"Because I do not know how to say what I have to say without nuance and subtext, but you will not understand that, which means I shall need to be very direct, and that is embarrassing."

"I am sorry I do not understand nuance and subtext. I do not want you to feel embarrassed. I do not want you to leave again."

"What *do* you want, Duncan?"

Duncan considered for a moment. "I want to be happy again, and I have been happiest when you have been here."

Hazel stretched her hands toward the stove, even though she

was not the one who had been in the rain for hours. "Do you understand what love is, Duncan?"

"Of course."

"Tell me what love is to you?"

"Love is . . ." This was difficult. Solid things you could touch or ideas that had already been written into words were much easier to explain. He thought for several seconds about what to say because Hazel had come all the way from King's Lynn, and he did not want her to leave again. And she had asked him a question, and he wanted to give the right answer.

Hazel shifted beside him.

"Is your foot hurting you, Hazel? Do you need to sit down?"

"No, Duncan, but I am scared."

He looked at her. "Scared of what?"

"What if you don't love me? What if you can't? What if I give up my school to simply be a discussion partner and a comfort to you?"

"You do not want to be a discussion partner or a comfort to me?" He was feeling the cracks in his brain again.

"Do you love me, Duncan?"

"Yes."

She looked at him, surprised. "You are so sure?"

"You think I do not know what love is?" Duncan asked, feeling as though he was starting to understand what Hazel meant.

"I worry that, yes. I worry that I will give up my independence to come back to the life we shared, and it—"

"Love is when I used to wake up in the morning and look forward all day to coming home from the office to see you again."

Duncan did not like to interrupt people when they were talking, though sometimes he did when he was very excited to say something regarding the conversation. This interruption was different. This was the most important interruption he had ever made.

"It is Da teaching me everything he knew about numbers. And Catherine taking care of me after Da died. And Delores keeping my dinner warm. Love is giving Elizabeth her full portion of fish even when I am hungry for it myself, and forgiving you for leaving Ipswich because I want you to be happy more than I want me to be happy."

Hazel was still looking at him. "Is it finding a cobbler who can make me a new boot?"

He looked at her feet, but her long skirts covered her shoe. "Do you need a different cobbler? Did Mr. Leavitt do a poor job repairing your boot after you stepped on Elizabeth's tail and bent the braces?"

"No, the boot is excellent."

Duncan relaxed. He had interviewed every cobbler in Ipswich to find the one who could best help Hazel. Mr. Leavitt was the most proficient, and Duncan did not know how he would find a better one.

"I love you too, Duncan. As it turns out, the year we spent together was the happiest time of my life."

"Forty-nine weeks and two days," he corrected.

"Yes," she said, her tone lighter. "The forty-nine weeks and two days we spent together was the happiest time of my life."

Hazel leaned toward him and lifted her chin. He resisted pulling away and instead kept his face very still until he realized she wanted to kiss him. In order for that to happen, he would have to lean down because she was too short to make up the difference, and because of her deformed foot, she could not stand on her toes, which was the typical way a person made up for their personal height deficits.

Duncan bent his head toward her and took a breath a moment before her lips touched his. It was like their wedding kiss all over again, except it was different too. He took a step closer to her, and then his hands were on either side of her face and her hands were holding his wrists, and the kiss changed even though he had not made the conscious decision for it to change.

He moved his arms around her back and pulled her close, and her arms came around his neck, and he pulled her closer still, and the kiss changed even more, and his body became filled with overwhelming sensations he did not want to run away from.

A sound came from Hazel, and he pulled his mouth back from hers, but he did not let her go. "Am I hurting you?" he asked.

She sighed a breathy kind of laugh. "No, Duncan. You never have hurt me, and I do not believe you ever will. Let tonight be a new start for us. Let us build a life we can enjoy to its fullest."

He kissed her again and let the sensations set the pace of what had become, without a doubt, the very best day of his life.

# Epilogue

"Someone to see you, ma'am."

Hazel took hold of the outer wheel of her bath chair and pulled it back sharply, causing the chair to pivot so that she faced the doorway where the nurse stood, holding a bundle of blanket that squirmed slightly in her arms. Hazel engaged the brake so the chair would not shift and put out her arms. "Thank you, Marjorie."

The nurse crossed the distance and transferred Baby Leon to Hazel's arms. She looked into the squinched face of her infant son and pulled down the blanket covering his chin.

"How is my darling boy this afternoon?" she cooed. Changing the tone of her voice, she addressed the nurse. "Would you take me into the parlor? I'll wait for Mr. Penhale there."

Marjorie walked behind the chair, released the brake, and took hold of the handles before pushing Hazel to the other side of the house where the winter sun shone warm through the western windows.

Hazel and Duncan had talked of acquiring a different house, and yet they were happy enough here at Lavender House that the talk never resulted in action. With Duncan sharing her bed-chamber on the main level, the baby and nurse could take the upstairs rooms. Duncan's green chair was now in the parlor, even though it did not match the other furniture, and Elizabeth's couch was in the servant's parlor, where the cat spent a great deal of her time. She and Cook got along quite well.

Though Hazel had sworn she would never use a bath chair, pregnancy had softened the ligaments of her hips and thrown off her center of gravity. She had talked to Dr. Randall about her options, and Duncan had found the bath chair in a single afternoon. She'd thought once the baby was born that she would dispose of the chair, but she loved holding her son when she was sitting. And she found that when she spent some of her day in the chair, walking for the other parts of the day was easier.

She and Duncan took "walks" together on fine days, him pushing her from behind and explaining every detail of the time they had been apart—who he had visited, what work he'd done that day, what updated reports and articles he'd read about the Stockton and Darlington railway system. He still did not have enough work to fill his office hours, but he was content with the work he did have and enjoyed the freedom his lower obligations gave him.

Hazel's initial awkwardness at having people look at them when they were out of the house faded until she barely noticed it anymore. Sometimes she worried about what her son would think of his odd parents as he grew, but she was increasingly at peace with the idea that if she could see through Duncan's peculiarities and he could see past her physical limitations and they could love each other well, surely their son would learn to love their beautiful imperfections too.

The nurse left Hazel sitting in front of the window but close enough to the bellpull so Hazel could call if she needed something. With the afternoon light falling on her, Hazel nursed Leon, content in a way that still felt impossible to her sometimes.

Who was she to be living this life? And yet, who was she not to? Like anyone else, she'd had to make sacrifices and accept her limitations, but her ability to choose her perspective and find joy in even the broken bits was as whole and as real as anyone else's too.

And while Duncan might have a more literal brain than most people, and some odd mannerisms, those things did not prevent him from being the best man she'd ever known. The people who cast him side glances and snickered at his out-of-context comments were far less important to her than those who were drawn to him. Delores. The people at church. Dr. Randall. Lord and Lady Howardsford. And, oddly enough, Harry, who came to visit every few months and had a grand time debating Duncan on whatever topic he'd tried—unsuccessfully—to educate himself on in the months between.

Duncan and Harry would never hunt together or race carriages or fence, but why was that the only way to build a relationship?

Why, indeed?

"I am returned."

She looked up to see Duncan standing in the doorway, hat in hand and shrugging out of his jacket. He hung the garment on the hooks he'd insisted be installed inside the doorway just like the hooks in his old rooms.

Leon had nearly fallen asleep, so she placed him on her lap and did up the buttons of her dress. "You're home early."

"As I have an early appointment in the morning, I thought it reasonable to come home early tonight to make up for the extra time I shall be in the office tomorrow." He crossed the room and sat in his favorite green chair beside her. He looked at their son a moment before looking up at her, staring slightly past her left ear. "I was very excited to see you today."

She smiled. "Were you?"

He met her eye. "I just said that I was."

"Right," she said with a laugh. Precise language. "Why were you particularly excited to see me *today*?"

"Because it was exactly two years ago today that you and I made vows to one another, which makes it a good day to reflect on the companionship we have enjoyed since that time. I bought you a gift." He reached into his pocket and pulled out a small box.

Hazel was embarrassed to have forgotten their anniversary, but then, in her mind, their marriage hadn't truly started that day. She shifted Leon so Duncan could hold him while she took the small box Duncan offered to her.

Duncan gently took the baby and rested him over his shoulder. Touching their child had not been a problem for Duncan, and he was completely delighted with fatherhood. Duncan stood and began to pace, patting his hand against Leon's back.

She opened the box to find a silver pendant in the shape of the infinity sign. A thin line of diamonds studded the surface and caught the afternoon sun with a thousand points of light.

"Duncan," she said softly as she lifted the necklace from the box. "This is beautiful. However did you find something this perfect in Ipswich?"

"It is not from Ipswich. It was crafted by a silversmith in Italy."

"Italy?" Hazel said, looking up as Duncan hit his seventeenth step and turned, still patting Baby Leon's back.

"I mailed the design and payment to the silversmith eight months, two weeks, and three days ago. It arrived in September.

Physical tokens can become a symbol of a person's devotion and affection, especially when given as an association of a significant date."

She looked from the symbol of eternity to Duncan. "This is a symbol of your devotion to me?"

"Yes."

"Because you love me."

"Certainly."

She fastened the chain around her neck, then fingered the pendant. "I love you too, Duncan."

"Wonderful."

The baby burped, and Duncan held him out at arm's length, hands under the baby's arms so they braced Leon's head. He smiled widely at the baby, who blinked back at his father.

"Life is a fascinating experience full of unexpected adventures and exciting discoveries." He pulled the baby back tenderly to his chest and turned to look at Hazel. "Would you be interested in physical intimacy tonight? Dr. Randall says that it is acceptable if you feel sufficiently comfortable, but that I am not to encourage you if you feel you need more time to properly recover from childbirth."

Sometimes it was all she could do not to laugh out loud. She shook her head at the thought of anyone overhearing their conversations. "I would like that, Duncan."

"Wonderful. Now I shall take Leon with me to see Elizabeth in the kitchen. Delores has sent her some fish."

He began to leave the room, then stopped and returned to her, bending down to kiss her. He pulled back slightly and met her eye. "You are the best thing that has ever happened to me."

And she knew he meant every word.

# Acknowledgments

I have loved writing the Mayfield Family Series and am so grateful for those readers who have enjoyed them as well. Hazel and Duncan's story was one I had looked forward to, as it provided me with new challenges and an opportunity to write unique characters. I loved showing how they grew together through their struggles and found that place where they could be the best version of themselves within a fulfilling partnership.

The wonderful Jennifer Moore (*Inventing Vivian*, Covenant 2021) and Nancy Campbell Allen (*The Matchmaker's Lonely Heart*, Shadow Mountain 2021) were, as always, my cheerleaders and brainstormers start to finish.

Brittany Larsen (*The Matchmaker's Match*, Covenant 2018) read the manuscript in its entirety and gave me essential feedback, as did my sister, Jenifer Johnson. She helped me get Duncan's character sorted out thanks to her experience as a Special Ed teacher. Leah Garriott (*Promised,* Shadow Mountain 2020) helped me find math puzzles as needed.

Each of these women helped this book become something I

could be proud of, and I am so grateful for their support, both professionally and personally.

Thanks to the team at Shadow Mountain—Chris Schoebinger, Heidi Taylor Gordon, Lisa Mangum, Heather Ward, Breanna Anderl, Troy Butcher, Callie Hanson, and Haley Huffaker.

This book was written during the most difficult period of my life, which perhaps makes me love it even more because it helped me remember that, though shadows come and dark corners exist within every experience, we can choose to find our way to brighter horizons and accept the beautiful imperfections of our lives.

I am grateful for the love and support of my children, my family and friends, and the dear readers who allow me to do what I love and love what I do. Much thanks goes to my Father in Heaven for helping me to see the step ahead, even if I only get to see one at a time.

# Discussion Questions

1. Did you find Hazel a likable character at the beginning of the book or did it take time for you to connect with her character? Was there a moment when your feelings toward her changed?

2. Have you had experience with someone like Duncan, who today might be diagnosed as being on the autism spectrum? If so, how did Duncan's character compare with your experience?

3. If you have read the other books in the Mayfield series, how did *Love and Lavender* compare?

4. Who was your favorite character in this story? Why?

5. There were several complex choices reflected in this story—Abigail choosing to leave, Catherine choosing to stay, Hazel choosing to return to Duncan, Harry and Hazel choosing to fortify their relationship as siblings. Did any of them stand out to you as particularly poignant?

6. How do you feel about Hazel's choice not to tell Duncan the truth about Abigail leaving?

7. Each book in the Mayfield series includes a flower in the title and as a token woven through each story. Do you have a favorite flower? What makes it special to you?

# About the Author

JOSI S. KILPACK is the author of several novels and one cookbook and a participant in several coauthored projects and anthologies. She is a four-time Whitney Award winner—including *Lord Fenton's Folly* (2015) for Best Romance and Best Novel of the Year—and a Utah Best in State winner for fiction. She is the mother of four children and lives in northern Utah.

You can find more information about Josi and her writing at josiskilpack.com.